"DO WOMEN FIND YOU ATTRACTIVE?" SHE PERSISTED . . .

"Now, what kind of question is that?" Longarm asked.

"An honest one." Amy got up and perched on the arm of the easy chair where Longarm was sitting. "Women who just can't keep from putting their hands on you. Like this." She stroked her hand up along Longarm's thigh. "Women who know you've got something they want and need." She was squeezing him now, and Longarm began to react to the pressure of her fingers. "Women whose lips are just thirsty for kisses."

Amy let herself fall backward into his lap, her robe parting . . .

Also in the **LONGARM** series
from Jove

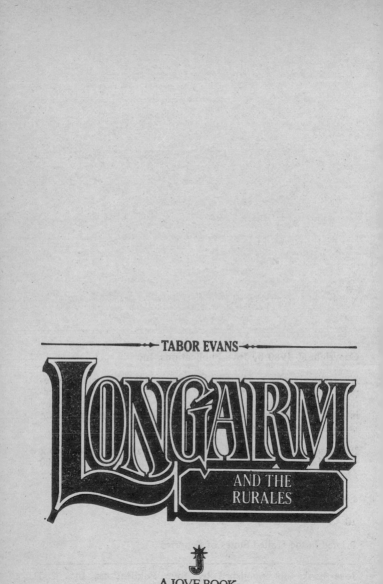

TABOR EVANS

LONGARM

AND THE RURALES

A JOVE BOOK

First Jove edition published December 1980

10 9 8 7 6 5 4 3 2 1

Printed in the United States of America

Jove books are published by Jove Publications, Inc., 200 Madison Avenue, New York, NY 10016

Chapter 1

There was no snow in Denver that morning, but the air had a definite bite to it. Longarm snapped awake at dawn, as usual, and told his stomach to quit growling until breakfast time. When his innards kept reminding him that he'd had a scanty supper the night before, he rolled out of bed. A bottle of Maryland rye with just a heel left in it stood on the bureau. Longarm swallowed the whiskey and started dressing. The air in his unheated room was too nippy even for a whore's bath, and in any case, he'd just drunk the whiskey he would have used to sponge himself down.

Dressed, with his Colt in its cross-draw holster belted on at the precise angle that suited him best, Longarm set his flat-crowned Stetson on his crisp hair and, with a final twirl of his sweeping mustache, set out to face the day. Breakfast came first, and he took his time. A second cup of coffee and a cheroot brought the morning around to the hour when George Masters would have his barbershop open for the day.

A half-hour later, shaved and trimmed, his tanned jaws still cool from a good rub-down with bay rum, Longarm was ready to see what his boss had on the docket. It was time, Longarm thought as he entered the Federal Building, that Billy Vail found something better for him to do than to cool his heels in Denver. And, after sweeping past the pink-cheeked young clerk who tried without much success to guard Vail's office door, Longarm passed on his sentiments to the Chief U.S. Marshal himself.

"Funny you feel that way," Billy Vail grunted, pawing through the ever-growing stack of paperwork that littered his desk. "I just got this on the overnight wire from Washington."

Longarm reached for the message, but Vail was already reading it over to himself. The wire was lengthy, and Longarm took out a cheroot and lighted it to pass the time. He'd smoked the thin cigar a third of the way down before Vail looked up and shook his head.

"Well, Billy?" Longarm asked.

"It's a good thing you've got a hankering to take on a job. This one is just about the right size to fit those number-twelve boots you favor."

"You going to tell me about it, Billy? Or am I supposed to read your mind?"

"Oh, it's not any secret. Seems somebody sneaked back into politics after getting himself a bad name in Washington, and he's trying to weasel himself back into a job there. The Attorney General himself's taking a hand in seeing that he won't make it."

"I'm betting you can't call names to me, though."

"You'd win your bet. But it's a name you'd be likely to remember, if I was able to give it to you. Which the boss says not to do, of course."

"You can tell me about the job, I guess?"

"Oh, sure. It's a little bit of a long story, so settle back and knock that ash off your damned cigar before it falls on my new carpet."

Longarm had been around Billy Vail so many years that he could read the signs of an ugly job, and this looked like one of them. Whenever an especially mean assignment came out of Washington, Billy began picking at him. Tossing the partly smoked cheroot into the brass spittoon at the corner of Vail's desk, Longarm settled back in the red morocco chair.

"Go ahead, Billy. Let's have it."

Vail looked at the message, knitting his bushy eyebrows worriedly. He asked, "Do you recall ever running into a Texas Ranger by the name of Maddox? Clayton Maddox?"

"Can't say I do. Which company's he with?"

"*Was* with. At the time we're talking about, it was A Company."

6

"In Austin, eh?" Longarm shook his head thoughtfully. "I never did spend a lot of time there. Mostly just stop-overs between trains. What's our interest in Maddox?"

"Back in '66, he was one of the Ranger renegades that joined the Texas State Police."

Longarm grunted. Every lawman in the West, no matter how late he'd come to wear a badge, knew about that sorry episode in Texas history during the Reconstruction years. When the carpetbaggers out of the East had taken over the white-pillared state house, they'd learned early that the Texas Rangers lived by a code that wouldn't allow them to carry out the kind of orders the Eastern conquerors were issuing to humiliate and subdue the spirits of those who'd supported the Confederacy.

After dissolving the Rangers, the Reconstruction government had replaced them with a motley crew of gunmen, thieves and scalawags that had been called the Texas State Police. This force was not only ready to carry out any kind of instructions the occupying rascals issued; its men were ingenious in evolving humiliations of their own.

Longarm said, "So Maddox turned his back on his own kind. Well, I reckon he wasn't the first one, and I don't suspicion he'll be the last. There's bad apples in every barrel, Billy. Even the Rangers. Hell, we both know that."

Vail nodded, leaned back in his chair, and ran a pink, thick-fingered hand across his shiny scalp. "Sure. Anyhow, Maddox worked around in the little jerkwater towns close to Austin—as city marshal, deputy sheriff, whatever he could find—until a year or so ago. Then he got the itch to go back to the Rangers again."

"And they didn't want him," Longarm guessed. "Well, he'd be a little bit long in the tooth for a Ranger, wouldn't he, Billy? The war's been over quite a while."

"Oh, Maddox wasn't all that old. He was on the light side of twenty when he first joined up. He'd only be a few years older than you are, right now."

"Which ain't all that grizzly, I reckon," Longarm said. "But I still don't see what all this has got to do with us."

"Just hold your horses. I'm getting there." Vail shifted his bulky frame in his chair and studied the message again

7

for a moment. "The last time he tried to rejoin the Rangers was about a year ago. And he wasn't in any mood to take no for an answer. When the captain he was trying to persuade kept turning him down, they got into a slanging match. I suppose they said a few things that they oughtn't. Anyhow, Maddox pulled down on the captain. Killed him."

"That's still not our affair," Longarm objected. "Hell, let the Rangers handle their own cases. Murder's not in our jurisdiction, Washington's told us that enough times."

Vail shook his head. "But Washington's not worried about the killing. It seems Maddox knows where there's two things that Washington wants real bad."

Longarm waited patiently. When Vail kept studying the message for the third time, Longarm lighted a fresh cheroot.

Vail finally looked up and said, "First of all, Maddox knows where there's God knows how many million dollars in carpetbagger loot hidden away. Graft money, most of it."

Longarm whistled. "That's enough to interest anybody, I guess."

"And along with the gold, there's papers tucked away that point a right dirty finger at two bigwigs who're getting ready to give the President a real bad time when election comes up next year."

"And that's the kernel in the nutshell, I guess?"

"Seems to be. So what we're supposed to do is locate Maddox and find out where the gold and the papers are."

"Well, now. That's a real nice job for somebody," Longarm said, keeping his voice noncommittal, as though he didn't know what was coming next.

"Glad you think so," Vail said amiably. "I don't guess there's any reason for you to put off leaving for Austin any longer than it'll take you to get your gear together."

"Now hold on, Billy!" Longarm objected. "If this Maddox killed a Ranger captain, the Rangers are going to be after him."

"That's right," Vail agreed brightly.

"And they know a lot more about him than I do, where he'd be apt to run to."

8

Vail nodded, and Longarm went on, "So how am I supposed to find this damn Maddox when the Rangers can't?"

"That's up to you," Vail replied, no sympathy in his voice.

"Damn it, Billy, this is a big country. I need a place to start from."

"Try Mexico, Washington says."

"Now come on, Billy! I was down there not too long ago, and there wasn't too many folks sorry to see me leave."

"All the information they've sent is that Maddox was heading for Mexico, the last trail of his the Rangers turned up."

"Hell, Mexico's almost as big as this country," Longarm pointed out. "How'm I supposed to know where to start?"

"That's what you're getting paid for," Vail said patiently, "but the word is he had a niece who lived with him 'round about Austin somewheres, and nobody's said anything about her going with him, so she might still be there. Maybe you can sniff her out. You got a reputation for being able to get all sorts of things out of fair young maids; maybe you can get some information out of this one."

"I'm grateful for what the good Lord sees fit to send my way," Longarm replied, smiling thinly.

"I don't know about the good Lord," Vail said, "but the clerk's got your orders ready about now, and a travel voucher. I don't see much reason for you to be wasting your time hanging around here."

"When you put it that way, Billy, neither do I." Longarm unfolded his six-foot-plus body from the red morocco chair, and stretched. "Seeing as Washington's in such an all-fired hurry, I figure I'd better be, too. Only one thing I need to find out before I go. You got any notions about where this Maddox started from to Mexico? Austin's a pretty big town now, maybe five or six thousand people in it. I'd waste God Almighty's length of time if I didn't have some kind of starting point."

Vail looked at the message again and shook his bald

head. "Not a clue in here. Not even the towns where Maddox worked before he did the killing. Just that they were all close to Austin. I guess you'll just have to pick one out yourself."

Longarm nodded. "As good a way as any, I reckon. Better than Austin, anyhow. You didn't mention it, but I got myself a hunch that if I go nosying around asking too many questions in Austin, there's going to be some Rangers run across my trail and come looking for me to find out why I'm interested in their renegade."

"It's your case from here on," Vail said. "Handle it any way you see fit. Just don't spend the Department dry finding Maddox. Don't forget, I'm the one that's got to account for whatever money you waste."

Longarm grinned. He touched the brim of his hat as he turned away. At the door, he looked back and said, "If you don't hear from me for a while, I'll still be on the job. I wouldn't want you worrying, you know."

Vail grinned back. "You worry about yourself. I'm damned sure not going to lose any sleep over you."

Walking down Champa Street on the way to his roominghouse to get his kit, Longarm moved at a faster pace than his usual city saunter. He carried most of the railroad schedules in his head, and if he hurried just a little bit, he could get the morning Fort Worth & Denver City southbound express to Fort Worth.

There, he'd make connections with a Katy local that would put him into Taylor to connect with an I&GN express to Austin. He could be in Austin by midnight. If he didn't shake a leg, though, if he lollygagged around and missed the morning express, it meant the milk train that night and a series of short hops on dusty, slow-moving locals, and he'd make Austin about noon tomorrow. He looked around for a hack, and saw one within whistling distance. As long as Washington was in such a stew, Longarm didn't mind adding a half-dollar in cab fare to his expense sheet.

He made the train with time to spare, checked his saddle through on the baggage car, and settled down in the

10

smoker. There was the usual array of drummers, ranchers, and men whose dress and actions gave no hint as to their occupations or interests. Longarm leaned his Winchester against the wall of the coach between his seat and the window and settled back to relax as the express pulled out of the depot, wound its way slowly through the growing city, and then gained speed as it hit the mainline south. He was leaning back with his eyes closed when the conductor came through collecting tickets.

"Longarm!" the trainman said, pleasure in his voice, when he stopped at Longarm's seat.

"Jim Pearson!" Longarm extended his callused hand to grasp the one the conductor extended. "It's been a while, ain't it!"

"A long while," Pearson agreed. "And I can't think of anybody I'd rather see on board today."

"Something bothering you, Jim?"

"There sure as the devil is. Fellow up in the day coach next to the baggage car. I've seen his face before, but I can't remember where. And I've got a hunch he's trouble."

"You want me to sashay up front and see if I recognize him from somewhere else, or from our wanted flyers?"

"I'd sure appreciate it. If he's a bad one, I want to keep an eye on him."

"Be a pleasure to help you. You sure helped me, that time the derailment just about had me whipped down, over in the Indian Nation."

Longarm stood up and started toward the front of the car. He was still some distance from the door when a man wearing a bandanna over the bottom of his face burst in, the big Navy Colt he was waving preceding him at arm's length.

Longarm didn't go for his own gun. Nobody but a fool would try to draw on a man who already had his weapon out and his finger on the trigger.

"Now, everybody just hold still, and don't do nothing foolish, and we'll get this finished up without you men getting hurt," the intruder said in a voice loud enough to reach the back of the coach. "All I want is your money and jewelry. I'm going on to the back, to give you time to

11

get your wallets and watches out, and to take off your rings and stickpins. When I pass by you, just drop your contributions in my hat, and that's all there'll be to it."

A buzz of voices rose in the smoker. The holdup man quieted them quickly by firing a shot through the coach roof.

"Do what I told you to. Now!" the holdup artist shouted in the silence that followed the shot. He started along the aisle as the passengers began fumbling in their pockets.

Longarm followed the example of the other men, holding his head down so his hatbrim would hide his face from the approaching bandit. If the robber was an old hand, there was a good chance he'd recognize a Deputy U.S. Marshal who managed to get around a good bit.

Turning his head without drawing the bandit's attention, Longarm kept his own face shielded and his eyes on the man's back as he went down the aisle between the coach seats. At the back, he took his hat off and began moving slowly up the aisle again, stopping beside each seat to let the passengers drop their tributes into the hat.

Jim Pearson had stepped up behind Longarm. The holdup man noticed Pearson for the first time when he reached the spot where Longarm stood. He said, "I was wondering where in hell you'd got off to, Conductor. First thing you better do is hand over your gun. And don't try to tell me you ain't got one, because I know better. Just take it out nice and slow and drop it in my hat, along with your money and that expensive railroad watch all you conductors wear."

Pearson complied without speaking. The gunman switched his attention to Longarm. "All right. You next."

To divert the man's attention, Longarm said mildly, "You're going to have to settle for just a watch off of me. I don't carry any money."

"Like hell you don't! Nobody travels on a train busted, mister, not unless he's a hobo, and sure as shit stinks, you ain't dressed like a bum! But I'll take your watch first, then I'll just go through your pockets myself while you hold my hat and see whether or not you're lyin'."

Longarm brought up his right hand slowly and hooked

his fingers around the watch chain. As he'd anticipated, the man's eyes followed the movement. The instant Longarm was sure the gunman's attention was focused on his right hand, he brought his left down with a flashing swoop that knocked the stickup artist's gun downward and to one side.

In reflex action, the man triggered the Navy Colt. The bullet smashed into the coach floor. By the time the gunman had recovered his wits and was trying to bring the revolver up again, his wrist was locked in the steel-tight grip of Longarm's hand, and the marshal's derringer was pressing its cold brass muzzle on the man's ear just above his bandanna mask.

"Now, then," Longarm said calmly, "suppose you just open up your hand and let that pistol drop to the floor. Then we'll take a look at your face and see if I don't know you from somewheres."

Though the bandit's eyes flashed hatred, he obeyed. Pearson picked up the fallen weapon and covered the man with it. Longarm returned his derringer to his vest pocket and jerked the mask down from the holdup artist's face.

"Well, if it ain't old Gus Posey!" he said. "You can't have been outa the pen more'n a few weeks, Gus. Wasn't it two years you got for that post office job I sent you up for the last time we locked horns?"

Josey replied sullenly, "Damn it, Marshal, a man gets turned outa the pen with ten dollars and a suit of clothes. He's got to make hisself a grubstake some way."

"You ever think about doing an honest day's work?" Longarm asked. When Posey didn't respond, he shook his head and said to the conductor, "Well, Jim, I guess if I handcuff old Gus, you can shut him up in the baggage car till we get to Trinidad, can't you? That'll be our last stop in Colorado. If you carry him any further, getting him accommodated in a jail's going to be a little more complicated."

"Don't worry, Longarm," Pearson answered. "I'll send a message ahead from our first stop, and there'll be somebody waiting at the depot to take him off your hands."

Longarm nodded. Then, raising his voice, he told the

13

passengers who'd been watching wordlessly, "Come claim your wallets and watches and jewelry, gents. This fellow won't have any use for them, not where he's going."

Austin looked just about as Longarm remembered it from his last visit.

And that was a while ago, he told himself as he walked along Lamar Avenue from the depot toward the Iron Front Saloon. He recalled the saloon very well indeed, and hoped it still had the big free lunch table that had fed him so well the last time he'd had to stop over in Texas' capital city. To his relief, the Iron Front was just the same. As far as Longarm could tell, there were even the same barkeeps handling the spigots that dispensed Pearl beer.

With a foaming stein in one hand, and a plate holding a generous assortment of cold cuts, cheeses, and pumpernickel in the other, Longarm glanced around to find an empty table. Everywhere he looked, all seats were taken, until he spotted a small table for two in a far corner of the barnlike building, with only one of its two chairs occupied. He threaded through the narrow aisles between the tables until he reached his objective.

"Mind if I join you?" he asked the occupant.

"If you've a mind to. Most people don't bother to ask."

As Longarm was putting his plate down, the stranger frowned. "Your face is familiar. I know I've seen you somewhere."

"Not likely, friend," Longarm said as he arranged thick slices of venison sausage on a slice of pumpernickel. "I don't get to this part of the country much."

"No, I don't think it was in Austin that I saw you before. Or even in Texas. It was——" the stranger snapped his fingers. "Of course! I remember you now! You're a U.S. Marshal. Denver. And your name's——"

Longarm had been studying his tablemate. He saw a youngish man with a full, twist-tipped mustache, carefully pomaded hair showing below the brim of a back-tilted derby, a rounded face with a suggestion of a beginning double chin, and dark, mischievously twinkling eyes. The man was dressed in the standard uniform of city dwellers:

14

starched white shirt with a high collar, a puffy black cravat, and a black broadcloth suit. He had neither the looks nor the attitude of a crook or a con man, so Longarm decided he'd be safe in admitting his identity.

"You've placed me right. But if I ever did see you before, I don't recall your face."

"We were never introduced. I was in Denver covering the trial of Texas Jim O'Conner. He was a local badman, and I thought we ought to give him a little notoriety."

"You're a newspaper fellow, then," Longarm guessed between sips of his beer.

"That's right. Porter's my name. Will Porter. But I sign most of my pieces with my pen name. O. Henry. You might've noticed it in my paper? It's called *The Rolling Stone*."

Longarm, his mouth full, shook his head.

Porter sounded disappointed as he said, "No. I guess you wouldn't. We only send a few copies up to Colorado. I suppose the only readers the rag's got in Denver are the exchange editors of the *Post* and the *Rocky Mountain News*."

"Hell, I don't even read the *Post*," Longarm said.

"Look here, Marshal," Porter went on. "I've been thinking about trying my hand at a few short stories about this part of the country. I'll bet you've had a lot of things happen to you that'd be new to people back East, where I come from."

"Things happen to just about everybody, I reckon," Longarm pointed out noncommittally.

"I don't mean just *things*," the young newspaperman explained. "I mean unusual things, funny things, even serious ones, that could only happen out here in the West." He saw that Longarm's stein was empty, and waved to one of the white-aproned waiters. In a few moments, the waiter set freshly filled steins in front of them.

"I'll tell you what," Porter suggested. "I'll buy the drinks if you'll do the talking. How does that sound?"

Longarm shook his head. "If I was feeling like seeing the elephant and hearing the owl, I might take you up on that, Mr. Porter. But I'm here on business, and I've got a long ride ahead of me tomorrow."

"Looking for a badman?" Porter asked.

"I reckon you might say that." Longarm suddenly had a thought. If young Porter was a newspaper reporter, he just might know something about Clayton Maddox. He said, "But before I get on with my business, I'd like to see an old-time Ranger and swap a few yarns with him. You might've heard about him. His name's Clayton Maddox. I disremember where he was the last time I heard. You wouldn't happen to know anything about him, would you?"

Porter looked at Longarm narrowly. "Clayton Maddox used to be a Ranger. But they're after him now, or didn't you know that? He shot Captain Elzey, right in his own office. Maddox was a town marshal up in Georgetown when that happened. He's on the run now. Nobody knows where he is, but the Rangers sure would like to."

"I'd heard he'd had some trouble," Longarm said. "I guess his niece is gone, too, then."

With a grin and a knowing look, Porter nodded. "You don't have to say anything more, Marshal. If you know Amy, I'd guess you're more interested in finding her than her uncle."

Longarm managed to look sheepish. "Georgetown, now," he said thoughtfully. "To the north a ways, as I recollect?"

"About forty miles. Well, Marshal, my invitation still stands. The night's just a puppy yet. Do me a favor and let's go out on the town together."

"No. I thank you for the invite, but I better not." Longarm stood up. "Fact of the matter is, I just stopped in here for a quick bite before I look me up a hotel. So I'll bid you goodnight and go find me one."

Longarm stopped at the bar and bought a bottle of Maryland rye to wake up with the next morning, then stepped out on the street.

As he looked around for a hackman who belonged to one of the half-dozen hire carriages that stood outside the Iron Front, he hummed softly to himself a bit of an old

16

song that came into his mind every time he found himself in Texas:

"Come all you Texas Rangers, wherever you may be,
I'll tell you of some troubles that happened unto me.
My name is nothing extra, so that I will not tell,
But here's to all you Rangers, I'm sure I wish you
well . . ."

Chapter 2

After Denver's chilly mornings, the warm sunshine of Central Texas was enjoyable. Longarm woke alert and rolled out of the almost-comfortable bed in the little hotel the cabbie had recommended, far enough from the I&GN depot to be out of the railroad-hotel class, but not close enough to Austin's center to be expensive. Bright sunshine streaked in around the edges of the window shade. He raised the shade to the top and looked out across the tops of the houses that stretched down to the Colorado River, a half-mile to the west.

From the shadows stretching toward the river, Longarm could tell that the morning was very young. He moved to the dresser and took an eye-opener from the bottle he'd bought at the Iron Front last night, and thought about Will Porter's statement that the last anybody had heard of Clayton Maddox, the Ranger renegade and his niece were living in Georgetown.

And that's better'n a half-day's ride, old son, Longarm told his reflection in the mirror. *If you're going to get there before the day's wasted, you better get moving instead of acting like a moon-calf waiting for its mama cow to come give titty.*

When he pulled up his livery-rented bay mare in front of the only saloon sign that showed on Georgetown's main street, the sun was indeed past its nooning. Longarm dismounted and took a quick glance into the saloon. It had no free lunch counter, so he looked along the unpaved street for a restaurant. The only signs of business that he saw were for Gus Koenig's Blacksmith Shop, Dreyfuss's

18

General Store, and the red and white striped pole of a barbershop. He stuck his head through the saloon's batwings.

"Is there someplace in town where a man traveling through can get a meal this time of day?" he asked the barkeep.

"Sure. Mrs. Rider's boardinghouse. It's just down the street a ways. Got no sign on it, but you can't miss it. Big white two-story place. It's past her regular serving time, but she'll almost always accommodate a traveler."

"Thanks. I'll be looking in on you later."

Longarm remounted and rode slowly along the street, taking a leisurely look-see at the town. Georgetown was an old settlement, as towns in Texas went. Fieldstone houses predominated, with high gabled roofs and narrow slits of windows; the heavy shutters on the windows were a reminder of the day not too far in the past when this was Texas' northern frontier, and settlers were fighting with the Comanches to decide which of them would live on the land. There were a few frame houses, and the big one just ahead had to be the one he was after, Longarm decided. He reined in at the hitch rail and knocked.

"You'd be Mrs. Rider, I reckon?" He asked the chubby, aproned woman who opened the door. She nodded, and he went on, "A man down the street said you might accommodate me with a meal. I've just rode in from Austin, and it's hungry time."

"Seeing as you're traveling, I'll be glad to. You can wash at the pump while I dish up. But it'll be potluck, and a quarter for the meal."

"That'll suit me fine, ma'am. I'm not a picky eater."

When Longarm went inside, he found one end of a long oak table spread with a clean cloth. Mrs. Rider was just finishing dishing up a platter of cold fried chicken, slices of hot fried steak, and side dishes of mashed potatoes, collard greens, lima beans, gravy, and a plate heaped with cornbread and biscuits.

"I hottened up the steak and vegetables," she told him. "Chicken's no good when it's warmed over."

"It looks mighty good to me, ma'am."

19

Longarm sat down and began eating. Mrs. Rider disappeared for a moment and returned with cups and a pot of steaming coffee.

"I'll just set with you and keep you company, if you don't object," she said, sitting down and filling both cups. "You're just going through, are you, Mr.—"

"Long, ma'am. And you might say I am and I ain't."

When Longarm went on eating and made no further response to her questioning look, she said, "Now, you eat some of those collards, Mr. Long. They're good for what ails you."

"Well, I'm mostly a meat-and-potatoes man, I guess."

"Just like my late husband. I told him time after time he'd better eat greens and cornbread instead of so much solid food, but he wouldn't listen."

Longarm took a spoonful of greens and a chunk of cornbread. He knew better than to displease a boardinghouse landlady, especially if he wanted to get some information out of her. The greens tasted better than he'd expected, and he ate them all. Mrs. Rider was still looking questioningly at him when he'd finished. He took a sip of coffee.

"As a matter of fact, I stopped off here to see if I could locate a man. You might know him. Clayton Maddox? Man about middle age. Most likely he'd be living with his niece, a young lady named Amy."

Mrs. Rider peered at Longarm with open curiosity. "Are you after him, or just looking for him? I guess you heard about his trouble?"

Longarm nodded. When he volunteered no further information, Mrs. Rider went on, "I suppose you know the Texas Rangers are looking for him?"

"I've heard. But I'm not a Ranger, ma'am."

"No. I'd know if you were. But you won't find Clay Maddox anyplace in Texas, Mr. Long."

"What about his niece? Would she still be here?" he asked.

Mrs. Rider's lips compressed. "That one! Yes, Amy's still here, lives in the little green house Clayton bought right after he was hired on as deputy town marshal. The

20

one back toward town, just behind Koenig's blacksmith shop."

"Do tell? Well, I just might stop off and visit with her for a minute. Maybe she knows something about where I might likely run into Maddox."

"Even if she doesn't, I'm sure you'll find plenty of other things to talk about, Mr. Long."

Longarm got a definite impression that it was time for him to go. He stood up. "That was a fine meal, Mrs. Rider. And I do thank you for taking the extra trouble to fix it for me." He dug change out of his pocket and placed a half-dollar on the table. Mrs. Rider reached into the pocket of her apron, but Longarm held up his hand. "No, ma'am. I don't look for any change. That meal was worth every penny of a half-dollar, so I'd be pleased if you'll accept it."

"Well . . . if you insist, Mr. Long. And if you're in town to stay awhile, my regular hours are seven o'clock for breakfast, noon for dinner, and six o'clock for supper. You'll be welcome anytime you want to come back."

A lighted cheroot clamped between his strong teeth, Longarm rode back toward the blacksmith shop. As the bay walked along the unpaved street, the lawman looked for the green house in back of the shop.

There was no mistaking it—a green house in a town of tan fieldstone and white paint. A hitching post stood in front of the little dwelling. Longarm draped the reins around it and walked to the door. The blinds on the front windows had been closed; the house looked blank and sightless.

He knocked, and when there were no sounds from inside, he knocked a second time, harder and longer. He'd just about decided to knock a third time and then give it up and go and wait in the saloon before trying again, when the door opened a slit. The eyes that peered sidewise through the slit were those of a woman, wide and long-lashed.

"Yes?" she questioned.

"This'd be the Maddox house, I guess?"

21

"Yes. But if you're looking for Uncle Clay, he's not here."

"I been told that. You'd be Amy, his niece?"

"Yes. Who are you, anyhow? I never have seen you around town."

"I reckon not. I'm from up north."

"You're not a Ranger. If you were, you wouldn't be wasting your time asking here for Uncle Clay."

"No. I'd like to talk with you a few minutes, though, if you can spare the time."

She laughed bitterly, a nasal, grunting chuckle. "You really are a stranger in Georgetown, or you'd know all I've got is time to spare." She paused thoughtfully, then said, "Maybe it'll do me good to talk to somebody I don't know. Come on in."

She opened the door wide enough to let Longarm enter, then closed it at once and threw the bolt. Longarm tossed his cheroot into the street and went in. After the bright sunshine, his eyes took a moment in adjusting to the dimly lit room. The girl noticed him blinking.

"You'll get used to it in a minute," she told him. "I like it this way. Do you mind?"

"No. Don't open the blinds unless you just want to. Like you said, I'll get used to it in a minute."

Longarm's eyes were adjusting rapidly. The room was sparsely furnished. A long table stood against one wall, and there were a settee, an easy chair and a pair of straight chairs set stiffly at angles to the sofa. A rocking chair was near the easy chair. The room had an unused feeling.

Now, too, Amy came into focus, a small girl, her head reaching barely to his shoulder. She had hair the color of clover honey fresh from the hive, and wore it in a fall down her back, framing her face. In the dusky light of the room, her eyes were wide, pale blue, almost colorless, rimmed in soot-dark lashes. Her lips stood out with startling clarity in the gloom, the kind of lips that since his childhood Longarm had heard called a bee-stung mouth. He got the impression of a face rounded rather than angular, and the loose wrap that she wore gave no hint as to her figure.

She indicated the easy chair. "If we're going to talk, I guess we might as well sit down. But I don't see why you'd want to talk to me. Everybody else just asks for Uncle Clay, and when I tell them he's not here and I don't know where he is, they don't waste any time in getting away."

"You set a lot of store by your uncle, don't you?"

"Uncle Clay was more my daddy than my real one was. Why wouldn't I think the world and all of him?"

"Nobody'd fault you for that, Miss Amy."

"Oh my God! Please, if you're going to call me something, don't make it 'Miss Amy.' I hear that until I'm sick of it. And I still don't know your name or what you want of me. You said you're not a Ranger. Who are you, then?"

Longarm had decided by now that he had nothing to lose by telling her. "My name's Long, Amy. And I'm a Deputy U.S. Marshal out of the Denver office."

"A U.S. Marshal? Does that mean you want to arrest Uncle Clay, too?"

"No. What the Rangers are after him for ain't a matter that's in federal jurisdiction. But I do want to talk to him before—" Longarm stopped short.

Amy finished for him. "Before the Rangers catch up with him and gun him down?" She laughed bitterly. "Because that's what'll happen if they find him. Everybody in Texas knows you don't stand trial for killing a Ranger, not if another Ranger gets to you first. Isn't that right, Marshal?"

"I've heard it said. But look here, if we're going to talk like friends, and I'm going to call you Amy, I guess you'd better call me something besides Marshal."

"Long, then? Isn't that what you said your name is?"

"Yes. But my friends mostly call me by a sort of nickname. Longarm."

"You think we can be friends? You're trying to run Uncle Clay to earth, and I'm trying to protect him. How can we?"

"I'm not looking for him with a gun pointed at him, or an arrest warrant. Don't you think that's enough reason, Amy?"

Amy thought for a moment and nodded. "Yes. I guess it is."

While they'd been talking, Longarm had been studying the girl as best he could, now that he could see her more clearly. She was not as young as he'd thought on first impression. Amy must be in her late twenties, he decided; either age or worry had begun to scratch tiny lines at the corners of her eyelids and from her nostrils to the corners of her pouting lips. She was old enough to be her own woman, he decided.

"Would you mind if I smoked a cigar?" he asked.

"Of course not. Uncle Clay liked cigars. It'd make me feel more at home if you did. I've been feeling strange in this house, all alone, ever since he left. I'd offer you a drink, but I don't have anything on hand."

"If you'd like to join me in a sip, I've got a bottle of Maryland rye in my saddlebag," he offered.

Amy debated for a moment; Longarm could almost see her mind at work. At last she said, "I think I'd enjoy a little drink, Longarm. I'll get some glasses and a pitcher of water while you go after the whiskey."

Amy was bringing in a tray with a pitcher and glasses on it when Longarm came back with the bottle. She put the tray on a table and Longarm uncorked the whiskey.

"I'll let you pour for yourself," he said. "I got the idea that water spoils the taste of good drinking whiskey."

For the first time, Amy smiled. "That's almost exactly what Uncle Clay always says." She poured a generous slug of the rye into her glass and added some water. "You know, a lot of people think it's depraved for a woman to drink hard liquor, but Uncle Clay taught me to enjoy the taste of it." She waited for Longarm to pour his drink and held out her glass for him to touch with his. "Well, Longarm, I still don't know what you're after, but I'm glad you knocked at the door. I feel like a human being again, and I haven't felt that way often the past several months."

Longarm didn't answer until he'd tossed off a good swallow of the rye in his glass and resumed his seat. He waited for Amy to sit down. He was very conscious that her eyes were fixed on him, studying him. He said carefully, "I think a woman—or a man—ought to do just about what pleases them, as long as it don't hurt somebody else."

"Try telling that to some of these old biddies around Georgetown," Amy said. "Why, a lot of them think I'm a scarlet woman just because I'm living here by myself."

"You don't really think your uncle's going to come back to Texas, do you?" he asked. "With the Rangers after him?"

"I don't know. All I do is hope." Amy looked off into the distance of her mind for a moment, then said, "You never have told me why you're looking for him, though."

"It's not much of a secret. I just want to ask him some questions about things that happened quite a spell ago, not anything that'll get him in the kind of trouble he's in now."

Amy finished her drink. There was a different timbre to her voice when she said, "If there was anything I could tell you, I would. You're the first person who's been halfway decent to me for a long time." She paused for a moment, and again Longarm was aware that she was studying him, a tiny frown rippling her brow. Abruptly, she asked, "What's your wife like, Longarm? Your job must take you away a lot. Does she object to that?"

"I haven't got a wife, Amy. Don't know as I'd want one, in my job."

"You must meet a lot of women, though."

"Oh, I meet a lot of all kinds of people."

"I'm not talking about just people. I said *women*, remember? Women who're—well, feeling out of sorts, lost, like I do."

"Sometimes," he hedged.

"Women who think you're attractive the first time they see you?" she persisted.

"Now, what kind of question is that?" Longarm asked.

"An honest one." Amy got up and perched on the arm of the easy chair where Longarm was sitting. "Women who just can't keep from putting their hands on you. Like this." She stroked her hand up along Longarm's thigh to his crotch. "Women who know you've got something they want and need." She was squeezing him now, and Longarm began to react to the pressure of her fingers. "Women whose lips are just thirsty for kisses." Amy bent to kiss him.

Longarm flexed his lips under the pressure of hers, and Amy's tongue darted into his mouth. He found one of her breasts with his calloused hand and started to caress and squeeze it. Her lips parted more widely, and the pressure of her hand squeezing on him became more insistent.

Longarm put his glass on the floor, shifting slightly in the chair as he did so. Amy let herself fall backward into his lap. Her free hand fumbled at the narrow sash that held her robe together. The robe parted, and Longarm's fingers encountered bare flesh, warmly vibrant.

Amy broke their kiss to whisper, "You do want to, don't you, Longarm?"

"Sure I do. If you're sure you do, too."

"I wouldn't ask you unless I did." Amy stood up and tugged at Longarm's hand. "Come on. It's just as dim and cozy in the bedroom."

Longarm let her lead him through the door at the back of the room. They were in the bedroom now. A tousled bed stood against one wall. Amy said, "Get undressed fast, Longarm. I'll go pour us fresh drinks while you're getting your clothes off."

Longarm's eyes scanned the room while he shed his coat and vest. He hung the vest on the bedpost, where the derringer in its right-hand pocket would be handy. He unbuckled his gunbelt and hung it over the vest, the butt of the Colt forward where he could grab it quickly. He was in no hurry. He was still just half-erect, and had taken off only his boots and shirt when Amy returned. She carried a glass in each hand.

"You're a slowpoke!" she exclaimed. She handed Longarm the glass containing the darker liquid and set her own glass on the dresser after taking a deep swallow. Her eyes were shining with anticipation when she turned back to Longarm. "Here. I'll help you undress."

Amy still had the robe on, gaping open in front and

hanging loosely from her shoulders. Longarm could see the softly rounded curves of her pink-tipped breasts, the tautness of her abdomen, the gentle swelling of her stomach and the blond, tufted triangle at the apex of her thighs. He cradled her breasts in his hands, squeezing them gently, while she unbuttoned his jeans and balbriggans and pulled them down below his hips.

"Oh my!" she breathed when she saw his erection spring up as the garments dropped. "You look like the best thing that's happened to me in a long time, Longarm!"

Longarm had bent his head to rub his lips and the wiry hairs of his moustache over the budded tips of her breasts. He stopped long enough to say, "You look pretty good to me, too."

He pulled her to him. Amy opened her thighs to straddle him, squeezing her thighs together, pressing her hips close to his and rocking against him urgently. Longarm kicked clumsily to get rid of the jeans and balbriggans wrinkled around his ankles. Amy was clinging to him, pressing down on his erection. He felt her moistness on him.

"About time we tried the bed, I'd say," he told her.

Together they shuffled to the bed. Amy turned around just as they reached its side. She let herself fall backward. Longarm fell with her, holding to their embrace. For a moment they lay motionless. Amy's breathing was gusty on Longarm's cheek.

She whispered, "I'm more than ready for you. But go into me slow, Longarm. Ever so slow. I want to feel every inch of you sliding in."

Longarm did as she'd asked. He took his time, letting himself down slowly until they were almost totally merged, then driving hard in a lunge that set Amy shuddering and breathing raggedly.

"Don't move for a little while," she whispered. "I'm so close to letting go. And I don't want to, at least not yet."

Longarm lay still. He watched Amy's face in the dim light of the shaded room until her lips stopped twisting and settled into a relaxed smile. Then he began to stroke, gently and steadily.

Amy exploded into a sudden frenzy of motion, twisting

and heaving beneath him until he had to pin her with the full weight of his body. She writhed beneath him until the breath rushed from her throat in a long, expiring moan and she quivered one last time before lying still.

For several minutes she said nothing, then she sighed. "I disappointed you, didn't I?"

"Not for a minute," he assured her.

"But you didn't—"

"No. But there's not any need to hurry."

"I tried to hold back, I really did. But I just had to let go. I could almost let go again right now, I've had to wait so long. Everybody's been afraid to come close to me, even to talk to me, since Uncle Clay's trouble."

"Let go whenever you feel like it," Longarm said. He began to thrust again, sinking himself into her hot readiness.

Amy rolled under him, brought up her legs and clamped them around his hips. He'd stroked for only a minute or two when she went into another spasm of ecstasy, more prolonged than the first. Longarm slowed briefly, then resumed his deep thrusts.

"Wait," she said after a moment. "I want to feel you deeper than you can go this way. Unless you—"

"Any way that pleasures you," Longarm told her.

She pushed him gently off her, and Longarm stood beside the bed while she positioned herself. Amy sat up on the bed and grasped an ankle in each hand, then fell back, pulling her feet above her head.

He knelt in front of her and leaned forward. Amy released her ankles, letting them rest on Longarm's shoulders. She grabbed him eagerly and guided him to her dripping crotch. He thrust forward and she gasped with a racheting of breath deep in her throat.

"Oh, that's it!" she cried. "Now drive on in! Let me take every inch of you!"

Longarm did as she asked. He braced his knees and lunged forward, feeling himself go deep. Amy began to babble incoherently within minutes. He kept thrusting, feeling himself building now, but holding himself back until at last Amy's garbled, throaty cries rose almost to a scream and he felt the muscles of her stomach contracting convulsively under his muscular belly.

"Right now!" she exclaimed. "Hurry! Hurry, Longarm! Come with me this time!"

Longarm let himself go. A thrust or two more and his body began shaking in rhythm with hers as he felt himself draining in a quivering spasm that matched hers. He held himself pressed hard against Amy's soft body until she stopped quivering and then stirred as though to move away. Then he got up and she stretched her strained legs out on the bed, her eyes dreamily half-shut. Longarm lay down by her.

"Thank you, Longarm," Amy whispered, kissing him softly on a corner of his lips. She frowned and asked, "You don't have to leave for a while, do you?"

"No. Why?"

"Because I'd like to nap a minute or two. Not long, just a little while. I've been alone such a long time, I haven't had a really good sleep—"

"Sure," he interrupted. "I know how it gets sometimes. You go on and sleep. I'll be right here by you."

With a contented sigh, Amy snuggled up to Longarm, her head on his shoulder. Within a few moments, she was breathing the deep, regular breaths of a peaceful sleeper.

Chapter 3

Longarm waited until Amy was sleeping soundly, then slipped quietly out of bed, easing her head off his shoulder and onto a pillow. She stirred and murmured, but did not wake up. Lighting a cheroot, he went into the living room and poured a fresh tot of Maryland rye, then returned to the bedroom where he sat studying the sleeping Amy.

He'd finished one cheroot and was on his second, puffing it thoughtfully, when Amy rolled restlessly on the bed. Her hands stroked the pillow, then ran down the sheet where Longarm had been lying. Her eyes opened and she sat up.

"Oh!" she sighed when she saw Longarm sitting naked in the chair beside the bed. "I couldn't feel you by me, and for a minute I thought I'd been dreaming." She stretched with catlike luxury before adding, "Except I knew it couldn't be a dream. I feel too good for it to have been."

"No. You weren't dreaming," Longarm said. "I just been sitting here studying you and wondering how much of what you told me I could believe."

Amy sat up, an indignant scowl on her face. "What do you mean, Longarm?"

"I mean your story don't hold together. You're not just a little girl that's lonesome for one of her relatives. You might call Clayton Maddox your uncle, but from the way you took on while we were taking our pleasure together, he must've been a lot more'n that to you."

She did not reply at once, but crossed her legs, Indian-style, and sat facing him. A thoughtful look was on her face. Finally, she sighed and said, "I suppose I might as

30

well tell you what you haven't already guessed. If I don't, you're the kind of man who'll start digging and find out all about it anyhow." She sighed again. "It's not much of a story, Longarm, but I need a little more Dutch courage before I can tell all of it. Will you get me another drink, please?"

Longarm brought the bottle in from the living room and poured an inch of rye into her glass. Amy took a thoughtful sip, studying his face. Longarm said nothing, but sipped from his own glass between puffs on his cheroot.

"Well, putting it off won't make things easier," Amy said at last. "I guess I'd better go back to the beginning."

Longarm nodded. "That's usually a pretty good place to start."

"I'll have to go back a while," she began. "You were right when you guessed that Clay's not my real uncle. He's family, but not blood kin. That didn't stop him from offering to take care of me when my mother died, and there wasn't anyplace I could go except to an orphan's home. And can you imagine what it'd be like for a girl going on fourteen in an orphan's home, Longarm?"

"Maybe not real good. But I can get a glimmering."

Amy nodded. "I think you might, at that. You're the kind of man who understands things. Well, to cut out all but what's really important, Clay put me through school, and fed me and saw I had decent clothes, and things like that. And I guess it would've happened sooner or later, the way I felt about him, maybe the way he felt about me. But we wound up—well, sleeping in the same bed."

"That's pretty much the way I thought it'd be," Longarm told her. "Something about the way you sounded when you talked about him. Go on."

Amy shook her head. "It's something I don't understand. About a year before Clay—" she hesitated before going on— "before Clay shot Captain Elzey, he didn't seem to be able to pleasure me anymore. Not that he didn't try. And so I took on a man or two—oh, hell, I spread my legs for anybody who looked at me, if you want the real fact of how it was. It wasn't quite the same as it'd been with Clay, but he wasn't any good to me." She

31

shrugged. "You know about the rest, I guess, or you wouldn't be here looking for him."

"Well, it explains about what I'd figured out. Not all of it, but mostly. I knew there had to be a reason for the way you acted. Not that it helps me much."

"You enjoyed it, though, didn't you?" Amy got off the bed and stood in front of Longarm. She looked down at him, sitting naked in the chair. "I know I did. It was just what I needed, especially with somebody who's got as much as you have to give a woman."

She dropped to her knees in front of Longarm and began to stroke him. Longarm felt himself stirring under the touch of her warm, soft hands.

Amy asked him, "Do you like to have a woman kiss you, Longarm?"

"I like whatever a woman enjoys."

"And I enjoy feeling a man get hard in my mouth."

Amy leaned forward and began to kiss him. Her tongue darted out over his flaccid tip. He began to grow hard. She took him into her mouth, deeply at first, then, as he swelled into a jutting erection, more shallowly.

Longarm enjoyed the sensation, but not the isolation. He liked to take part when he was pleasing a woman. He put his hands in Amy's armpits and lifted her. She resisted at first, as though reluctant to stop, but he brought her up bodily, held her above him until she opened her thighs, and then, as he lowered her slowly, Amy's hand snaked down to guide him. She sank down with a throbbing sigh as he penetrated deeper and deeper, then began to rock back and forth above him.

Her breasts were level with Longarm's mouth. He kissed their budded tips, taking them between his lips, caressing first one, then the other with his tongue, and occasionally rubbing across their hard pinkness with the wiry bristles of his mustache. Each time he caressed her breasts, Amy shuddered with delight. Her head was flung back, her honey-gold hair cascading down to Longarm's knees.

Longarm was not holding back, this time. Amy's preliminary caresses had aroused him well. He began to thrust upward as the speed of her rocking gyrations increased and the tempo of her movements became spasmodic. She cried out—a long, keening wail—and Longarm brought his hips upward in a sustained thrust. Then Amy melted into trembling limpness as Longarm jetted and sank back on the chair. She sagged forward against him. Their bodies were both moist and trembling.

Amy sighed after a moment, breaking the silence of the dimly lit room. She stood up slowly and stepped back. Longarm started to rise, but she put a hand on his chest and pushed him back to the chair.

"No. Sit still a minute, I'll be right back."

She disappeared through the bedroom's rear door, and Longarm heard the muted clanking of a cistern pump. In a moment, Amy came back carrying a pan of water and a towel. She knelt in front of Longarm and washed him, the water cold on his crotch. Putting the pan on the bureau, Amy slipped on her robe and belted it.

"I'll see if I can find us something to eat, while you dress," she said. "I imagine you're hungry, and I know I'm starving."

Longarm picked up his scattered garments and put them on. He heard Amy rattling dishes in the kitchen, and went out to join her. She was standing in front of the open cupboard, holding a link of summer sausage and a box of soda crackers. She turned when she heard Longarm's footsteps.

"I guess this is all I've got to eat. I haven't paid much attention to food lately."

"It'll do fine," he said. "I'm not all that hungry, anyhow, I had a big meal at the boardinghouse just before I started out to find you."

"Well, I'm starved. Sit down, Longarm. I'll slice the sausage and we can visit while we're eating."

Amy ate hungrily, but Longarm did little more than nibble at a slice of the sausage and a cracker or two. He gave Amy time to satisfy her own hunger before he went back to his interrupted questioning. This time, he had a little more to go on.

"Clay Maddox must've been a pretty shrewd man," he suggested. "He must've left some kind of hint where he was going and what he was going to do. With the way things were between you and him, he wouldn't've just pulled stakes. He'd've let you know, somehow, what he had in mind."

Amy shook her head. "He didn't, though. Not a single word. He left the day he—the day of the shooting—and all he said was that he was going to Austin to see about rejoining the Rangers. I didn't know what happened until the next day, when the Rangers came looking for him."

"And he never sent you a letter? Not even a postcard?"

Amy's face took on a puzzled frown. "He did send me a postcard. I got it about two weeks after the Rangers had been here. It didn't say anything that made sense, though."

"Where'd he mail it from?"

"Uvalde. And there was just one line on it. It wasn't even signed, but I knew Clay's handwriting, of course."

Longarm's instinct told him he'd cut a trail of some kind. He wasn't quite sure what it was, yet, though. He asked, "What did that one line say, Amy?"

"I told you, nothing that made sense. All he wrote was just that one sentence. 'Look where it is hidden.'"

"And that was all?"

"Every word."

Longarm dropped the slice of sausage he'd been nibbling on and took out a cheroot. He flicked a sulfur match across his thumbnail and lighted the long, thin cigar. His eyebrows were pulled together in a frown.

That's got to mean something, old son, he told himself, ignoring Amy's questioning stare. *Uvalde's west of here, west of Austin, and maybe the fastest way to Mexico, where Billy said the Rangers had trailed him. But Amy's right. What he wrote don't make a bit of sense. Unless—*

He turned to her and asked, "Amy, did your uncle talk Mexican?"

"Spanish?"

"Same thing. Did he know the lingo?"

"Yes, of course. I think he was stationed on the border at one time, when he was a Ranger."

Longarm racked his brain, summoning up his half-

34

forgotten bits and scraps of Spanish. He started to ask Amy another question, but thought better of it. He was suddenly impatient to get back on his interrupted trail.

He stood up and said, "Amy, it's time for me to be moving again. Not that I want to go, you understand, but I've got to."

Her smile had begun to fade the instant Longarm stood up. She said, "I was hoping you'd stay with me tonight, at least. The nights are worse than anything, you know."

Longarm nodded. "I can see how that'd be. But I've got to get back to Austin, see if I can't find a trail to pick up."

"I'm sorry I couldn't help you."

"Oh, you did. More than just helped."

As Longarm started to leave, Amy hurried to his side. "Longarm . . . will you let me know if you find out anything about Clay? Whether he's all right, how he's doing. Just anything at all."

"You know I will. Don't look for too much too fast, though." Longarm bent to kiss her upturned face.

"No. I'm used to waiting now . . . as much as anybody ever does get used to it."

She stood in the doorway to watch Longarm ride off. He turned once to wave at her. She'd closed the door by then, except for a crack. His last glimpse of Amy was like his first, an impression of dark eyes gazing from a darkened room.

Back in Austin, with the sun already down and the last flush of a red sunset fading behind the banks of the Colorado River, Longarm stopped first at the I&GN Depot; it was the first railroad station he passed on his way into town. He'd been going over his newborn theory, wondering whether he was being too hasty, whether he'd jumped to a false conclusion on the basis of a hunch and a hope. After hitching the livery horse to the long rail in front of the station, he went in. He found the agent in charge and introduced himself.

"I'd imagine you've got a bunch of maps around here that'd help me," he told the agent. "Think you could drag out a few for me to look at?"

"We've got plenty of maps, sure. But what're you looking for?"

"Whichever one takes in the most of Mexico."

"That's easy. Our surveyors are always looking for routes down there, even if we don't have much luck getting any trackage laid south of the Rio Grande. Come on up to the drafting room."

Out of the half-dozen maps the station agent brought out of the big, flat files, Longarm selected one that showed the northeastern section of Mexico in large scale. He pored over it under the bright carbide lamp, following the few roads that showed. Finally his finger stopped. He studied the map for a minute, then turned to the agent.

"You talk any Spanish?" he asked.

"Some. Around here, you've got to, just about."

Longarm nodded at the spot where his finger rested. "Maybe you can tell me if I'm right about what this means."

Peering at the map, the station agent muttered, " 'La Escondida'? That what you're talking about?"

"That's it. What does it mean in English?"

"Why, as near as I can translate, it means 'the hidden,' or maybe 'the secret.' That what you're after?"

Longarm nodded. "I read it that way, too, but I've damn near forgot what little of the language I know. I just wanted to make sure I was right." Longarm handed the map back to the agent. "Thanks, friend, you've been a real help. Now all I got to do is figure out the easiest and quickest way to get there."

Looking at the map, the agent told him, "That's not much of a trick. Take the SP to Eagle Pass, and then get on the Mexican railroad to Monterrey. That'll put you in about sixty or seventy miles from La Escondida, as close as I can tell, looking at this map."

"And I'd guess I can get a livery horse in Monterrey to take me the rest of the way?"

"You sure won't get past Monterrey on any railroad I know about, Marshal. They're pushing iron as fast as they can to connect up with the Mexican railroad mainline that runs to El Paso, but they've still got a ways to go.

36

Pretty rough country southeast of Monterrey. Mountains, not much water. Anyplace beyond Monterrey, you'll have to get to on horseback."

"Well, that's my problem, ain't it? Thanks again for your help, friend."

At dusk, two days later, his bones aching from the jolting of an antique day coach on the Ferrocarriles Nacional de Mexico, Longarm swung off the dilapidated railroad car in Monterrey and walked forward along the train, carrying his saddle in one hand, his rifle in the other, and his saddlebags slung over one shoulder.

He'd put in the three hours of waiting at Eagle Pass between the SP and the Mexican National Railway by requisitioning a cavalry horse at Fort Duncan. Longarm wasn't sure a Mexican livery horse would understand his limited Spanish vocabulary.

With the cavalry roan saddled, he swung on and rode down the Calle Morelos to the Plaza Zaragoza, following the directions he'd been given by the Mexican conductor, and had no trouble identifying the arched facade of the Posada Ancirra. The plaza was just coming to life. Longarm heard the strains of a mariachi band, and saw figures strolling around the plaza in the gathering dark, but put aside the temptation to sample Monterrey's attractions of the evening.

Old son, he told himself, *you just better keep your head low and your peter in your pants while you're here. That hotel looks like it's a real nice place, and maybe there won't be too many bugs in the bed. You still don't know whether you're just making a harebrained trip with nothing at the end of it, following a damn wild hunch. There's a pretty good ways to go to get to La Escondida, and trouble's got a way of following you.*

Following his own sound advice, Longarm ate a quiet supper in the Ancirra dining room and went to bed.

Midmorning found Longarm well on the way to his destination. He'd been shifting in the saddle since shortly after daybreak as the roan followed the climbing, winding road

—more trail than road, in reality—near the spine of the Sierra Madre Oriente. It was a deserted road, though well marked by the hooves of horses, mules, human feet, and even the ruts of the two-wheeled carts he remembered from his earlier visit.

These were younger mountains than the Rockies, where Longarm felt at home, younger and much farther south, on the edge of a tropical zone. On both sides the peaks rose jagged and bare in the beating sunshine. There was no shade except for that of an occasional thin *ocote* pine, or the feathery branches of an acacia. In places, the trail skirted the rim of a deep *barranca*, and in some of these wide, craggy valleys, Longarm could see the signs of abandoned mines.

Now and then the hairs on the nape of Longarm's neck prickled and rose. The feeling was familiar to him from all the times he'd traveled through areas populated by Mexicans; he attributed it to the *miradores*—the Watchers—whose presence could be felt everywhere on Mexican trails and roads. In any other place, such a feeling would have triggered his sharply honed instinct to rein in and reach for his Winchester in its saddle scabbard, but he knew that the most he would be likely to see of the enigmatic *miradores* would be a distant figure silhouetted against the sky on a high ridge. Maybe. It was far more probable that he would see nothing at all. So, even though he searched the sparsely vegetated landscape with eyes sharpened by the countless times he'd ridden across a strange and alien countryside, he only spotted, once or twice, the white rump of a small deer as it bounded away down one of the slopes.

He stopped at noon to eat, and to give the roan a longer rest than he'd allowed the horse since he'd started from Monterrey, then rode on steadily until dusk. Just before dark, he came to a saddle in the road, a dip between two steep slopes. It was as good a place as any to stop for the night; he wasn't sure how much farther he had to go.

Supper was a repetition of lunch. He'd been able to buy only local provisions for his trip: thin corn tortillas; some links of dry-cured *salchicha*, heavily spiced with red pepper; a few puffy *bizcochos*. Still, he was making a meal, Longarm thought as he chewed on the peppery sausage, taking big bites of tortilla to cut the tang of the spicy meat.

Back on the trail at sunrise, Longarm found the going easier as the winding pathway threaded through a pass and began to descend the slope into a wide valley. From his height on the upper slopes, Longarm could see the stream meandering along the valley floor. It was a creek, not really big enough to be called a river, but it provided water through a gridwork of irrigation *acequias* to keep green the fields that lay between the irrigation ditches.

Descending the slope, Longarm caught an occasional glimpse of a cluster of houses huddling on a small rise beside the stream. The distance he'd covered, judging by the length of time he'd been traveling, meant that the village must be La Escondida, he thought. He kneed the roan to a little faster pace on the gently sloping trail.

Rounding a sharp bend in the trail, he suddenly found himself approaching a small building just beside the path, which was beginning to show signs of turning into a road. A saddled horse was tethered outside the little structure. As Longarm came closer, a man carrying a rifle at ready stepped out of the hut. He wore the crossed bandoliers and ornately decorated sombrero that to Longarm meant only one thing: *rurale*. He signaled with his rifle for Longarm to halt.

"*Buenas dias, senor,*" the sentry said.

Longarm reined in and nodded. "The same to you, *amigo.*"

"*Gringo, no? Americano?*"

"That's right. Sorry I don't savvy your lingo. But all I'm interested in is getting on to that town up ahead," Longarm replied. He'd learned that it was better never to let a *rurale* know that he could speak and understand a little of the language.

"You go to La Escondida, *sí?*" the *rurale* asked.

"If that's the place up the road," Longarm nodded.

"You got papers, no?"

"Some. Depends on what kind."

"So, you got some. You go to *la cuartel general*, in La Escondida. You onderstan'?"

"I guess you mean the *rurale* headquarters?" Longarm asked.

"Ah, *sí*." The sentry smiled, nodding. *"Habla con el Capitán Sanchez, sí?"*

"Sí. Your boss? *El jefe?"*

Smiling broadly, the sentry nodded and waved Longarm on.

Longarm returned the wave and rode on down the trail. It was a road now, with occasionally a smaller trail branching off it. Ahead, the houses of La Escondida were growing larger.

Well, old son, Longarm told himself as the roan continued to carry him closer to his destination, *if you was the prayerful kind, you'd be making a couple of prayers right now. One being that your hunch was right. And the other one being that you don't run into none of the* rurales *you tangled with the last time you was in Mexico.*

Chapter 4

This La Escondida sure ain't such a much of a town, Longarm thought as he rode past the first houses. The place seemed only one street wide, though here and there a house or two straggled back from the others.

All the houses he passed at first were single-story dwellings, little better than shacks. Most of them were made of adobe, some of adobe bricks, others simply by plastering the brown mud itself into the spaces between poles driven into the ground in a rough square or rectangle. Thatched roofs were the rule, and many of them looked less than waterproof.

Windows were unglazed; doors, if they had doors other than a gaping opening, were a few boards held together with cross-slats and hung by leather straps or loops of wire. In most of the yards, scrawny chickens scratched in the baked soil. Goats were tethered beside a few of the houses, but Longarm noticed only two or three cows. There were almost as many children as chickens.

Women lounged in some of the doorways, and occasionally there were two or three women standing together, gossiping. The character of the dwellings improved as Longarm rode on. More and more of them were adobe bricks with linteled porticos, some paved with brick. Many of the houses bore decorations of colorful tiles set into their walls as borders for doors or windows, and all the houses were larger.

Longarm entered the plaza, the central square around which the lives of most villages in Mexico centered. Around the square were stores, a *posada* with a sign reading *Hotel Grande del Oriente,* and two buildings with the

41

swinging batwing doors that had either migrated south from the U.S. or north into the U.S. These boasted wooden plaques over their doorways with *Cantina* burned into the wood. Streets radiated from the corners of the plaza, and Longarm could see other houses of a substantial nature facing them.

It had been a long, dry ride. The sun had already dropped behind the mountain crests west of the town, and lights were to be seen in most of the buildings and dwellings. Longarm reined the roan in at the hitch rail before one of the cantinas and pushed through the swinging doors.

A pair of kerosene lamps fought the gloom of the narrow, low-ceilinged barroom. The bar that stretched the full length of the room was respectable enough, made of native wood instead of the traditional mahogany, and there were open shelves along the backbar, which lacked the usual mirror. A lone barkeep lounged at one of the tables scattered around the room. He stepped behind the bar when he saw Longarm, and waited.

"Buenas tardes, señor. Qué quiere?"

"Whiskey. Maryland rye, if you got some."

"Americano, no?" the barkeep asked. He smiled. "I talk it a little the English. Wheesky, I onderstan', but thees marieland rye, *qué es esto?*"

"Oh, hell, just pour me the best whiskey you got," Longarm said. "It'd take too long to explain about Maryland rye, and I'm thirsty."

While he'd been talking to the barkeep, another customer had entered. As the newcomer stepped up to the bar, Longarm saw that he was an American. Longarm scanned him without seeming to do so, a quick flicker of his eyes with his head turning so slightly that his movement would pass unnoticed.

"Well, well!" the man said. "Welcome to La Escondida, friend. My name's Sam Ferris, and since you're the newest American in town, the drinks are on me."

He tossed a silver peso on the bar and said something in Spanish to the barkeep before extending his hand.

Longarm took the outstretched hand. It was firm and as

calloused as his own. Custom now allowed him to size the newcomer up openly, and he did so as they shook hands.

Ferris was a chunky man, shorter than Longarm, though almost as broad. His face was as chunky as his body. His jaw was a block of bone and muscle, his cheekbones high, his eyes slitted above them. Judging from his eyebrows and blue eyes, Longarm guessed that his hair would be sandy. Ferris wore duck jeans tucked into miner's boots, a tan shirt, and a flat-brimmed, Dakota-creased hat. His gunbelt sagged from the weight of a holstered Remington worn low on his right hip.

"Long," Longarm said succinctly, releasing Ferris's hand.

"You here on business? Or just passing through?" Ferris asked.

"That depends. Guess you'd say I'm sorta looking for a reason to stop. If I find one, I might stay a while."

Ferris nodded. "Well, there's just a few of us here. Always glad to see a new face, Long." The barkeep had placed glasses and poured their drinks while the two talked.

Ferris raised his glass. "Here's how," he said brightly.

Longarm nodded. They sipped the whiskey. It was better than Longarm had expected. He fished out a cheroot and lighted it.

Ferris went on, "Have you had supper yet?"

"Not yet. I just this minute blew in, needed a swallow to cut the trail dust. You got a good place to eat here?"

"If you like the native grub. But I was just thinking— the lady I work for's having a little blowout tonight. Just for us Americans, of course. Outside of two or three saloon bums, there's only five of us from the States in this damn place. I know she'd be mad at me if I didn't invite you."

Longarm didn't hesitate to take the opportunity to meet La Escondida's American colony so easily, but courtesy demanded a suitable hesitation. Besides, he didn't want his eagerness to show.

"You sure about that?" he asked Ferris.

"If I wasn't sure, I'd've kept my jaws shut."

"Then, I reckon it'd be my pleasure to join you. And to thank you, I'm buying the next round."

Ferris was as punctilious as Longarm in observing protocol. It was a time when some men changed names oftener than their shirts, when today's outlaw might be tomorrow's lawman, today's gambler tomorrow's city official, or vice versa. Politeness barred personal questions being asked by men meeting for the first time on strange territory. He was as silent as Longarm while they downed their drinks.

When their glasses were emptied, Ferris looked questioningly at Longarm, who nodded. Ferris led the way outside.

Darkness was nearly full by now, the sky a deep, rich blue in the east, fading to a narrow strip of pale azure in the west. The peaks of the Sierra Madre Oriente cut the skies on all sides of the wide valley in which the town lay, irregular black chunks, their flanks already in the darkness.

Ferris jerked a thumb at the cavalry roan. "Yours?"

Longarm nodded. "I guess there's a livery here where I can board the critter?"

"No. But there's room for it in our stable. You can keep it there and welcome."

"That hotel back there," Longarm remarked as he followed Ferris, leading the roan along the quiet evening street, "I guess it's the only place to stay?"

"You guess right, Long. It's not too bad, though. There'll be plenty of time for you to get settled later on."

At the corner of the plaza, Ferris led the way down one of the streets that led off the square's corner. Longarm was peering around as they walked, trying to get oriented, to get the feeling of the town. There were only a few others on the street: men in loose suits of coarse cotton, pants with a blouse worn dangling to their hips, low-crowned straw hats with broad, ragged brims. No women seemed to be abroad now.

"What the hell does this town live on?" he asked Ferris.

"Oh, they raise some maize, and a little bit of cotton, and beans. And there's grassland where there's not enough water for crops, *el Patrón* runs some cattle on it. Of course, we hire a few men out at the mine."

"You're getting ahead of me," Longarm said. "Who's

this *el Patrón*? And what kind of mine is it you're talking about?"

"Time enough for that later," Ferris told him. "We're here."

They'd passed three or four houses, and now Ferris stopped in front of the next, a large dwelling made of adobe bricks. Like the others, it presented an almost blank front to the street: two high, narrow windows with shutters that now swung open, and a sturdy wooden door. Only a faint light trickled through the windows.

"We might as well go around and in through the patio," he told Longarm. "I'll get one of the boys to look after your animal."

He led the way beyond the house, along a high adobe wall, and turned into a narrow passage that separated the wall from the next house. A wide gate broke the fence after they'd walked a few yards; Longarm followed Ferris through it, into a flagstone-paved patio. Lights from the house spilled through wide open windows and a broad double door into the enclosed area. At the back of the patio, Longarm saw two smaller houses and the yawning opening of a stable.

A young Mexican, wearing the same costume Longarm had noticed on the street, came running up. Ferris shot a stream of Spanish at the youth; he spoke too fast for Longarm to follow.

"Juanito'll take care of your horse," Ferris said. "You've got truck in your saddlebags, I guess. Don't worry about it; it'll be safe. Come on in and meet my boss."

A table spread for a meal stood in the center of the large room they entered from the patio. The woman bending over the table turned around when Longarm and Ferris came in.

"Oh, Sam," she said. "I thought it was about time for you to get here."

"I'm a little bit late, I guess," Ferris replied. "Julia, this is Mr. Long. I didn't think you'd mind if I asked him to dinner."

"Why, that's wonderful!" she exclaimed, extending her hand to Longarm. "We're delighted, Mr. Long. A new face

45

is a real treat, here in La Escondida. And Sam didn't mention it, but my name's Wheatly."

Longarm took her hand and studied her as he shook it. Julia Wheatly was, he judged, at the far edge of her thirties, perhaps past them by a year or two. She wore a plain black satin dress with a lace collar its only relieving note. A brooch of gold and diamonds was at her throat.

She was a tall woman, and her body had the fullness of maturity, a sturdy richness of flesh without fat. Her face was round; it was a pleasant face, unremarkable, with even features, still unlined except for shallow frown-wrinkles on her high brow and smile-creases at the corners of her generous lips. Her hair was black and showed no gray strands, and was worn in a loose bun low on the back of her head.

"I'm right pleased to meet you, Mrs. Wheatly," Longarm said. "Ferris told me you were having some folks in for supper. I hope me being here won't upset your party."

"Of course it won't. The others will be as pleased as I am. And it's not a formal party, just a little birthday celebration for the young son of the only real family of Americans who live here in La Escondida."

"That eases my mind," Longarm said. "It's nice of you to make me welcome."

Mrs. Wheatly turned to Ferris. "Sam, why don't you show Mr. Long where to put his hat and wash up? The others should be getting here soon."

Walking down a short hallway to the bathroom, Ferris said, "She's a real nice lady, Mrs. Wheatly. Husband died a little less than a year ago, and she went right on with the gold mine he'd been developing. Kept me in my job, too."

"You'd been with her husband a long time, I guess?"

"For a while, sure. Nice of her, just the same." Ferris pointed to a door. "Bathroom. You can find your way back all right, I guess."

Feeling better for the removal of several layers of trail dust, when Longarm returned to the spacious *sala*, he found that the other dinner guests had arrived. His professional suspicions had already been aroused by Ferris; the man was a bit overly affable, which he'd learned in several

46

of his cases served as a good device for fugitives to avoid the impression that they had anything to hide. And Ferris had been almost deliberately vague about the length of time he'd worked for the dead Wheatly.

After introductions, when they settled at the dinner table, Longarm took little part in the conversation. He watched and listened, filing away the characteristics of the two men of the party, trying to pick the most likely candidate to fit the sparse details he knew about Clayton Maddox.

George Blanton, a stolid, somewhat soft and peaceable-looking man, seemed the least likely of the two. Longarm got the impression that Blanton was exactly what he seemed to be, a Protestant missionary to Catholic Mexico. For one thing, Blanton's plump, pleasant wife, Dora, and their young son, Bobby, pretty obviously lacked the ability to play the roles they'd have had to assume. Still, Longarm reminded himself, fugitives seemed to have an uncanny ability to acquire families in order to ward off suspicion. He wasn't yet ready to write off Blanton, but he rated the plumply affable, balding man as an outside prospect at best.

Terrance Barns seemed a likely choice, as Longarm studied him across the dinner table. Barns was the type of young-old man who could be any age from thirty to fifty. His hair was an indeterminate sandy blond, a shade in which a few gray strands would go unnoticed either on his head or in his full mustache. Barns's eyes were a pale gray, his eyebrows sparse, his skin the ruddy sort that became a deeper hue without tanning. His chin was firm, his frame sturdy, though he was not a large man. Mentally, Longarm marked down Barns for a much closer look.

There was little local gossip passed across the dinner table. For the most part, the conversation was devoted to semi-humorous remarks directed at Bobby Blanton, the age-old gibes about wine and women directed to any youth when he reaches his sixteenth year. After dinner, when the party moved from the table in the candlelit patio into the main *sala*, the attention was centered even more directly on Bobby as his gifts were bought out.

Bobby accepted the attention and the gifts with grave

47

courtesy; he was, Longarm thought as he looked on, a biddable boy, though a bit young for his age. Belatedly, it occurred to Longarm that a churchman's son might avoid the forced growth common to so many Western boys.

With one exception, the gifts were predictable: a hat and shirt from Bobby's parents, a new jackknife from Sam Ferris, a hand-tooled belt from Barns. All these were shaded when Julia Wheatly produced her present, a well-used but handsome rifle.

"Oh, golly!" Bobby exclaimed as he took the rifle and looked at its silver frame and polished, blued barrel and walnut stock. "I never thought I'd have a gun as fine as this one!"

"It belonged to my husband," she said. "I thought you might as well be using it. Better than having it rust away in a closet."

"Well, I sure won't let it get rusty," Bobby assured her. He began moving from one to the other to display his treasure.

"That's a real good gun you got there, Bobby," Longarm said when his turn came to inspect the rifle. "It's a .44-40 Winchester, same as mine, except it's got something mine ain't." Longarm put a finger on the words engraved in scrolled letters on the top strap of the gun's frame. "You know what that means?"

Bobby read the legend aloud. " 'One of One Hundred.' No, sir, Mr. Long. Can you tell me?"

"That's what the Winchester people put on their best gun, the ones that've got the smoothest action and shoot straightest. They say only one out of a hundred is a special rifle. There's only one better one, and that's the rifle marked 'One of One Thousand.' And I'll tell you for a fact, there ain't too many of either kind of these around."

"Golly whillikers!" Bobby breathed. "Mrs. Wheatly, I sure do thank you. More than ever, now that Mr. Long's told me about my new rifle."

"You're very welcome, Bobby," she replied. "I hope you enjoy it and use it wisely."

An idea popped into Longarm's head. He said, "Bobby, I guess I'm the only one here that didn't bring you a present. How'd it be if I made up for it by taking you hunting? I know there's deer in the hills hereabouts, saw quite a few on the trail coming in."

"Oh, I'd really like that, Mr. Long!"

"Unless your folks don't want you to grow up to be a hunter." Longarm looked questioningly at George Blanton.

"Hunting is a very healthful pursuit, Mr. Long," Blanton said. "I certainly approve of it. And I know Dora doesn't have any objections." He looked at his wife for confirmation and she nodded promptly.

Longarm said, "I thought maybe because of you being a preacher—"

"My belief, Mr. Long," Blanton said, "is that the good Lord put animals on earth to sustain man by providing food. No, if you want to teach Bobby how to use his new rifle, by all means take him hunting."

"When can we go, Mr. Long?" Bobby asked. "Tomorrow, maybe?"

Longarm thought quickly. His offer to take Bobby hunting hadn't been altruistic; the boy might be a valuable source of information about the Americans living in La Escondida.

He said, "I don't see a thing wrong with tomorrow, Bobby. I need a little rest from traveling, and that's as good a way as any to get one."

"I'll be ready whenever you say," Bobby offered eagerly.

"Well, we don't want to start too late. Deer like to bed down around sunup." He looked at Mrs. Wheatly. "Sam told me you wouldn't mind me keeping my horse in your stable. I'll see to his feed, of course."

"Don't worry about that, Mr. Long. There's plenty of room and feed both, and no lack of help to look after him."

"I'm grateful," Longarm told her. Then he said to Bobby, "Say we start right after dawn. If Mrs. Wheatly don't mind, we better meet here." He looked at her again. "Would it disturb you, ma'am, us getting away so early?"

"Goodness, no! Sam gets his horse early most mornings, and the servants will be up. I'll tell them to have your breakfast ready."

"Now, that's imposing too much, Mrs. Wheatly—"

"Nonsense! Besides, unless you like a breakfast of tortillas and goat cheese, there's nowhere else in town to go at that time of day."

"Well, thanks again." To Bobby he said, "It's all fixed, then. We'll go see just how good you can shoot with that new rifle of yours."

The presentation of Bobby's gifts seemed to signal the end of the party. Sam Ferris stretched and stifled a yawn and said, "I guess I'd better be getting along. We're pushing as fast as we can out at the mine right now."

"That's a pretty good idea," Longarm agreed. "I sure enjoyed the dinner, Mrs. Wheatly, but Bobby and I are going to be getting up as early as Sam. I'd best be moving, too."

"You do have a place to stay, don't you, Mr. Long?"

"Oh, I'm taking Sam's word that the hotel on the plaza's as good as any I'll find here."

"It is. And don't worry about your horse. It'll be quite safe. My stable boy is very good."

"I won't worry. And thanks again. I'll have to stop by the stable and pick up my saddlebags, then I'll head for the hotel."

"Did you stop at the *rurales'* office when you first came in, to register?" Ferris asked.

"Come to think of it, I didn't. Don't know how it slipped my mind. They had a guard of some kind along the road in, and he told me about it."

"I'd advise you to go there before you go to the hotel, Mr. Long," Terrance Barns said. "That's something the *rurales* are very particular about."

"They are," Blanton confirmed. "I'd heard of them pulling people out of bed at the hotel if the hotel reports an unregistered guest."

"I'd better take care of it, then. Glad you reminded me of it, Sam."

"You know where the office is?" Ferris asked. When he saw Longarm starting to shake his head, he went on, "It's right on the corner of the plaza. Big dressed-stone building, the only two-story one in town besides the hotel. You can't miss it."

His saddlebags weighing down one shoulder, Longarm walked the short distance to the plaza. Ferris had been right; in the small town of ground-hugging, flat-topped adobe structures, the Palacio Federal was unmistakable. It looked like any government office building in any town Longarm had visited north of the Rio Grande—a stolid, institutional appearance. He went inside and looked around; the only open or even lighted door was at the end of the corridor.

A pistol-belted man leaned back in a chair inside the door. The hat pulled over his eyes to shield them from the light of the oil lamp that burned on a battered desk was the braid-decorated, high-crowned sombrero that was the trademark of the *rurales*. Longarm cleared his throat. The man pushed his hat up and stared at him.

"Qué quieres, hombre?" he growled.

"I just come to town and I hear I got to sign some kind of book here." Longarm followed his usual policy of giving no signs that he knew a bit of Spanish.

"Registrar?" the *rurale* asked.

"Sí." Longarm thought he'd allow himself that much leeway.

"Norteamericano?"

This time, Longarm settled for a nod.

Reluctantly, the *rurale* stood up. *"Momentito,"* he rumbled. *"Es necesario para los norteamericanos hablar con el capitán."* He disappeared through a door in the back of the room.

Longarm eased the saddlebags from his shoulder as the wait lengthened. The *rurale* returned, followed almost at once by an unshaven man who had on both the gold-embroidered *charro* jacket and the braid-lined trousers that officers of the *rurales* wore. He stopped in the doorway, yawning and rubbing his eyes, and glanced without interest at Longarm.

"Norteamericano a registrar?" he asked.

Then the glance became a stare, and a frown formed on his face. When Longarm's eyes opened in surprise, the

51

rurale captain took a step forward into the brighter light. "You do not remember me?" he asked.

"Can't say I do. Maybe I ought to, and I might, if you'd tell me your name," Longarm replied.

"Bartolome Sanchez," the *rurale* gritted. "And your name you are not need to tell me." The *rurale*'s voice grew grim. "I am watch you in Los Perros where you are murder *mis amigos* Ramos and Molina. *Se llama* Long, and your countrymen call you Longarm. *Sí*, I remember you! I remember you very well indeed!"

Chapter 5

For several stretched moments the two men stared at each other. Longarm tried to recall having seen Sanchez's face during that hectic period on the border, but couldn't remember it. There'd been an entire *rurale* company present at the shootout in Los Perros when he'd outdrawn and outgunned Ramos and Molina, and since then, other faces and places had crowded the border fight out of Longarm's memory. He didn't doubt Sanchez's statement that he'd been there, though. The *rurale* captain had to have been present to know about the affair and to recognize him.

Longarm said, "That's past and gone, Sanchez. We'd both better just forget about it."

"It is sometheeng I find hard to forget, Longarm." Sanchez grinned wolfishly. "You see? I remember even the name your countrymen call you." He snorted. "And our *rurales*, too. They still talk of *Brazolargo*."

"Well, maybe I ought to feel flattered, but I don't. Look here, Sanchez, all I come in for was to sign your register, the way I'm supposed to do. I been in the saddle all day, and my butt's starting to drag. Now, trot out your book and I'll put my name on it. Anything else can wait till tomorrow."

Sanchez shook his head. "Is not so easy as that. Before I let you sign the *registro*, is better we are talk."

"I don't see we got much to talk about."

"Mira! Already we do not agree!"

Sanchez indicated a chair across the room. Longarm shrugged and sat down. Waving the *rurale* sentry out of the room, Sanchez himself sat down in the chair behind the battered desk, facing Longarm. He took corn husks and a tobacco pouch from his pocket and spent a moment rolling himself a cigarette. He watched Longarm's face during the time the operation consumed. Longarm sat expressionless, puffing his cheroot.

"Bueno," Sanchez said. *"Hablamos."*

"You're the one wants to talk," Longarm told him.

Sanchez's face showed that he wasn't too pleased, but he asked, "You 'ave just get to town, no?"

"Yes. Oh, I stopped to have a drink and a bite of supper. Then I remembered what your man on guard duty had told me about coming in to register, so here I am." Longarm didn't think it would be wise to let Sanchez know where and with whom he'd had that supper.

"Why you do not come here first, as my sentry have tell you to?" Sanchez asked, frowning.

"Because I was hungry and thirsty, damn it! A man that's been in the saddle all day disremembers things, when his belly tells him it's time to fill it up."

A smile flickered over Sanchez's face, but vanished into his former stern expression. "You are yet of the *policía federal* of your country, no?"

"Yes."

"And you are look for *un fugitivo* here in La Escondida, no?"

"Well, I guess you can say I'm looking. I don't know rightly whether the man I'm after's here or not. Not till I've looked around some, which I ain't had time to do yet."

"You are bring the papers you need to arrest this man, to take him back to your country, yes?"

"Now, damn it all, Sanchez, you know as well as I do that all the papers a lawman needs in a case like this is his badge."

Sanchez considered this for a moment. *"Quizá que sí, quizá que no.* This one, he is guilty of no crime in my land?"

"None that I know about." Longarm decided it was time for him to counterattack. He said, "Look here, Sanchez, you and me are on the same side of the fence right now. This ain't a case like that one up at Los Perros. Why don't you just forget about that time. It's over with. Let's start fresh."

Sanchez's lip curled and he snorted. "So easy it is for you to say this thing, *Brazolargo*. Me, I do not forget that I have watch you kill *mis compañeros*."

"It was a fair shootout. At least for my part, it was." Longarm didn't see much point in reminding the *rurale* that it had been his dead companions who'd broken the rules. He went on, "Anyhow, that business in Los Perros didn't seem to hurt you none. It opened up a way for you to get promoted, I see. You wasn't anything but what? A sergeant? A corporal? And I reckon you'd still be one, if Ramos and Molina were still around."

Sanchez started to smile again, but did not allow himself to soften that much. He said, *"Tal vez. There is truth in what you say." He shrugged. "Bueno. Let us say I make you what you call in your country the deal. Agradable?"*

"Sure. If it's reasonable."

"I propose you this, Longarm. You stay from the way of my *rurales*, no?"

"I got no reason to mix your men up in it. Not now, anyways."

"So, we agree this much." Sanchez busied himself rolling another corn-husk cigarette. Longarm matched his stalling by lighting another cheroot. Through the smoke clouds that hung between the two men, the *rurale* captain looked at Longarm narrowly as he went on, "I do not ask you to sign the *registro*. If you do so, too many people in La Escondida will come to know you are a *policía federal norteamericano*. This is maybe not so good for you. You look here for the man you are seek. You find him, you bring him first to me, so I know he is wanted for no crime in my country. If he is not, you are free to take him back to yours."

"That sure sounds fair enough to me, Sanchez. I'll go along with you on it." Longarm started to extend his hand to seal the bargain, but thought better of it. Sanchez might not consider a handshake a binding agreement, he reminded himself. He stood up. "Well, I guess now that's settled, I can go get some shut-eye."

Sanchez frowned. *"Shoot-eye?"* Then his face cleared and he smiled. This time he did not wipe it off. "Ah, *dormir, no?"*

"Yeah. Sleep. I bid you goodnight, Sanchez. I'll be at that hotel around the square if you want to ask me any more questions."

Walking around the plaza to the hotel in the suddenly cool night air, Longarm went over his impressions of the three men he'd met at Julia Wheatly's dinner. George Blanton still seemed the least likely of the three to be Clayton Maddox, but it was a toss-up between Sam Ferris and Terrance Barns.

But tomorrow's another day, old son, he reminded himself. *You just might hit paydirt when you're out with the boy tomorrow. Just take it easy, now, and don't let this business with Sanchez get under your skin, either. You got about as much time to figure out who's who as you need. This little town's one place where Billy Vail can't send you a telegram trying to get you to hurry up.*

He was so amused by the picture in his mind of Vail trying to send a wire to La Escondida that he was still grinning when he swallowed a nightcap of Maryland rye from the bottle in his saddlebag and turned in for the night.

"Don't you think we ought to see a deer pretty soon, Mr. Long?" Bobby asked.

For a moment, Longarm didn't reply to his young companion's question.

"Mr. Long?" Bobby repeated.

"Oh. Well, now, Bobby, deer ain't real predictable critters, especially when it's so near a town. Best we can do is ride along and keep our eyes peeled. A little bit later, when we get up higher on the hill, we'll tether our nags and do some still-hunting."

"What's still-hunting?" Bobby frowned.

"That's when you find a spot where a deer likely won't

56

think to look for you, and hunker down and wait for a deer to come by."

"Oh. Is that a better way, Mr. Long?"

"Maybe not better. It depends. Oh—Bobby, while it's on my mind, I wish you'd go easy on that 'Mr. Long' business. Most of my friends call me Longarm, and I've got so used to it that I answer to it better'n any handle with a 'mister' in front of it."

"You mean you want me to call you Longarm?"

"If it's all the same to you."

"But isn't that a nickname?"

"I reckon you'd call it that."

"Father and Mother say it's impolite for somebody my age to call older folks by a nickname."

"Now, I don't mean to say they're wrong, Bobby. But I'd say it's all right when any of us older folks would rather be called by a nickname than by our proper names."

"I guess that's right. If you want me to, then, Longarm, that's what I'll call you."

"Thanks."

They rode on in silence. The pair had been out for nearly two hours, riding at an easy pace across the wide valley and up its gently sloping western side to where the trees and brush began. Longarm hadn't yet started to question Bobby about the three men of La Escondida's tiny American colony; he'd wanted to make sure first that the youth knew which end of a rifle to put to his shoulder. Once he'd satisfied himself that Bobby understood at least the rudiments of rifle-handling, they'd stopped on the lower slope while Longarm helped the boy sight in the weapon and get accustomed to its sight-picture. Only then had he announced that it was time for them to start hunting in earnest.

He said, "You know, Bobby, I don't blame you for being proud of that new rifle. It's a mighty fine one. Sorta surprising that Mrs. Wheatly'd give it to you instead of— well, maybe somebody like Sam Ferris. Sam worked for her husband a long time, didn't he?"

"Well, it wasn't really such a long time, I guess. Mr.

57

Wheatly's been dead about a year now. Mr. Ferris only started to work for him a little while before he died."

"But they knew each other before, the way I got it last night."

"Oh, that was somewhere else, back in Idaho or Butte or someplace like that. Mr. Ferris just came to La Escondida two or three months before Mr. Wheatly passed away."

"But you and your folks were here for a good while before that, weren't you?"

Bobby frowned. "Let's see. The Wheatly's were here first. Then we moved here, then Mr. Barns, then Mr. Ferris. That's the way it was, Mr.—Longarm."

"Ferris came from someplace up in the mining country, you said. Montana or Idaho. Where'd you and your parents come from, Bobby?"

"Why, we were in Santa Fe. Father had a mission to the Pueblo Indians, then."

"You like it better here than you did there?"

"Oh, I don't know. It's warmer here, but it rains more. The people are alike a lot, except that the Chihuahua Indians aren't as nice as the Pueblo people are. Why, they still fight like the American Indians used to do in the old days. At least that's what Father says."

"Has your daddy always been a church missionary?"

"Since before I was born, I guess. He has as long as I can remember."

Longarm figured he'd just crossed one off his list of suspects. Giving himself good marks for the time spent, he turned his full attention to hunting.

"Guess it's about time for us to still-hunt awhile," he told Bobby. "Late in the morning this way, deer like to bed up for a while, rest and sleep, before they go out for their evening graze."

"You sure know a lot about hunting, Mr.—Longarm," Bobby said. He followed Longarm's example, reining in, tethering his horse to a tree. Then, as Longarm started upslope on foot, Bobby kept close beside him.

"Oh, I wouldn't say I know all that much," Longarm replied. "Not near as much as some fellows I could introduce you to. But they're outdoors all the time, in wild country where you got to have game if you want to go on eating meat. Why, I know men who can look at a deer's hoofprint and tell you what the critter was browsing on two hours ago."

"Jiminy! How do they do that?"

"I wish I knew, myself," Longarm grinned. He'd forgotten how serious young people could be, how they tended to believe the exaggerations that were a part of yarning. "But we better walk quiet now, and not talk. We're getting up in the brush, and there's likely to be a deer jump up out of any of these patches we come to."

"Like that one up ahead?" Bobby asked.

"Any of 'em. Big or little." They were approaching a thicket, a sprawl of young acacias.

"You think there might be a deer—" Bobby began.

Before he could finish the question, a young spike buck leaped out of the brush and bounded upslope. Bobby got his gun up faster than Longarm had expected him to. He waited for the youth to fire, then triggered his own rifle at almost the same instant. The two shots blended into one. The buck leaped higher than his earlier bounds had taken him, took a few staggering steps and collapsed. Bobby began running toward the fallen animal. Longarm stopped him with a shout.

"Hold up, Bobby! Take your time and keep your gun ready. That critter might not be dead yet."

Bobby skidded to a walk and Longarm caught up with him. They approached the fallen deer together.

"He's dead, all right," Longarm said as they drew closer. "That was a mighty nice shot you made, young fellow."

"But you shot at the same time I did. How do we know which one of us really got him?"

"We'll take a look. If there's two bullet holes in him, we both claim credit. If there's only one, I'd say you get full claim, because I was a mite later on the trigger than you."

When they inspected the carcass of the young buck, turning it over to be sure, they could find only one bullet hole.

"It's your deer, then, Bobby," Longarm said. "Like I

59

told you, I was late shooting. You'd got him before my shot was off."

"Are you sure? Maybe we could tell if we cut out the bullet and looked at it?"

Longarm shook his head. "Wouldn't tell us a thing. Your rifle's a .44-40 Winchester, same as mine. Same size slug, same lands and twist. There'd be no earthly way to tell which one of us got off that shot." Longarm had no intention of diminishing Bobby's confidence in his marksmanship or in his new rifle. He knew, of course, where his own slug had hit.

"Whillikers!" Bobby exclaimed. "I've really got some gun here, haven't I, Longarm?"

"You sure have. All the rifle a man could want. See you take good care of it, now. Clean it soon as you can after we get back, and be sure you don't leave shells in the magazine too long. Oil gets in around the primers if you do, ruins the powder. Now, then, let's get this fellow bled and then we'll bring the horses up and start back. Maybe we can get your mama to fry us up a platter of fresh liver for supper tonight."

They were loading the carcass on Bobby's horse, their rifles already put away in their scabbards, when the shot rang out and a slug kicked up a puff of dust from the ground between the horses' hooves. Longarm drew, but when he saw the muzzle of the old '71 Mauser leveled between his eyes, let his gunhand sag slowly downward. The man holding the rifle on them looked like any of the Mexicans Longarm had seen around La Escondida except for the bandolier of cartridges looped over his shoulder.

"*¿Qué haces en la tierra del Patrón?*" he demanded.

Longarm hesitated momentarily as he summoned up his long-unused Spanish and asked, *"Quién es usted?"*

"Soy un guardabosque. Este venado toca el Patrón!"

To Longarm's surprise, Bobby answered the rifleman in Spanish as fluent as the man himself had used. He said angrily, *"Este venado toca a mí!"*

"Hold on, Bobby," Longarm cautioned. "You know this fellow?"

"No, sir. He says he works for *el Patrón*, guarding the

60

forest. I guess maybe he is; he said the deer doesn't belong to us, but to his boss."

"Let's don't rile him, then, seeing he's got us dead in his sights. Now, who is this *Patrón* fellow?"

"*Señor* Mondragón. He owns all the land around the town for I don't know how many miles."

"You acquainted with Mondragón?"

Bobby shook his head. "My folks are, but I just know him when I see him."

"Well, you know the ropes around here better than I do. Why don't you see if you can get him to take us to his boss? I got a hunch we'll do better talking to *el Patrón* than to one of his men."

"I'll try," Bobby said, his voice showing his doubt. To the rifle-wielder, he said, "*Queremos hablar con el Patrón.*"

Astonishment spread over the guard's face. He gasped, "*Cómo?*"

His voice sharp, Longarm said, "*El Patrón, hombre! Pronto!*"

For a moment, it appeared to Longarm that the guard was going to refuse. The man was conditioned to obey, though. After hesitating, a puzzled frown wrinkling his face, he said, "*Porqué no? Vengamos, hombres.*"

"Looks like we won this round," Longarm said under his breath to Bobby. "Where's this *el Patrón* hang out? In town?"

"I know he's got a house in town, but I don't think he really lives in it. He's got a lot bigger house down in the valley that everybody calls 'the hacienda,' and that's where I think he stays most of the time."

Although the guard had agreed to their demand to see his master, he did not relax his vigilance. He kept his rifle on Longarm and Bobby while they mounted, and rode behind them after he'd pointed at the vestigial trail that led down the valley slope. When they reached the floor, he came abreast of them and pointed out the direction they were to take, a branch off the road along which the two hunters had ridden on their way out, but leading away from La Escondida.

For a mile or so, the narrow dirt road paralleled the

base of the valley's wall; occasionally Longarm caught a glimpse of the wide valley floor, checkered with fields in which men and women were working. Abruptly, the road turned back toward the wall and entered a narrow arroyo. After a hundred yards or so, the arroyo opened out into a huge box canyon, carpeted with grass and wildflowers, and dominated by a sprawling house, built of limestone blocks, that towered three stories high above the canyon floor. Behind the huge house at a distance there were a score of smaller structures.

"If this is where *el Patrón* lives," Longarm said in a half-whisper to Bobby, "I'd say he's got a real fancy layout."

"I guess this is his place, all right," Bobby replied. "I never have been out here before, though. I reckon Mrs. Wheatly and Mr. Ferris are the only Americans who have."

Longarm's mind had been busy while they were riding. As they drew closer to the house, he said to Bobby, "I want you to listen to me real good, now."

"Is something the matter, Longarm?"

"No. Not now. And if we handle this right, likely there won't be. But I'm going to ask you to keep a secret with me. Think you can do it?"

"Sure. I'm old enough to know how to keep quiet."

"All right. Now, have I got your word you won't say a thing to anybody about what I'm going to tell you?"

Bobby's reply came unhesitatingly. "Yes, sir."

"I'm a deputy United States marshal, Bobby. I'm down here on official business, and I don't want anybody to know about it yet. Now, I might have to tell this *el Patrón* who I am. If I do, I'll ask him to keep quiet about it. And right now, I'm asking you to do the same."

"A real, live U.S. marshal?" Bobby's eyes were wide as he asked the question.

Longarm smiled. "I feel pretty alive, so I guess I am. Now remember, you ain't going to give me away. Not even to your folks."

"I won't forget," Bobby promised. "Golly whillikers!"

They were within fifty yards of the mansion's door

now. Someone inside must have been watching the area and reported their approach, for before they reached the wide steps leading up to the door, the door opened and three men came out.

Those in the rear, Longarm spotted at once as being *pistoleros*. They wore pistol belts, each belt sagging under the weight of a pair of holstered revolvers. The one in front, he was sure, must be *el Patrón*.

He was a younger man than Longarm had expected to see, not much past thirty. *El Patrón* was tall, just an inch shorter than Longarm, but exceedingly spare-framed. His complexion was olive, a tone lighter than the dark tan skin of the men behind him. His hair was jet black, combed straight back from his wide forehead. His nose was high-bridged and thin, his eyes brown. He had long sideburns in addition to a waxed and curled mustache. His lips were full, with a downward twist at their corners. He wore a suit of dark purple velvet, cut *charro*-style, a short jacket over a frilled shirt, and tight-fitting trousers that flared at midcalf over highly polished black boots.

"Qué tenemos aquí, Gomez?" he asked the guard.

"Cazadores, Patrón," the man growled.

Longarm decided to waste no time. "Just a minute, *señor*," he said. "I guess your man here said we was trespassing, or something like that. Thing is, we were out hunting, to try out a new gun the young fellow here had just got for his birthday. We didn't start out to step on no toes, or go where we hadn't ought to be. There wasn't any way we could tell we were on your land, if that's what the trouble's about."

"I see," the man said in excellent, almost unaccented English. "You must be recently across the border, and not aware that land in Mexico is not open to everyone, as it is up there."

"Well, we respect private land, when we know it's private," Longarm replied.

"You, young man," the *Patrón* said to Bobby. "You, I have seen in La Escondida. Your parents, they are the Protestant missionaries, are they not?"

"Yes, sir."

"Your name is . . . Blanton, Roberto Blanton, is my memory correct?"

"Yes, sir."

"And your friend, here?"

Before Bobby could reply, Longarm said quickly, "My name's Long, Mr. . . ."

"Mondragón, *Señor* Long. Ramón Mondragón." He bowed, a small bow which managed to convey the impression of a formality given to one not quite his equal. "If you have not already learned this, I am the *hacendado* of La Escondida, and everything in this valley is under my proprietorship. The land, the game, the tame animals, the houses, the crops, the people. It is not, I think, in accord with your North American customs."

"No, Mr. Mondragón," Longarm replied, trying to keep the grimness out of his voice. "No, it sure ain't."

Mondragón shrugged. "Well, that is a small matter. Of course, I would not embarrass a visitor to our nation over such a small matter as the shooting of a deer. I make you and young Roberto welcome to my hacienda, *Señor* Long. Dismount, please, and come inside. We will drink a glass of wine together and chat for a moment, if you are in no hurry."

Chapter 6

Mondragón led them into the hacienda. Beyond the high, arched entrance door, a wide hallway stretched for what to Longarm seemed something like a quarter-mile to another doorway. Sunshine streaming in through the second door brought highlights from the polished flagstone floor that stretched through the wide passage.

Halfway down the hall, Mondragón opened a door and gestured for them to enter. Longarm and Bobby followed him into a large square room with a high ceiling that showed the raw beams under a herringbone pattern of boards that formed the ceiling. Books lined one wall. A richly patterned Oriental carpet glowed on the floor, and chairs were scattered about. A massive desk stood in front of tall windows that looked out over the valley. The center of the wall opposite the bookcase was taken up by a head-high fireplace. Over the mantel hung the somber-toned portrait of a grandee of old Spain.

"My father," Mondragón said, indicating the painting. "He fought with Díaz in the battle at Tecoac. He was the *hacendado* here before me, just as my son will be *hacendado* after I am gone."

Bobby asked, "And everything in the valley will belong to him then, just like it belongs to you now?"

"Of course," Mondragón replied, his voice casual. He saw the small pucker that appeared between Longarm's brows. "You do not approve of our system, *Señor* Long?"

Longarm needed time to frame his reply; he made it by lighting a cheroot. Mondragón waited patiently. When the cigar was glowing satisfactorily, Longarm said, "It ain't

65

for me to like it or not, Mr. Mondragón, seeing as I don't have to live with it."

"Ah, but you do—as long as you are in La Escondida, or in my valley. By the way, how long are you planning to stay?"

"I don't rightly know. About the only way I can give you an answer to that is to say, till I move on. Or maybe I ought to be more polite, you being the boss here, and ask if I'm welcome."

"Of course you are welcome." While they talked, Mondragón had moved to a tall, carved cabinet at one side of the room. "Outside, I invited you in for a glass of wine, but it is my observation that *norteamericanos* do not always enjoy wine. Would you prefer something stronger? Whiskey, perhaps? Cognac? Or our native tequila or *habanero*?"

"Well, I got a real liking for good Maryland rye whiskey, if you happen to have a bottle."

Mondragón frowned. "This is a whiskey of which I have not heard, *Señor* Long. I must tell my *mayordomo* to lay in a supply. But let me offer you some of your own country's whiskey of the kind you call bourbon. Will that be adequate?"

"Why, sure, Mr. Mondragón. Just fine."

Mondragón turned to Bobby. "And you, Young Roberto? A sherry, perhaps? That is what I propose to have, myself."

"Is that like liquor?" Bobby asked.

"It is a wine. A strong wine, to be sure. Yes, I suppose it could be called liquor. Why do you ask?"

"Because if it's liquor, I can't have any. I promised my folks I wouldn't drink any liquor until I'm twenty-one."

A woman's voice broke in from the doorway. "Perhaps the *joven* would share my morning chocolate, Ramón."

Longarm turned to look. The woman in the doorway was young, not past her early twenties. She had a short, thin nose that brought her upper lip up in a half-pout above a lower lip that was a trifle too full. Her chin was rounded, her cheekbones high, her eyes a deep, lustrous black. Her hair was blacker than her eyes, and cascaded

66

down her back. It was gathered at the neck by a loop of gold. She wore a floor-length morning gown of cream-colored satin. The gown was belted into a high waist and did nothing to hide full breasts and flaring hips.

She asked Bobby, "You are Roberto, the missionaries' boy, no?"

"Yes, ma'am. Bobby Blanton."

"Of course." Turning to her husband, the young woman said, "You must see that the boy is too young for wine, Ramón."

"I had not thought of it, my dear Corazón. When I was his age, my father allowed me wine, mixed with water, of course. But, I am forgetting." To Longarm he said, "*Señor* Long, allow me to present my wife, Corazón. This gentleman is visiting La Escondida from the north."

Corazón inclined her head. "*Señor* Long."

Longarm swept off his hat and offered her a half-bow. "Mrs. Mondragón, I'm glad to make your acquaintance."

A woman servant brought in a silver tray holding a china pot and a cup and saucer. She put the tray on the desk and turned to leave.

"Bring another cup, Adelita," Corazón said. The woman nodded and went out. Corazón waved a hand at the chairs and said, "Now, let us sit down."

They found chairs. The servant returned with a cup, and Corazón poured chocolate for herself and Bobby. There was one of those awkward pauses that occur when strangers with no common ground, meeting for the first time, search for an inoffensive topic of conversation.

Ramón Mondragón broke the silence. "*Señor* Long and young Roberto hunted deer this morning. Gomez heard them shooting and brought them here."

Corazón nodded. "Yes. I saw them ride up from my window." She looked at Longarm. "Do you enjoy hunting in your own country, *Señor* Long?"

"Not all that much, Mrs. Mondragón. When I'm out in the field, traveling where there's not any towns, and I need fresh meat, I'll shoot a rabbit or whatever's handy."

"Longarm—Mr. Long, that is—was showing me how to use my new gun this morning," Bobby volunteered. "Honest, Mr. Mondragón, we didn't know we were on your land."

Mondragón shrugged. "As I have said to you, a small deer is of no importance." He turned to Longarm. "Your job requires that you travel, then?"

"Sometimes."

"And it is your work that brings you to La Escondida?" Mondragón persisted.

"Oh, my work takes me to a lot of places." Longarm looked through the tall windows, across the valley floor. The checkerboard fields he'd glimpsed only occasionally earlier, when he and Bobby started out, were now busy with people.

He asked, "How many people you hire to keep this place of yours working, Mr. Mondragón?"

"Hire?" Mondragón looked puzzled, then his face cleared and he said, "Perhaps you did not understand what I told you when you arrived. I hire no one. Those are my *peons* working in my fields, Mr. Long. I feed them, clothe them, allow them to build their *jacales* on my land. They want for nothing. Is that not true, Corazón?"

"Of course, Ramón. They have everything they could wish for."

"Except money," Longarm suggested.

"Why would they want money?" Mondragón asked. He sounded genuinely puzzled. "If they wish something other than what they receive regularly, they have only to ask me, and I provide it."

"Just as you provide for me, Ramón," Corazón smiled. "I need no money, you tell me, as long as I have only to mention to you that I need or want something."

"True," Mondragón nodded. "I'm glad you have finally realized that, my dear."

Longarm put his glass down and stood up. He saw the danger of pursuing the line of talk he'd unwittingly begun, and had no intention of angering Mondragón.

"We'd better be getting back to town, Bobby," he said. "Your folks might get worried if we don't show up pretty soon."

"There is no need to hurry," Corazón protested. "We

have visitors so seldom here. I had thought perhaps you would stay and join us at luncheon."

"*Señor* Long knows best what he must do, Corazón," Mondragón said curtly. He, too, stood up, as did Bobby. "I will walk to the door with you, *señor*. Then there will be no arguments from my people when you and your young friend ride off with the deer I have given you."

Longarm kept his voice neutral. "We thank you for the deer, Mr. Mondragón. We'll know better than to hunt on your land, next time."

"Nonsense. I am glad to share my deer with my friends." Mondragón paused before continuing. "*Señor* Long. You have been very careful to avoid mentioning your reason for visiting La Escondida. I have not pressed you for it, you notice. But I will remind you that the ways of Mexico are not those of the United States. If you have difficulty in the future, I hope you will inform me."

"Well, now, that's right nice of you to offer," Longarm said. "I'll sure keep it in mind."

Mondragón smiled. "Do so. And remember, if you know those with position in Mexico, anything can be arranged. For a price."

As Longarm and Bobby rode back to La Escondida, the deer lashed behind Bobby's saddle, the youth asked, "Longarm, was that all true, what Mr. Mondragón told us? About him owning everything in sight, even the people?"

"I guess in his way of looking at things it is, Bobby."

"But how can he *own* people? He sure don't own me!"

"Or me, either," Longarm said with a smile. "These Mexican folks, now, that's something else. I'd say they agree with him, or they wouldn't keep on working for him without getting paid."

"Then it's just like it used to be down South, at home, isn't it?"

"Pretty close to being, I'd imagine. And I guess the same thing's apt to happen here someday that happened back home a few years back."

"You mean the War?"

"Yep. But that ain't our worry, Bobby. Best thing we

69

can do, it not being our country, is to stay clear of getting mixed up in somebody else's troubles."

"Longarm, what's it like, being a U.S. marshal? Do you ever get into fights with bad men?"

"Now and again, when I can't bring 'em in peaceful. The law's got to be fought for, Bobby, just like most things." Longarm decided it was time to change the subject. He said, "Now, you remember what I told you about not letting on what my job is. And the best way not to let something slip out is just to forget I ever told you what I did, then you won't say something you'll be sorry for."

"Oh, I won't let anything slip." Bobby squirmed around in his saddle to look at his trophy. "Can we go hunting again sometime soon, Longarm? I really enjoyed it, this morning."

"We'll see. Don't forget, we'd have to get Mr. Mondragón's permission next time."

Bobby's face fell. "I don't think I'd want to ask any favors from him, Longarm. I . . . well, I don't guess I like Mr. Mondragón."

"You know something? I feel just about the same way, myself. But now you've got the feel of your new rifle, you can do some practicing on a target."

Bobby's face brightened. "I can, at that. But I'm glad you were with me the first time I shot it. It's a real good gun."

George Blanton was almost as enthused at Bobby's success as the youth was himself. While they were waiting for Dora to fry the fresh deer liver for a late lunch, he told Longarm, "I'm not much of a hand with guns, Mr. Long. I do appreciate what you did for Bobby this morning."

"I enjoyed it as much as Bobby did, I reckon. He's a fine boy, Mr. Blanton."

"Well, Dora and I think so, too. But we're probably prejudiced, Bobby being our only child."

"I understand you were in New Mexico Territory before you came down here," Longarm remarked casually. With equal casualness he added, "I don't suppose you've spent any time in Texas, have you?"

70

"No. Indian Nation, now, we were there when Bobby was born. Then we got the mission in Santa Fe, and now we're here."

Longarm was pleased that Blanton's replies were prompt and factually identical with the information he'd gotten from Bobby earlier.

In their table-talk during lunch, he managed to confirm the rest of the information Bobby had unwittingly passed on about Ferris and Barns. He noticed Bobby's face now and then knotted into a frown, and wondered how far he could trust the youth not to reveal his identity. It didn't suit Longarm's plans for either Ferris or Barns to learn that they were under suspicion at this point.

Halfway through lunch, Bobby began to yawn, and Dora Blanton's eyes took on the glaze of sleepiness as well. As they rose from the table, she told the boy, "Siesta time, Bobby. Off to your room, now. You're not used to tramping over the hills all morning."

"Neither am I," Longarm remarked. "If you folks are used to taking a siesta, I guess I better go on over to the hotel and take a little bit of a nap myself."

"It's the custom of the country," Blanton said apologetically. "Not that we weren't accustomed to it even before we came here. Santa Fe's as much Old Mexico as it is New."

Like all houses in the village, the Blantons' dwelling was only a few steps from the plaza. Longarm, unlike the cowboys who rode their horses everywhere, even across a street from one saloon to another, did not mount to ride to the hotel. He walked, leading his horse. Tying the cavalry roan to the hitch rail, he took his saddlebags and rifle and went to his room.

Sleep came easily, after he'd sipped a shot of Maryland rye while removing his boots, jeans and shirt. In his balbriggans, he stretched out on the bed to finish his drink and enjoy a cheroot. He did manage to toss the cigar butt into the spittoon that was a standard feature even in Mexican hotels, before slumber overtook him.

A tapping on the door roused him. He didn't know how long he'd slept, but from the glare of sunshine beating on

71

the drawn window shade, he knew his nap couldn't have been a very long one. He called, "Who is it?"

"Julia Wheatly, Mr. Long. I . . . I desperately need to talk to you about a very disturbing development."

There was a note of urgency in her voice. Longarm rolled off the bed and started pulling on his shirt and jeans while he was replying, "Just a minute, Mrs. Wheatly. I'll be right there."

"I don't like to disturb you during the siesta hour," she began when Longarm opened the door. "But—"

He broke in, "Maybe you'd better come inside while we talk, Mrs. Wheatly, if it's anything you want kept private. You don't mind just the two of us being in a hotel room, do you? And me with my boots off?"

"Goodness, no! I got over that kind of silliness a long time ago."

She came in and Longarm closed the door. It was apparent to him that Julia Wheatly was upset, and obvious that she'd dressed hurriedly. She had on a long dress that sat unevenly on her white shoulders, and her hair was not as smooth and carefully groomed as it had been the night before. She was frowning, a worried crease between her eyebrows.

She said, "Normally, I'd talk with Sam about this, but he's out at the mine and . . . well, since it concerns you, I decided I'd just come and ask you myself."

"You're all agitated," Longarm said. "Maybe you'd feel better and it'd smooth your nerves if you had a little sip of something. All I got is Maryland rye . . ."

"That'll be fine," she broke in. "I don't drink whiskey often, so I suppose rye's just about as strong as the other kind."

"There's not much difference in the strength," Longarm said, making conversation to distract her while he poured them each a drink. "Now, then . . ." He handed her the glass and took his own. "You take the chair, and I'll just perch on the side of the bed."

He lighted a cheroot and sipped while he watched her down the whiskey in one throw. Her eyes watered and she

72

gulped for a moment after her heroic swallow. Longarm waited until she'd recovered.

"Whenever you feel like talking, Mrs. Wheatly, I'm listening," he told her.

"Well . . ."she seemed reluctant to begin.

She studied Longarm's face for a moment, raised her glass nervously, and found it empty. Longarm reached across to the table, picked up the bottle, and poured her a much smaller portion than the first. This time she sipped the whiskey.

"Well," she repeated, "I might be foolish, coming to you this way, because there's always a lot of wild servant talk floating around in a little place like La Escondida. But the fact is, I've been worried for a long time, and so has Sam, ever since that new vein was found. In fact—"

"Worried about what?"

"Why, the mine."

Longarm frowned. "I guess I don't quite follow you."

"Perhaps not. I did mention it when we first met, but you haven't been here while all this was developing, and I don't know how familiar you are with the situation in Mexico right now."

"I was here not too long ago. Not here, of course. Further north, and on the border. But it was right wild then, and I don't reckon it's changed much."

"It's like a jungle, Mr. Long. The people in power, Díaz's people, know that Díaz has said he won't run for reelection as President. Right now, all of them—and I'm sure that includes Díaz himself—are grabbing everything they can before his term expires."

"And you're afraid they're going to grab for your mine?"

"Yes. If this new vein turns out to be a rich lode, the mine will be worth a lot of money. And I don't know whether you understand what a woman's place is here, but Mexico's a man's country, and any widow, like myself, is fair prey."

"I've seen a little bit of that," he said, nodding.

"Right now, here in La Escondida, power's pretty evenly divided between el Patrón—that's Ramón Mondragón, the

73

hacendado—and Captain Sanchez, who's in charge of the *rurales*."

"I've met both of them," Longarm said.

"Yes. So I understand. And which one are you going to side with, Mr. Long?"

His eyebrows rose, and he scratched the back of his neck pensively.

"Side with? I guess you lost me somewhere."

Mrs. Wheatly's eyes sharpened angrily. "This may be just servant talk—you might as well know that's my source for it, that's what got me so upset. And maybe I'm foolish even listening to it. But I didn't think you were that kind of man, Mr. Long, or I'd never have invited you into my home, even if Sam Ferris did bring you with him!"

"Hold on, Mrs. Wheatly," Longarm said, holding up a rawboned hand. "You got me all confused. I don't quite savvy what you're getting at."

"Are you sure?" she snapped. "Your little visit with *el Patrón* this morning didn't help you make up your mind, after you'd talked with Captain Sanchez last night?"

"I can see you're accusing me of something, Mrs. Wheatly, only I ain't quite sure what. Maybe you just better start over again, from the beginning, and talk to me in plain English."

"I . . . I guess I'm not making much sense, am I?" Julia's anger was ebbing now; her calmer tone showed it. She went on, "I'd better start at the beginning."

"I've always found that to be the best place," he agreed.

"I'll have to go back a little while. Both *el Patrón* and Captain Sanchez would like to get their hands on my mine. And that's not servant talk, Mr. Long. My husband told me that, just before the vein he'd thought was going to be such a rich one petered out. Of course, they lost interest then."

"But now that the mine looks promising again, they're acting greedy?" Longarm asked.

"Yes. Of course, the one who's in best with Díaz will get it in the end, even if they take it away from me."

"I still don't see what all that's got to do with me."

74

"You did go to the *rurales'* office to register last night, didn't you?"

"Sure. You knew I was going there when I left your house."

"And you stayed there a long time, talking to Captain Sanchez."

"Turned out me and Sanchez had tangled one time—the time I mentioned to you a minute ago, up north, on the border."

"Oh? I didn't realize you'd known him before."

"I didn't *know* him, Mrs. Wheatly. I didn't even remember him. He remembered me because—" Longarm stopped short. He didn't want to bring up the border business, because that would mean giving away his reason for being in La Escondida. He improvised, "—because I stepped on a lot of *rurale* toes that time, and his was one set I had to tromp on."

"I see. And your visit to *el Patrón* this morning?"

"That wasn't a visit. Me and Bobby went hunting, you'll remember. We fixed up to go last night."

"Yes. Of course I remember."

"We shot a deer. One of Mondragón's men jumped on us and took us to his house out in the country to talk to his boss. That's all there was to that."

"And you weren't offering to hire out to them as a gunman, to help them take my mine over?"

"Is that what all this is about?" Longarm said incredulously.

"Yes." Julia was on the defensive now. "Nobody can hide much of anything in this town, Mr. Long. I heard about your lengthy visit with Sanchez at breakfast, and about your visit to the Mondragón *hacienda* at lunch. Servants gossip, and the word spreads fast."

"It sure must!" Longarm chuckled. "Well, you can rest easy, Mrs. Wheatly. If it comes to somebody taking that mine away from you, and I got to choose up sides, there's only one side I'd want to be on, and that's yours."

She looked at him for a moment. "Why . . . you really mean that, don't you, Mr. Long?"

"I don't generally say things I don't mean."

"And you're not a hired gunman?"

Longarm decided that he'd better come out with the facts. When she wasn't worried about her mine, Julia Wheatly seemed sensible enough. Besides, if he didn't assure her, she might retain some shadow of doubt that he was telling the truth.

"I'm going to tell you something, Mrs. Wheatly," he said soberly. "But before I do, I want your solemn word that you won't pass it on to anybody else."

"Why, of course I won't repeat anything you tell me in confidence!"

"I know that. Now, then, the fact of the matter is—" He stepped over to the hook where his coat was hanging and took out the wallet that held his badge. "I'm a deputy U.S. marshal, and I'm here on a case that's got nothing to do with mining."

Opening the wallet, Longarm showed her the badge with his name engraved on it. She gasped and ran a finger over the raised insignia.

"Why . . . you really are! Oh, Mr. Long! You don't know how happy that makes me! My God, I feel so good I could kiss you!"

To Longarm's surprise, she threw her arms around him and pressed her lips to his. Her action was so unexpected that Longarm responded as he would to a lover's kiss. His tongue pressed against her lips. She opened her mouth to accept it. They clung together, standing beside the bed, prolonging the kiss, her lips working under his, her tongue twining furiously in his mouth.

Then they broke the kiss and drew apart, looking intently into one another's eyes.

Chapter 7

Their eyes stayed locked for a strained moment, each trying to read a message. At last she said, "I . . . I'm not sure that I meant what that kiss seemed to promise, Mr. Long."

"It seemed to pleasure you as much as it did me."

"I'm not a loose woman, you know. I don't go inviting every man I meet to . . . to . . ."

"I never thought you did."

"But I won't deny I found it pleasing. And exciting. And I haven't found a man who's really excited me since my husband died."

"That's been a while, I recall you saying."

"Yes. Too long, perhaps." She looked at him, a plea in her eyes. "I'm a mature woman, Mr. Long."

"And a right handsome one, too. Man gets to my age, little scrawny girls in pigtails don't draw him much."

"That's something I'll never be again. I'm just as glad, I suppose. Growing up is a thing you should only have to go through once."

"But you've got to go through it to come out a handsome woman like you are."

"I'm glad you think so." Julia extended her glass. "I think I'd like just a drop more, please."

He splashed more whiskey into their glasses. Julia's eyes questioned him over the rim of her glass as she drank. Longarm emptied his own glass in one swallow and put it down. He stood waiting for her to finish. She took her time, gazing at him thoughtfully. At last she put her glass aside and smiled at him.

Longarm bent to kiss her again. This time her response

was quicker than before. She clasped her arms around him and pressed her full breasts to his chest. Longarm ran his hand down her back and pressed her to him. The warmth of her body made itself felt on his groin. He began to come erect.

Julia released one of her arms. Slowly, almost reluctantly, she ran her hand down his side and worked it between their close-pressed bodies. Longarm felt her fingers on his growing erection. He twisted his body to one side to give her hand more play. She squeezed him softly. He began to caress her breasts with his palm, feeling the nipples beginning to harden as he stroked her.

She broke their kiss and whispered, "I'm not sure yet that I want to go through with this, Mr. Long."

He smiled gently. "Seeing as how we're getting a trifle familiar, you can call me what most of my friends do; this 'mister' business gets purely awkward. Call me Longarm. But we'd best stop now, if you can't make up your mind."

"But I don't want to stop, either . . . Longarm."

"Don't then."

Julia's hand was exploring Longarm's crotch. "Yes," she said decisively. "I do want this."

Her lips sought his again. Longarm pushed his fingers under the cascade of long dark hair that streamed down her back and found the buttons of her dress. He began unfastening them. Julia released him and started to unbutton his shirt. She reached his waist and went on working buttons free, now the buttons of Longarm's trousers.

He'd worked his way down her dress buttons to her waist. Julia was unfastening the buttons of his balbriggans. She pulled the underwear free, down to his hips, and then stopped long enough to shrug her shoulders as Longarm worked her dress over them. She helped him by sliding her shift down over her shoulders before returning her attention to him.

They stood together now, skin touching skin. Longarm bent to kiss the large brown rosettes of Julia's breasts. Their tips came to life under his tongue, thrusting forward. Her hands were still busy pulling down Longarm's underwear. She got the balbriggans down to his thighs, freeing his erection. She drew a deep breath as she wrapped her hand around him and closed it in a firm grasp.

Longarm, still caressing her breasts with his lips and hands, heard her whisper, "I didn't expect you to be so big. Why, you're huge!"

When Longarm did not reply, she pulled his erection up against his belly and twisted her body, pressing close, to trap it between them. Longarm felt a film of perspiration forming on Julia's soft skin. Her breasts were crushed against his chest, and he felt a quiver run through her body.

"This isn't enough," Julia whispered. "The bed, Longarm!"

They were only a step away from the bed. Longarm lifted Julia free from the tangle of cloth around her feet, kicked himself free of his own tangled garments, and took the step that brought them to the bed.

They lay side by side, still in their embrace. Julia brought a leg up across Longarm's hips. She still held tightly to his erection. Now she brought its tip to her, and Longarm felt the soft, moist roughness of her pubic hair as she eased him shallowly into her.

She broke their kiss to whisper, "Go in slow, Longarm. You're so big, I'm afraid you'll hurt me."

"I'll be easy," he promised.

He moved his hips carefully, entering her with gentle firmness. Julia gasped as he sank into her, and he felt her body quivering under his hands. When he was in her fully, Longarm lay quietly for several moments, letting her wet warmth surround him, and then he began stroking, slowly, easily, until he felt her relaxing.

Still he moved slowly, never thrusting, as the tempo of Julia's breathing grew faster, and the inner muscles of her thigh across his hips began to grow taut. Longarm moved faster now. Julia's body began turning, and her hips responded to his faster stroking, jerking to meet him as he went in.

"I'm holding back," she breathed. "I can't wait much longer, though. Aren't you almost ready?"

"It takes me a while," he replied. "Go on, Julia. Let go and take your pleasure. I can wait for mine."

She was trembling now, and Longarm went into her faster, with longer strokes. Julia's trembling became a quaking, and her breathy sighs turned to moans, then to a final throaty cry as her body convulsed and her hips jerked wildly for a moment before she exhaled a last gusty sigh and grew limp.

"Ohh!" Julia sighed. "It's almost a sin to feel so good!" Then, as Longarm stirred and raised his body a bit, she added quickly, "Don't move yet, Longarm. I like the way you feel."

"Oh, I won't be moving much, not for a long time. Just easing my weight off you a little bit."

"I don't want that kind of easing. At least not until you've finished. You can hold on a little longer, can't you? Just until I get my second breath?"

"Sure. Rest as long as you like, Julia. I like being where I am right now, too."

Julia leaned forward and kissed him. Longarm opened his lips to her tongue and they melted together once more. Her body was moistly slick now. He stroked her sides and lifted himself a bit to rub her breasts, their tips still protruding firmly from the rosettes. She began to breathe faster.

"If you're ready now . . ." she whispered.

"Whenever you are."

She responded by raising the leg that still rested across Longarm's hips. He sensed what she wanted him to do, and lifted himself to let her free the leg on which he lay. She planted a hand on Longarm's chest and pushed his back down to the hard mattress, and then moved to straddle his hips.

"I'm not afraid you'll hurt me anymore, not now," she told him. "But I'd like to be on top this time. Unless you mind."

"Whatever pleasures you most," he replied.

Julia arched her back to raise her hips until only the tip of Longarm's shaft was still inside her. She let herself down gently, her eyes upturned in their sockets as she sank lower and still lower until she'd taken him completely into her. She began rocking her hips back and forth, bearing down hard on him.

Her position brought her breasts within reach of Longarm's face. They were big, but not pendulous, firmly full and pillow-soft. He raised his head and took a tip between his lips, sucking it into his mouth, working his tongue over the nipple and the pebbled skin of her rosette.

Julia shuddered as the satiny skin of her breasts felt the scratching of the day-old bristles on Longarm's cheeks. She twisted her shoulders to drag both breasts over the sandpapery surface of his jaws. He raised his head to let her scrape as much as she wished, then moved his lips quickly to the other breast and caressed it, too. Julia began moving her hips in a quicker tempo, moaning softly as she rocked.

Longarm brought his hips up in rhythm with Julia's rocking. He slid his hands down her sides, rubbing her silky soft skin, moist with perspiration. The aroma of woman filled the warm room, and Julia's breasts now tasted pleasantly salty as Longarm's tongue caressed them.

"I'm doing better this time," she panted. "I don't want to hurry and I want you to enjoy this, too, but can you stay hard a while longer?"

"You keep on just as long as you feel like it. I told you, it takes me a while."

"Is there time for me to stop and rest a minute?"

"Plenty. However long you feel like it."

"I feel like I want to rest and fuck at the same time," she said, then blushed. "Or do you think I'm being vulgar?"

"Oh, I've heard the word before. Used it a few times myself, I guess, too."

"You're a strange man, Longarm. What is there about you that makes me feel like I can do or say anything I want to?"

"I can't rightly give you a reason, Julia. But I'm glad you feel that way."

"Well, I do. And now I feel like going on."

Julia began rocking her hips once more. Longarm let her

set the tempo of her movements until he felt himself building. Still in control, he began thrusting up to meet her, and his response inspired her to move faster. She was soon past the stage of being satisfied with rocking. She crouched over him on her hands and knees, offering her breasts to his waiting lips, raising her hips high and dropping on him quickly, heavily.

Then she was in her final spasm, and Longarm let himself go, sank his fingers into her soft buttocks and pulled her to him while he arched his back in his own shaking orgasm. Julia fell forward on him and lay quietly, the sweat from her exertions bathing both of them.

After a while she said, "I think this is the nicest siesta I've ever had, Longarm. But it can't go on forever."

"Too bad it can't. It's been a real fine one for me, too."

"Finding out you're on my side has helped a lot. You've eased me in more ways than one." She rolled away from him. "But I'm going to have to go now. I know you'll want to rest, too. You must've gotten up early, to take Bobby hunting."

"Oh, I'm not all that tired, if you want to stay a while longer."

Julia rose from the bed and began untangling her clothes from the jumble in which they lay on the floor. She said, "I'd like to, but I'd better not. You'll come to dinner tonight, though, won't you?"

"If that's an invite, I sure will."

"I'm expecting some good news from the mine. Maybe we'll have something to celebrate."

"Does Sam Ferris think he's getting close to that new gold vein you've been hoping to strike?"

"He says it's looking good." Julia was dressed now. She leaned over the bed to kiss him softly. "Until dinner, then."

She slipped out the door and was gone. Longarm lay still for a few minutes, then got up to light a cheroot. He went to the window and pulled the shade aside to gaze out on the plaza. It was still deserted, the siesta hour quiet, undisturbed. He lay back down and finished the cheroot. Then he went to sleep.

Sounds of yapping and snarling woke him. The light on his windowshade was a deep amber now. Longarm rolled out of bed and pulled the shade away from one side of the window to look out. On the side of the plaza catty-cornered from the hotel, a half-dozen of the town's pack of stray dogs were having an argument over some scrap of food. He watched the animals for a moment, until the most aggressive of them got sole possession of the bit of meat they'd been arguing about, and the argument ended.

Long shadows from the westering sun had put most of the plaza in the shade. With the afternoon heat diminishing, La Escondida was slowly coming back to life. A woman walked along the far side of the plaza, her full skirts swaying as she moved her hips to balance the bulging basket that she carried on her head. A trio of children appeared from nowhere and vanished to the same place in some childhood game of chase. A man pulled a protesting goat across a corner of the square and disappeared into a narrow passageway between two of the squat, blocklike adobe buildings.

On the far side of the plaza, Longarm saw Terrance Barns turn the corner from the street and disappear into one of the cantinas. It seemed as good a time as any to have a talk with Barns. Longarm disentangled his clothes and donned them quickly.

Barns was sitting at a table in a corner of the dim barroom, a glass of some deep brown liquor on the table in front of him. He saw Longarm and lifted his glass in greeting. Longarm didn't wait for a further invitation. He crossed the room and sat down with Barns.

"I feel like it's getting to be that time of day myself," he said, indicating Barns's glass.

"It's as good a time as any for a drink," Barns agreed.

Longarm looked for the barkeep, but Barns had already beckoned him to the table. The barkeep was on his way to them, carrying a wicker-encased jug and a glass. He placed the glass in front of Longarm and filled it to the brim. Longarm dug out a half-dollar and put it on the table. The barkeep looked at him, smiled, and put the jug in the center of the table between the two men. He picked up the U.S. half-dollar that Longarm had put on the table, replaced it with a silver Mexican peso, and returned to the bar.

"Hell, I was going to buy the drinks," Barns said, frowning.

"You were here first," Longarm said. He lifted his glass and smelled the liquor it contained. "What in hell is this?"

"*Habanero*. It's a Cuban-style rum, not as raw as their local *aguardiente*. Good-tasting, or at least it is to me now, but it's got one bad habit. It sneaks up and hits you like a ton of bricks before you know you've drunk enough to feel it."

Longarm tasted the liquor and found it unpleasantly sweet. He put the glass back on the table and said to Barns, "I guess I'll stick to whiskey. This tastes like syrup to me."

Barns had already drained his glass and was refilling it from the jug. He said, "It takes a little while to get used to, but it suits me better than tequila."

Longarm waved the barkeep to the table. "You got American whiskey in this place?" he asked.

"*Sí, señor. Pero es muy costamente.*"

"If *costamente* means what I think it does, I don't much care what the price is, as long as I get some decent drinking liquor," Longarm told the man. "Suppose you just trot out a bottle of your best and we'll talk about the price after I look at the label."

Barns saw the Mexican barkeep's bewilderment and said quickly, "*Tome una botella del licor Americano, ni un pizca el precio.*"

With a shrug, the barkeep started back for the bar. Longarm said, "You speak the lingo down here pretty good, Barns. You been here long?"

"Not very long, this trip. A year or so. But I've been in Mexico before."

"Got a business down here, I guess?"

"No. Just living here awhile." Barns hesitated and added, "It's a lot cheaper here than at home."

He drained his glass and refilled it from the jug. Before

Longarm could ask the next question he had in mind, the barkeep returned carrying a bottle. The label on it was water-stained and faded, but Longarm recognized the orange-and-green border and his face widened into a smile.

"That's something I ain't seen in a coon's age," he said to Barns. He was fishing money out of his pocket as he spoke. When the barkeep reached the table, he asked him, "How much?"

"*Por la botella?*" the man asked. He shook his head. "*Muy costamente, señor. Un peso veintecinco centavos Americano.*"

"A dollar and quarter, U.S.," Barns translated. "Hell, Long, that whole jug of *habanero* only cost two bits Mex."

"That's cheap," Longarm replied. He handed the money to the Mexican. "I'd pay double that right now for ten-years-in-the-wood Maryland rye, when I'm running as low as I am on real drinking whiskey."

Barns was refilling his glass. He swallowed half of its contents in a gulp. Looking at Longarm with a puzzled frown, he asked, "What brings a man like you to La Escondida, Long? Julia Wheatly and Sam Ferris—I can understand them being here. And the Blantons, too. But you're not the kind of man who travels for pleasure."

"Oh, I guess you could say I'm sorta looking," Longarm replied. He'd uncorked the whiskey and now took his first satisfying sip.

"Investments? You're interested in the Wheatly mine? Scouting for some big company back home?"

"Well, now, Barns, if I was, that'd be my own affair, wouldn't it? You wouldn't look for me to make a big blow about it, if I wanted to keep things quiet."

"No. I suppose not. I didn't have any business asking. I beg your pardon, Long."

"No offense." Longarm tipped the bottle up again. "I don't get mad or nervous when a man asks me a question. There ain't any law I ever heard of that says I got to answer him if I don't feel like it."

"No. I guess not." Barns was twirling his glass nervously. He drained it with a gulp, put it back on the table and stood up. "I'm getting drunk too fast tonight. You'll

85

pardon me, Long. I'd better be going before I make a fool of myself." Picking up the almost-full jug of *habanero,* he hurried out of the cantina before Longarm could reply.

Longarm lighted a fresh cheroot before he took another small sip of the whiskey. He was looking at the swinging doors, which were still flapping gently after Barns's abrupt departure.

There's something eating on that man, he mused. *Now, it might be he's wanted for something besides killing a Ranger captain, and it might be he's just running away from some sort of canker that's eating at his mind. But he's one that'll do to keep an eye on until you can find out one way or the other.*

Beyond the batwings, Longarm noticed that darkness had settled in. There were a lot of questions he'd planned to ask Barns, but they'd have to wait. His stomach was telling him it had been a while since noon, and even a good bait of fresh deer liver wouldn't stay with a man all day.

He picked up the bottle and pushed through the swinging doors. Just outside the bar, one of the local *peluqueros* had set up shop on the plaza, his scissors and razor on a rickety stand, a straight chair with one leg wired together standing ready for his customers. Longarm rubbed a hand over his jaws. Two days of stubble made a man feel grubby. Resigning himself to a scraped face, he sat down.

Twenty minutes later, surprised that the itinerant barber's razor had been sharp after all, and having dropped off his fresh bottle of rye in his hotel room, Longarm started for Julia Wheatly's.

She greeted him with an enthusiastic hug and a warm kiss. "I was hoping you'd get here early. Sam stopped by on his way to his room, to get cleaned up. It looks like the vein that Edgar—my husband—uncovered just before he died is going to be very rich indeed."

"That ought to make you feel real good, Julia. I'm right glad to hear it, for your sake."

"To tell you the truth, Longarm, between our siesta and the good news Sam brought, I'm simply walking on air. I hope you don't mind drinking your champagne warm. There's no ice in La Escondida at this time of year, but I thought that when Sam comes back we ought to open a bottle before dinner to celebrate."

"That's a fine idea. I'd like to hear what Sam has to say, too."

"He didn't tell me much. He'd been mucking in the new shaft all day with the *obreros*, and he was terribly dirty. But we can open a bottle for ourselves and have a glass while we're waiting for him to get back."

"Whatever you'd like, Julia. I know you must feel pretty bucked up about things."

Although champagne wasn't one of Longarm's favorite drinks, and the warm champagne that he and Julia sipped to toast the new ore vein tasted a bit flat, he managed to put up a show of enjoying it. They were on their second glass when Sam Ferris came in. He hesitated in the door of the *sala*, seeing Longarm and Julia sitting with glasses in their hands.

"Come join us, Sam," Julia invited. "I've been telling Lo—" she caught herself in time and amended, "—telling Mr. Long about the new vein. Sit down and have a glass of champagne with us before we have dinner."

An embarrassed frown on his face, Ferris said, "I'll sure do that, Julia, but . . . well, I won't beat around the bush. I brought somebody with me."

"Terrance? Or George?"

"Neither one of them. You see, I stopped in for a little drink to celebrate, and ran into this American who'd just rode in, and we had a drink or two, and . . . well . . ."

"It's all right, Sam. You know how I feel about making newcomers welcome. Where's our guest? Why don't you bring him in and introduce him?"

Ferris turned and said, "Come on in, Tom."

A tall, thin man appeared behind Ferris in the doorway. His face was deeply tanned, and his concave cheeks needed shaving. His mouth was concealed by a full mustache. He wore a brown corduroy jacket, a pair of duck riding pants, and fancy-stitched boots with stirrup heels. In his hand he carried a broad-brimmed cream Stetson with a

San Antonio crease. A revolver butt was outlined in the bulge the jacket made over his right hip.

Ferris said, "This is Tom Dodd. Tom, this is Mrs. Wheatly and . . . and Mr. Long."

Dodd acknowledged the introductions with a half-bow to Julia and a nod to Longarm. He said apologetically, "I sure hope I'm not busting in on something. I tried to beg off coming, but Sam wouldn't take no for an answer."

"I'm glad he didn't, Mr. Dodd," Julia told him. "I'm glad he brought you."

"Tom's here on business, I think, even if he didn't say so," Ferris put in. "But if I followed his line of work, I guess I wouldn't be in much of a hurry to talk about my job, either. Tom's a Texas Ranger."

Chapter 8

For several moments after Dodd's announcement, no one spoke. Julia broke the silence. "Why, how interesting, Mr. Dodd. A Texas Ranger. You know, Mr.—" She stopped suddenly and brought her hand up over her mouth.

Dodd stood expectantly, waiting for her to continue. So did Longarm. Finally, Dodd asked, "What was it you started to say, Mrs. Wheatly? Mister who?"

"It really wasn't anything important. I just thought about a man who . . . who used to be a Ranger. But he was a friend of my family, a long time ago, when I was a child." She stood up. "I'd better tell Estella to serve dinner. Mr. Long, why don't you pour a glass of champagne for Sam and Mr. Dodd? It'll go flat fast, not being iced. I'll be right back."

Longarm made himself so busy finding glasses and pouring the champagne that neither Ferris nor Dodd had a chance to talk to him until Julia returned.

"We'll be ready to sit down in a few minutes," she said. "Mr. Dodd, I'm sure you'd like to wash up. Sam will show you where to go."

Ferris motioned to Dodd and the two left. Julia waited until she was certain they were out of earshot before saying apologetcally, "I'm sorry, Longarm. I almost gave you away, didn't I? I suppose I'm not used to keeping secrets."

"You didn't hurt a thing. Dodd's sure to find out who I am pretty soon, anyhow. If he hasn't already guessed."

"Will it hurt your chances of doing what you're here for?"

"I don't reckon so," Longarm said thoughtfully. "Might be that Dodd's here for the same reason I am."

"Does that mean you can work with him, then? Or him with you? Whichever way it'd be."

"Maybe, maybe not. A lot's going to depend on how fast I can work, now that Dodd's here. It might even help me a little bit, him getting here. Like the barrel told the box, two heads is better'n one."

"Well, I'm glad I didn't give you away, just the same."

"Dodd didn't notice. But he might if you forget again."

"I'll be careful."

Dodd and Ferris returned. Julia said, "I'm sure we can go in to dinner, now. I hope you'll enjoy the local food, Mr. Dodd. Most of us who live here have gotten used to it."

"Hungry as I am, Mrs. Wheatly, I know I'll find it good," Dodd assured her.

Julia's cook had done very well with the local food. There was *cabrito,* crisply succulent from long spit-roasting, sauced with a mild concoction of onions and young green chilis that had not yet gotten red and hot. A salad of tender young corn with the small local tomatoes in a mild vinegar dressing stood beside each plate, and there were the inevitable refried beans and thin tortillas, steaming hot.

When the edge had been taken off their appetites, Longarm said to Ferris, "I hear you did real good out at the mine today, Sam."

"Good, yeah. Not as good as we'd hoped, but I think the lode's going to get better as we go deeper into it."

"We've been trying to follow this vein for months," Julia explained to Dodd. "And it looks like Sam's finally hit it."

"Mining's a chancy business, I guess," Longarm observed. *Chancy ain't the word,* he thought, remembering his recent experiences with the highgraders in California's High Sierra country, and the labor warfare he'd had to wade through among the coal miners in southern Colorado. He figured he'd had enough experience with mines and mining to last him a long while, but once again he decided it might prove to his advantage not to appear too knowledgeable.

90

"Almost as chancy as Dodd's business is, I guess," Ferris replied. "Chasing gold's like running after a man who's hiding from the law."

"About the only difference is that the law has a better chance to catch up," Dodd remarked. He looked directly at Longarm. "You know what we say in the Rangers. Sooner or later we always get our man."

"I've head that said," Ferris replied, smiling.

"You must've spent some time in Texas, then, Ferris," Dodd said, "Not many except Texans know about our Ranger brag."

"No," Ferris replied quickly. "I never have even been to Texas, but I've been a lot of other places." -

Dodd frowned. "Now, that strikes me as odd. How the devil can you get to Mexico without going through Texas?"

Before Ferris had a chance to reply, Julia said, "If we're all through eating, why don't we go back to the *sala* for our coffee? I know Sam's got more to tell us about the mine."

Longarm didn't think much of the idea, but didn't see any way of changing the situation gracefully, so he stood up and followed them out of the dining room. While the others—chiefly Ferris—talked gold and mining, he watched Dodd covertly, and when not watching the Ranger, he spent part of his time wondering why Ferris had been so quick to disassociate himself from Texas and why Barns had been so quick to leave the saloon earlier.

Julia caught Longarm's eyes with a secret look once or twice, and there were several occasions when Longarm noticed Dodd glancing at him speculatively.

Longarm was relieved when the conversation dragged to a virtual standstill. There were still questions in his mind about his aborted conversation with Terrance Barns earlier in the day, and if Barns ended up as he'd started out, the chances were good he'd be in one of the two cantinas on the plaza, probably drunk enough by now to drop the guard he usually kept on his tongue. And there were still the two saloon bums to be questioned. Unlikely suspects though they might be, he still had to satisfy himself that neither of them was Clayton Maddox.

He took advantage of the first long pause to stand up and say, "If it's all the same to you, Mrs. Wheatly, I better be on my way. I got started on that hunting trip before breakfast this morning, you know."

"We'd enjoy your company," Julia replied, just the right note of friendly regret in her voice. "I know you've been busy, and if you feel you have to go . . ."

"I'd better, much as I'd like to set and visit some more."

Dodd said, "I hate to be an eat-and-run guest, Mrs. Wheatly, but I'm in about the same boat as Long. I've had a long day in the saddle, and I don't think I'd be very good company. And from what Ferris told me earlier, he's got a lot of business to talk about with you. So I'll just walk along to the hotel with Long."

Julia nodded. "I understand quite well, Mr. Dodd. Do feel free to stop in for a visit anytime you can. And there are some other Americans in La Escondida you'll want to meet if you're staying long. I'll have an all-American dinner in a few days, and you'll get a chance to meet them then."

"I'll look forward to that, Mrs. Wheatly. And I certainly thank you for a fine dinner."

Longarm and Dodd had walked only a few steps down the dark, quiet street toward the plaza when the Ranger said without any preamble, "You're a deputy U.S. marshal out of Denver, aren't you? The one they call Longarm."

Longarm didn't see much point in trying to evade Dodd's point-blank question. It was against his code to lie outright, and a lie in this case would be a waste of words.

"Yep. I figured you had me spotted two minutes after you'd stepped into the house."

"And you're down here trying to find Clay Maddox, aren't you?"

"If you weren't pretty sure I am, you wouldn't toss his name at me, now would you?"

"I'm going to take him back with me, you know, Long. I don't know why you federals want Clay, but I guess you know why us Rangers do."

"I know."

"Murder's a more serious charge than anything you could want him for. Why don't you just go on back up to Denver and leave me to run Maddox down, then?"

"You think you've got any better chance to find him than I have?"

"Sure. I'll tell you, and you see if you don't agree. First off, I know exactly what Maddox looks like. Next, I know pretty much what his habits are. And finally, I don't intend to let the Ranger force down by going back to Austin without him."

Longarm avoided an immediate answer by fishing out a cheroot and flicking a match over his thumbnail to light it. When the cigar was glowing satisfactorily, he said, "You're overlooking a thing or two, Dodd."

"Such as?"

"I reckon you've heard about the *rurales?*"

"What the hell kind of question is that, Long? Sure I have."

"They don't like Texas Rangers any better than they do U.S. marshals."

"Meaning what?"

"Meaning that if you ain't registered with the *rurales* yet, and they find out about you being here, you're in a heap of trouble."

"Damn! I'd forgotten all about that sentry outside town. All right, I'll go register. Now, what's your next argument?"

"When you do register, you're going to find out that the *rurales* will want extradition papers and all kind of red tape."

"That's all right. I've got the papers."

"Sanchez—that's the *rurale* captain here—he's not going to be satisfied with papers alone. My own hunch is that he's looking to make some money on a payoff from any fugitive you or me or any other lawman from the States tries to take back there."

Dodd grunted. "Hmph. Well, I'll find a way to get around Sanchez. Go ahead. What's next?"

"Me."

"You intend to give me trouble, then?"

"I intend to take Maddox back with me. He wouldn't be the first man the Rangers wanted that I've got through Texas with and on up to Denver."

There was reluctance in Dodd's voice when he said, "Yes. I've heard about some of your cases, Long. But that won't cut any ice with me."

"Look here, Dodd," Longarm said. "I don't blame you for wanting to get the man you're after. Thing is, I want him, too. Now, you got a point when you say murder's a bigger charge than what we want Maddox for. But after we get through with him, he can still be handed over to the Rangers on your murder charge."

Dodd thought this over for a moment. "I'll tell you what, Long," he said. "I won't say no and I won't say yes, right this minute. You give me a little while to think it over. Maybe your idea's not such a bad one, after all."

"You do your thinking, then. I'll go on about my business tonight. We'll have a drink together tomorrow, and see what we can work out."

Leaving Dodd to his own devices, Longarm angled across the square to the cantina where he and Terrance Barns had been earlier in the day. Barns was not there, as Longarm had hoped he'd be, but the same Mexican barkeep was on duty. He stared blankly when Longarm asked him, "Has my friend Barns been back here since he left earlier?"

"No entiendo, señor," the man said, shaking his head. *"Quiere whiskey norteamericano otra vez?"*

With a mental sigh, Longarm summoned up his fragmented Spanish. *"Mi amigo Barns. ¿El aquí anoche?"*

"Señor Barns!" the man exclaimed brightly. Then he shook his head. *"No ha vista, señor."*

"Whiskey, then," Longarm said. He took the glass of bourbon, wishing it was Maryland rye, and found a seat at one of the unoccupied tables. Barns might return, he thought, or one of the saloon bums he wanted to question might wander in.

Longarm was generally a patient man when stalking a wanted criminal, but Dodd's presence in La Escondida had made him restless. He sat through two solitary

94

whiskeys and three cheroots before deciding to try his luck at the cantina across the plaza.

At first glance, the second cantina was as hopeless as the first. The barkeep did know a bit of English, though his answers to Longarm's questions were discouraging.

"*Señor* Barns? Ah, *sí*. He comes here often."

"Today?"

"Early, *sí*. Tonight, not yet."

"How about the other Americans?"

"*Señor* Ferris? Ah, *sí*. *Señor* Blanton?" A shrug.

"There's a couple of others in town here."

"*Seguro, señor*." Another shrug, more expressive than the first. "*Son nadas, Borrachos, vagabundos.*"

"I know they're no-good drunks," Longarm said, exasperated. "But do they come in here regular?"

"*Seguro.* When they 'ave *dinero*."

"Either one of 'em been in tonight?"

"*Anoche,* no. But later, maybe."

Drawing on his reserve of patience, Longarm got a glass of bourbon and went over to a table to wait. The evening was well along, and with any luck, one of the three men he was looking for should show up reasonably soon. It was about time for his luck to change.

Halfway through his second whiskey, it did change. One of the saloon bums—Longarm hadn't had time since he'd arrived to find out the name of either of the two men —wandered in. He looked around the small group of drinkers, all Mexican except for Longarm, and made unerringly for the table where his fellow countryman was sitting.

"Good evening, my friend," the man said.

Longarm looked at him, judged him to be only half-seas over. The man was about the right age to be Maddox, but didn't fit Longarm's mental picture of the renegade Ranger, even allowing for a year or so of wear and tear. He was of middle height, with a paunch that was too big for his pants; he wore his belt low, his belly hanging over it. His face was as bloated as his stomach, his blue eyes almost hidden by puffy lids, his brown hair sparse and tousled in greasy locks above a high forehead. An aroma of unwashed sweat and stale *mescal* wafted from him.

"You are a stranger here, I see," the man continued. Longarm nodded.

"And a fellow American, in a strange land. Perhaps I can help you to get acquainted with the people and the customs. My name is Alexander Dumas."

"Funny," Longarm said. "There's a Frenchman I've heard of by that name. Writes books."

"Ah, yes. One of my ancestors, no doubt. I didn't catch your name, sir."

"Maybe because I didn't mention it. Name's Long."

"I am overjoyed to meet you, Mr. Long." Dumas looked yearningly at Longarm's half-empty glass. "What do you think of my offer, sir?"

"I ain't had time to study on it yet." Longarm had already weighed the probability of the man's being Maddox, and had decided the chance was small. Still, he had to do his job and make sure. He said, "Sit down and have a drink and we'll talk about it."

Dumas waved to the barkeeper first, then sat down. While the barkeep was crossing to the table with Dumas' drink, the batwings swung inward and an oversized Mexican swaggered up to the bar. He wore the braid-encrusted sombrero and stitched boots that identified him as a *rurale*. His jet mustache, like everything else about him, including the big Dragoon Colt on his pistol belt, was a bit larger than life-size.

"*Momentito, Zoribal!*" the barkeep called out as the *rurale* strode toward the bar. "*Tan pronto como sierve el borracho.*"

Hurriedly, the barkeep placed a tall glass of water-white liquor in front of Dumas, dropped a handful of ten-*centavo* pieces on the table in return for the American quarter Longarm handed him, and returned to serve the *rurale*.

Dumas drained half the glass of *mescal* before returning his attention to Longarm. He said, after exhaling a gusty breath that almost knocked Longarm off his chair, "Now, sir, my proposal. I can show you the attractions of La

96

Escondida with the experience of one who has spent years in this lovely valley."

"How many years?"

"Four, Mr. Long. Four years without a single moment away from my adopted home."

Longarm was watching the *rurale*, Zoribal, out of the corner of his eye. The big man was standing with his back to the bar, a glass in his hand, his eyes fixed on Longarm and Dumas. A bit belatedly, Longarm asked, "You'd have to be able to show me a lot more than I've seen here so far. About all—"

Zoribal took two long steps that brought him from the bar to within a foot or so of the table where Longarm and Dumas sat. He raised his voice and asked, "You are the one they call *Brazolargo*?"

"I've heard that's how they put my name into your language," Longarm answered mildly.

"We of the *rurales* have small love for you, *Brazolargo*," Zoribal sneered. "I have heard of the treachery you used to kill our men in Los Perros." He spat on the floor. The blob of spittle landed an inch from the toe of Longarm's boot. "I see you choose your friends from your own level, *Brazolargo*. *Mentiradores, puercos y perros*!"

Longarm looked at the big *rurale* with cold eyes. "Let's see, your name'd be Zoribal? Seems I heard the barkeep call you that, anyhow."

"I am Zoribal. Why?"

"Well, now, I don't quite follow your lingo, Zoribal, but I get the idea you weren't being very complimentary in what you just said."

Zoribal grinned nastily. "I do not compliment *gringos*! I spit on them!" He spat again. This time, the blob landed on Longarm's boot.

Longarm wasn't anxious for a brawl, but there was only one way to handle a bully. He eyed the big *rurale* coolly and said, "You ain't worth wasting a bullet on, Zoribal, even if you are trying to get me to draw on you. You got the guts to lay your gun by mine, here on the table, and we'll settle this man to man?"

97

Zoribal measured Longarm's size with his eyes. *"Mano a mano?"* he asked. *"Seguramente!"*

"Let's just make sure we move at the same time when we put our guns down," Longarm said. He circled the table to face Zoribal across its top and pulled his coat lapel aside. The *rurale* stepped up to the table, his hand well away from his holstered revolver. The eyes of the two men locked. The undertone of chatter that had filled the cantina had died when Zoribal first approached Longarm; now it burst forth again in a brief spate of sound.

Longarm nodded and brought his hand up to the butt of his Colt, holding it with only his fingers. Zoribal grasped his revolver butt in the same fashion. With his free hand, Longarm motioned to Dumas to get out of the way. The saloon bum wasted no time in scurrying to the side of the room.

Again Longarm nodded, and both men lifted their revolvers with their fingertips and laid them on the table. They stepped back and moved sidewise so that the table was no longer between them. Zoribal lunged first. Longarm stepped aside and let him rush through thin air. Zoribal whirled almost as quickly as Longarm did. The *rurale* had time to evade Longarm's counter-rush, and as Longarm went by, Zoribal thrust out his foot. Longarm tripped and fell.

As he went down, Longarm grabbed Zoribal's ankle. The big *rurale* fell heavily. Longarm kicked Zoribal in the jaw. The Mexican's head snapped back, and then slumped to the floor. Zoribal lay dazed, barely able to move his arms. Longarm grabbed a wrist and flipped Zoribal on his face. He put a knee in the small of the *rurale*'s back and pulled his wrists together. Kneeling on the still-dazed Mexican's wrists, Longarm snaked his handcuffs from his coat pocket and snapped the shackles on the groggy *rurale*.

Longarm's knee had encountered something hard when it was on Zoribal's forearm. Investigating, Longarm pulled a dagger from the *rurale*'s sleeve. He tossed it on the table with the guns.

Until Longarm stood up, few of those in the cantina

realized that the fight was over. Now an angry buzz rose from the tables. Longarm picked up his Colt and casually let its muzzle traverse the room as he holstered it. The buzzing died down quickly. A bellow of anger sounded from the floor as Zoribal came to his senses.

"Shut up!" Longarm snapped. "You was the one wanted to fight. Now I don't want to hear you yelling no more!"

Zoribal subsided and struggled to his feet. His face was smeared with grime from its contact with the floor. He glared at Longarm with murder in his eyes.

"What we do now?" he asked.

"We go see your boss."

"*Capitán* Sanchez?"

"Unless you got more'n one boss, he's the man I'm talking about. Come on, Zoribal, *vamos!*"

Longarm stuck the *rurale*'s revolver in his belt and dropped the knife in his coat pocket. He took hold of the chain linking the handcuffs' wrist loops and twisted it, just to show Zoribal what could happen if he began giving trouble. Then he marched the *rurale* out of the suddenly silent cantina and down the dark street to the Palacio Federal.

It was still early enough in the evening for Sanchez to be at his desk. His eyes goggled when he saw Longarm escorting Zoribal into the office. Then, when he saw the handcuffs on his man's wrists, his jaw tightened and a red flush of anger darkened his olive skin.

"What is this about?" Sanchez demanded.

"Your man wanted to fight," Longarm replied. "I obliged him. He lost." Longarm tossed the gun and knife he'd taken from the *rurale* on Sanchez's desk. "Here. I figured he better not be carrying these while I brought him back to you."

Zoribal broke in with a stream of Spanish sputtered out so quickly that Longarm could not follow it. Before the *rurale* had slowed down, Sanchez waved him to silence. When Zoribal cut off his diatribe, Sanchez turned back to Longarm.

"You have the keys for your handcuffs, Long?"

"Sure."

Sanchez was obviously controlling his anger. "You will release Zoribal at once, then. He will not attack you."

Longarm shrugged. He took out the handcuff keys and freed the big *rurale*'s wrists. Zoribal glared at him, but made no move to attack.

Sanchez lifted Zoribal's gun from the desk as though to hand it to its owner. Instead, he spun the revolver by the trigger guard and Longarm found himself looking down the Colt Dragoon's yawning muzzle.

"Now, Long, or *Brazolargo,* as you seem to enjoy being called, you have commit a serious offense against *los Rurales de la Republica de Mexico.* This is a very good chance for you to enjoy my hospitality. Zoribal, take his guns and call Mateo. Then see that he is put in a suitable cell in our jail!"

Chapter 9

Longarm's only previous experience with a *rurale* jail had been in the primitive country across the Rio Grande from Los Perros. He discovered that there was little difference in the jail to which he was now taken. It was in the cellar of the Palacio Federal; the underground area could not be called a basement, for basements are dry and clean.

This excavation was neither, though walls and floor were both of crudely dressed stone blocks. The floor was ankle-deep in debris left by a succession of occupants. The walls were damp and inscribed with scratched-in *graffiti:* names of prisoners or their girlfriends, dates, suggestions that the reader perform unconventional and often physically impossible sexual feats, patriotic slogans, and insults to *rurales* and others.

There were eight cells in the jail, four along each side of a wide central corridor, and all were empty except the one occupied by Longarm. Iron bars spaced in a gridwork of four-inch squares divided the cells from the corridor and from each other. Each cell was provided with a wooden bunk padded with a thin, straw-stuffed mattress, and a bucket. A lantern hanging from the ceiling in the middle of the corridor shed almost enough light for Longarm to see his hand a foot from his face.

Before being taken to the cell, Longarm had been thoroughly searched, stripped of his coat and vest, and his pockets emptied. The derringer on his watch chain had created a great deal of comment on the part of Sanchez and Zoribal; its discovery was something Longarm regretted, but could do nothing to avoid. His supply of cheroots and matches had also been confiscated, as well as his badge. The thought of his possessions tucked away in a cloth bag in Sanchez's desk drawer made Longarm angry each time he remembered his humiliation.

You got yourself into a real pretty mess, this time, he mused, stretched out on the unyielding mattress of the wooden bunk. *And it's your own damn fool fault, not being smart enough to walk away from a scrap. Now, seeing as you got yourself into this jackpot, you better look up your sleeve and find the cards to play that'll get you out of it.*

Clasping his hands behind the back of his head for a pillow, Longarm began racking his brain for a solution. The thudding footsteps that sounded through the wooden floor of the *rurales'* offices and quarters that formed the ceiling above the iron grid that topped his cell diminished and stopped.

After a while, the quiet began to grate on Longarm's nerves. He sat up, then stood and began to pace the cell, first from side to side, then around the perimeter. The scraping of footsteps in the corridor drew him to the front of his cell. Longarm recognized the newcomer, and after a moment of thought recalled his name. He was Mateo, the jailer.

"You wish for something, *Brazolargo?*" he asked. Mateo's skin was dark, an indication of mixed Indian-Spanish ancestry. His features were blunt and craggy; he was of what had already begun to be called, in Mexico and elsewhere, the *tipo Benito Juarez.* He went on, "Water, maybe? A *cigarillo?*"

"How much?" Longarm asked. He had a poor opinion of jailers; most of those he'd encountered always put a high price on the small services they offered prisoners.

"For you, *Brazolargo, nada,*" the jailer replied.

"How come?" Longarm asked suspiciously.

Mateo shrugged. "We have a saying, *'Favor hace favor.'* If I do something for you, then you do something for me, no?"

"That'd depend on what you'd expect me to do. If you was . . . well, if you was to get me some of my cigars and matches outa the drawer Sanchez put 'em in, up-stairs . . ."

"That is a big favor, *Brazolargo*," Mateo frowned. "*Capitán* Sanchez would be angry, very angry, if I took something from his desk."

"Maybe. *If* he was to find out about it. But I figure you'd be smart enough to bring me just a few. I don't imagine he counted 'em real careful. Just tossed 'em in, as far as I could tell."

Mateo nodded slowly. "I remember, it was as you say. So, if I do this thing for you, you will repay my favor?"

"How?"

"A small thing. A very small thing, *Brazolargo*. I have some friends who want to talk to you. I would bring them here soon, while it is still quiet, and you will talk to them. No one will know about this, you understand."

"What'd we be talking about?"

"My friends will tell you. It will be better that way."

Longarm thought quickly. He'd have nothing to lose by talking to Mateo's friends and seeing what they had in mind. And a handful of cheroots would ease the monotony of waiting. He said, "All right, Mateo. You bring your friends along, and my cigars, and we'll have us a confab."

Mateo nodded, smiling. "*Gracias, Brazolargo*. You will not regret that you do this thing, I promise you."

Apparently, Mateo's friends had been anticipating a quick reply, and were waiting nearby, for only a few moments passed before Mateo returned. With him were two men, both younger than the jailer, but both showing the strong strain of Indian ancestry that was apparent in Mateo. He handed a half-dozen cheroots and a few matches through the bars to Longarm, who wasted no time in lighting up.

Mateo told him, "Now I have done what I say I will. These are the friends you have say you will talk with, *Brazolargo*. Cristobal Flores and Luís Zaragoza. And I will stay and talk as well. I too have interest in what you say."

Flores and Zaragoza had been studying Longarm with open interest. Now Flores said, "We have hear of you,

103

even so far away as here from Los Perros, *Brazolargo*. How you make fools of *los rurales*, and send them running *como perros con colas entre sus pies*. We are come to ask you—"

"Now wait a minute," Longarm interrupted. "If you've come looking for me to take on Sanchez and his crew, that just ain't—"

Zaragoza broke in on Longarm's protest. "*Momento, Brazolargo*. It no is *los rurales* of which we are speak. It is *el Patrón*."

"Mondragón?" Longarm asked.

"*Sí*," Mateo said before Zaragoza could continue. "*El Patrón*." He spat. "The robber of our work, the one who takes our women for his pleasure."

"Maybe you better tell me more about the why of all this," Longarm suggested, puffing on his cheroot.

Zaragoza shrugged. "It is the same what happen all over our country, *Brazolargo*. *Los hacendados* own the land. Even the little bits where we make our houses they own." He shrugged, and the corners of his mouth drew down.

"And the houses, too," Flores added. "*Mira*. We are the *peons*, the *campesinos*. We work in the fields for *el Patrón* each day, except for Mass on Sunday. He give us a little bit of the crop we plant and till and harvest. We dig *las acequias* to bring us water and to water the fields, and when we drink the water it taste bitter, because *el Patrón* say the water she is his, too."

Longarm frowned. "You mean he don't pay you in money?" He remembered, now, how Mondragón had referred to "his" people, "his" land. It had not struck him then that the *peons* were little more than Mondragón's slaves.

"What is money like, *señor*?" Flores asked. He plunged his hands into the pockets of his shapeless feed-sack trousers and turned the pockets out. "These are empty, all the time empty. And so are the pockets of the other *campesinos*."

"What was it you said about women a minute ago?" Longarm asked. "Does this *Patrón* fellow take them, too?"

Zaragoza's voice was a snarl when he replied, "*Sí*. It is

our daughters he takes, the *jovenas*. On them he try to make the *niños* he cannot make with his own wife." He grinned—a twisted, ugly grin. "*El Patrón* he is not tell nobody, but that he get no *niños* on no woman he fuck it is him to blame, not her."

"But that don't stop him from messing with yours," Longarm said.

Flores shook his head. "No, *Brazolargo*. *Mira*. Two daughters I have with my wife. Today, they are too young for *el Patrón* to want, but I think of tomorrow, when they grow up."

"That's a pretty big job you're looking at," Longarm warned them. "Mondragón's got bodyguards and land patrols, to judge by what I seen the only time I was out there. And guns. You figured on all that?"

Zaragoza nodded. "We are not *estupidos*, *Brazolargo*. But we know the men of the land patrols are few, and come only seldom to *la hacienda*. They do not worry us."

"What about Sanchez and the *rurales*?" Longarm asked. "Won't they be on Mondragón's side?"

"We do not forget *los rurales*," Flores said. "But they are not Díaz's men. The *rurales*, they belong to the *hacendados*."

"What about Díaz? Won't he help Mondragón? When I was out there, he told me his father and Díaz were pals."

"*El Patrón* is make *fanfarron*, *Brazolargo*. It is—how you say?—brag. He want all to think he stands high with *el Presidente* Díaz because Díaz and father of *el Patrón* had great friendship. But Díaz is far away, and Díaz is for Díaz before all others."

"That still means you're going to have the *rurales* mixing in on Mondragón's side," Longarm pointed out.

"*Verdad*," Zaragoza said. He smiled craftily. "This is where we are count on you."

"To take on Sanchez's crew while you go after Mondragón? That'd be a fool's game. They'd cut me down fast, if I went up against 'em by myself."

"We do not expect you to fight Sanchez and his men, *Brazolargo*," Flores explained. "But to take them away

105

from La Escondida while we and our people deal with Mondragón."

"Just how in hell you figure I can do that?" Longarm asked. "Take a look around you and remember where I am, Flores."

Mateo spoke for the first time. "We don't forget. I will see that you do not stay here longer than is needed for us to make ready."

"You mean you can get me out of here?"

Mateo shrugged. "I have the keys. But if you take them away from me when I bring you *desayuno*—the breakfast —and perhaps hit me on the head so I become unconscious, who can blame me, a poor jailer, if the famous *Brazolargo* has overcome him?"

His voice enthusiastic, Zaragoza took up the argument. "We have it all planned! *Entiendes, Brazolargo!* An ordinary prisoner, Sanchez might not chase. You, he must go after, and all the *rurales* in La Escondida must go with him."

Longarm shook his head. "It's a mighty pretty scheme, I'll give you men that. But there's something you ain't thought about. I'm here on a job. If I start running from the *rurales*, the only real place I got to go is the border. When I get out of here, I aim to finish my job in La Escondida."

Mateo shook his head sadly. "No, *Brazolargo*. *El Capitán* Sanchez will not let you do that. He does not follow your laws, you he will judge by *la ley del fuego*. Do you know what this means?"

"I've heard about it, even in my own country, Mateo. A prisoner gets shot when he tries to escape. That what you're talking about?" Mateo nodded. Longarm asked, "How come you know what Sanchez has got in mind?"

"There is no record you were ever arrested," the jailer told him. "There is no list of your belongings on the jail's book. There never is one kept, when the *ley del fuego* is to be used."

"That dirty son of a bitch!" Longarm spat. "Damned if I wouldn't bet Sanchez sent Zoribal to pick a fight with me, just to have an excuse to get his hands on me!"

106

"I do not think you would lose such a bet," Mateo agreed. "That is why I am remember the thing Cristobal and Luis are trying to do. It is why I bring them here tonight."

Longarm lighted another cheroot to give him time to think. His sympathies were with the *peons*, but he wondered if they'd really thought of the odds against them. In Díaz's Mexico, all odds were with the ruling clique, and groups at the top had a way of overlooking differences between themselves when threatened by unrest among the mass of people they exploited.

Your own odds ain't much better, though, old son, he reminded himself. *There must be twenty, twenty-five men that'd be riding with Sanchez. But even the* rurales *ain't all that good shots, and if you got your own horse and guns, you oughta be able to give 'em a pretty good run. And if you're going to get shot in the back unless you do something, even a slim chance is better'n none.*

"All right, Mateo," he told the jailer. "Looks like you and your friends have got yourself a deal. When's it going to be?"

Mateo looked questioningly at the other two Mexicans. They nodded in unison. The jailer told Longarm, "If we are to do this thing, it is better to do it at once. Luis and Cristobal have only to pass the word to our people at the *hacienda*. We can be ready to act by dawn, if it is agreeable with you, *Brazolargo*."

"It can't be too quick to suit me. You're a good fellow, Mateo, but this place you run ain't the most comfortable one I've ever spent any time in. You go on and pass the word. I'll be ready whenever you say."

Flores and Zaragoza left at once, after Longarm cut short their effusive thanks. Mateo went with them, promising to return as soon as the *rurales'* office upstairs was deserted except for the lone night sentry.

"You will have no trouble with that one," he assured Longarm. "He is *un dormilion* who is only half awake, even in the daytime. And I will tell you everything you need to know when I come back to let you tie me up and lock me in this cell."

Longarm stretched out on the bunk again. It did not seem as hard as it had felt earlier, now that freedom was only a few hours away. It was freedom with a big *if* attached to it, of course, but even that kind of freedom looked good when compared to the alternative. He wasted no time making plans, for there were no plans to be made.

About all you can do, he warned himself, *is to keep your nag's nose up and stay ahead of Sanchez and his crew. And in the kind of country you'll be riding over, that sure won't be too hard to do.*

Longarm was sleeping when Mateo came back, but his finely tuned senses brought him rolling off the hard bunk and onto his feet with cat-quickness at the first small sound of the jailer's *huaraches* scraping on the stone floor. The jail was as silent as a grave, and Mateo's warning finger pressed across his lips wasn't needed to caution Longarm to move silently.

In the lowest of whispers, Mateo explained the floor plan of the first floor, and told Longarm exactly where his belongings were—coat, vest, hat, weapons and other items that Sanchez had taken from him.

"I will wait until I am sure you have gone," he said, "And give you time to get to your horse and saddle it. Then, all you must do is let the *rurales* see you. They will gather all their men before they ride after you. The *rurales* fear you even more than they hate you, *Brazolargo.*"

With Mateo's help, Longarm tore strips off the mattress-sack and tied the jailer to the bunk. He fashioned a loose gag, one that Mateo could easily dislodge when the time came for him to give the alarm. He started to wrap the gag around Mateo's jaws when the jailer stopped him.

"First you must hit me. It must be a mark that will show when they find me," he said.

"Damn it, Mateo, I don't want to hurt you."

"It will hurt but a short time. My people have been hurting for many years. Here. Take off one of my *huaraches* and hit me with it."

Reluctantly, Longarm did as the jailer asked. Mateo did not flinch when the blow landed, though an angry red weal on the side of his face began to rise at once. "Now, the gag," he told Longarm. "And—*vaya con Dios, Brazolargo*. You are doing a good thing, and He will be with you, be sure of that."

Getting out of the Palacio Federal was easier than Longarm had thought it would be. He crept up the stairs, keeping his feet close to the edges of the steps to avoid noises that might arouse the sentry. As Mateo had predicted, the guard was dozing. Longarm stepped silently behind him, clamped a calloused hand over the *rurale*'s mouth, and knocked him out with the guard's own revolver. The sentry sank noiselessly to the floor.

Fewer than five minutes of silent prowling were all that Longarm needed to find his Colt, derringer and watch, his wallet with the badge still pinned inside its fold. A quick minute more of rummaging through the wardrobe cabinet in the main office brought to light his vest, coat and hat. He spent another minute checking his guns to make sure they were still loaded, and running his hands through his coat pockets to assure himself that his emergency gear was still intact.

Then, holster adjusted to the exact angle that would put his Colt in his hand with a single rapid sweep, hat riding jauntily on his head, Longarm stepped out into the dark gray of the false dawn.

At that hour, even the night-prowling cats and dogs that haunted La Escondida's streets had gone to bed, and the town's few inhabitants had not awakened. Longarm made his way along the unpaved street to the hotel. Without the spare ammunition that his saddlebags contained, he'd be a cripple in any shootout with the *rurales*.

He entered the *posada* quietly, went to his room and picked up the saddlebags and left as silently, turning at the corner of the plaza toward Julia Wheatly's house, where his horse was still stabled. There was a horse in the stable he hadn't seen before. Longarm decided from its brand that it must belong to the Ranger. His saddle with his rifle still in its scabbard was lodged on the rail of the stall his horse was in. He was absorbed in getting the animal saddled as quietly as possible and had no idea that he was not alone until a man's voice spoke behind him.

"Long, where the goddamn hell have you been? And where do you think you're heading for at this time of day?"

If the speaker had not called his name first, Longarm would have drawn as he whirled. His catlike crouching turn placed him facing the front of the stall. Tom Dodd stood there watching. The Ranger's wide-brimmed hat was pushed back on his head, his hands on his hips.

"Well, damn you, Dodd, I might just ask you a question or two myself. How come you're out of bed and why the hell are you sneaking up on a man? That's a good way to get yourself shot."

Dodd grinned. "I asked you first, Longarm. You know, I went to both of this damn town's saloons last night, looking for you. Heard at the second one you'd been in a fracas with a big *rurale*, so I went on over to see about it. That captain of theirs, Sanchez, said you'd brought one of his men home after you'd swapped a few punches with him. Then Sanchez told me the last time he saw you was when you walked out of his office door."

"Sanchez lied to you. I been in his stinking jail all night. Or most all night."

Dodd sniffed. "I thought something smelled pretty high. Didn't figure it was you, thought maybe one of the horses had colic. How'd Sanchez come to let you go?"

"He didn't."

"You mean you busted out of a *rurale* jail?"

"It's been done before. It ain't such a much of a trick." Longarm went back to finishing his saddling job.

"No. I seem to recall some tall yarn about how you did it once before. But damn it, man, they'll be after you like possums after persimmons!"

"Sure. That's why I'll be grateful if you'll stop pestering me. I need to get the hell out of here as fast as I can."

Without a word, the Ranger stepped into the adjoining stall and slung the saddle on the rail over the back of his own big bay.

"Where you think you're going?" Longarm asked.

"Damned if I know. But if you got any ideas about riding out of here by yourself with a full company of

110

hornet-mad *rurales* after you, you've got another think coming!"

"Now hold up a minute, Dodd—"

"Hold up, my ass! There weren't any Texas Rangers at the Alamo, but there were sure a lot of them fighting when we whipped Mexico in '39, and finally got free from them. I figure any Texan's still got a few scores to settle with 'em."

"I'm not asking for any help from you."

"I wasn't listening for you to. Now finish up with your saddling and let's get to riding. You don't know where you're heading for, and I damn sure don't, either, but wherever it is, there's pretty sure to be a fight when we get there, so I'm going with you!"

Chapter 10

"If that's the way you want it," Longarm told Dodd. "You're old enough to know what you're getting into."

"I'm old enough to know when I'm being a damn fool," Dodd said. "But I guess a man's entitled to be one, now and again." He pulled the last strap tight and tested the saddle with a healthy tug on the horn and pommel. "I'm ready. Which way do we head? I haven't had a chance to scout the ground around here."

"Northeast's my choice. We get to high ground ahead of 'em in that direction."

As they mounted, the Ranger said casually, "When we've got some time to spare, you might tell me why you're setting yourself up this way."

"What makes you think I am?" Longarm asked, reining the cavalry roan out of the courtyard and leading the way to the plaza. He looked to the east. The sawtooth peaks of the Sierra Madre Oriente were outlined now against a line of pearly grey.

"Hell, Long, you're not pulling any wool over my eyes. If you were really on the prod, you'd've been gone while I was getting saddled. You act like you want the *rurales* to spot you."

"It's too much of a story to go into now. We'll have time to gab later on."

Longarm was watching the street that led to the Palacio Federal. There was no sign of activity there as yet. The building, in the hush of the beginning dawn, was as quiet as a mausoleum at midnight. He guided the horse down the middle of the street away from the headquarters building, turning in the saddle to keep an eye on the structure. Dodd looked back, too, but made no comment.

Ahead of the two riders, the dirt street became a narrowing trail a half-mile ahead before it began curving into the slope that rose from the flat floor of the valley. They rode on silently, Longarm looking back now and then. He saw Sanchez leading the first *rurales* around the end of the Palacio Federal just before the curve in the road began.

"All right," he told Dodd. "Let's kick 'em up. They're coming out now!"

They kicked their horses into a gallop. Longarm looked back. The *rurales* had seen them, of course. There were about twenty of them, give or take three or four. Sanchez was in the lead, standing in his stirrups, waving his men on. They could hear the shouts of the *rurales* through the quiet morning air. Longarm judged that their pursuers were a little more than a mile behind them. Then they could no longer see their pursuers, as he and Dodd went into the curved section of the road and began mounting the slope.

"I sure hope you know where we're going," Dodd called above the thudding of hoofbeats on the loosely packed dirt of the road. They could see far up the treeless rise now, past the last of the scattered *jacales* of La Escondida. They were about three miles from the area where the road narrowed into a trail that swept in easy arcs to the first rock outcrops that lay between the unvegetated valley and the zone of brushy undergrowth.

"It don't make a hell of a lot of difference," Longarm called back. "All we've got to do is keep ahead of them *rurales* until we get to someplace where they can't see down into the valley and where we've got enough cover to dodge around in."

"We've got time," Dodd said. "As long as they can't see us, they're going to have to slow down and watch for tracks to see if we leave the trail."

"That's about how I figured it. We still better make time, though, and keep as far ahead as we can."

Dodd nodded, and they devoted their attention to searching the terrain ahead for a suitable spot to pull in. Behind

113

them, the *rurales* were neither gaining nor falling behind. Dodd's horse stumbled, but regained its stride.

"Let's begin looking for a place to hold them off," Dodd suggested. "We can't keep this pace up very much longer."

"I won't argue that," Longarm agreed. "We've got a long day ahead, too. Best plan I can see is for us to keep ahead a little ways longer, till the country gets rougher, then take cover. It'll take that bunch a while to catch up, give our mounts time to breathe. Then we can take off while theirs are still blowed."

Dodd grinned. "By God, Long, you're talking like a Ranger. I was just thinking the same thing myself."

Both Longarm and Dodd devoted all their attention to the terrain now; they knew that the pace of the chase had been established. They concentrated their attention on the landscape ahead, looking for a spot that would give them the greatest advantages of cover and height and a clear field of fire, while still keeping the sun ahead of them and in the *rurales*' eyes.

By this time the morning was in full blossom, with the sun rapidly turning from its sunrise red into the orb of blazing white that it would remain until late afternoon. Until it rose much higher, it would glare into the eyes of a shooter sighting into it on the upsloping ground.

Both men spotted the kind of place they'd been looking for at about the same time. A score of yards off the winding trail, a knoll rose above the level of the ground. A crest of rocks topped the little hump. There was no cover other than thin-branched acacia brush within good rifle range. In unspoken agreement, they guided their horses to the knoll, rode behind it and dismounted.

Longarm opened his saddlebag. "There's plenty of time before they get here," he said, taking out the Maryland rye. "I been saving this all the way from the border, because they don't have it in these saloons down here in Mexico. But I figure we're entitled to a snort right now."

He offered the bottle to Dodd. The Ranger drank and pursed his lips. "That's sure as hell not a whiskey for boys."

Longarm drank and restored the bottle to the saddlebag. "No. But it's a pretty good tipple for a man who likes a bite in his liquor."

Dodd was pulling his rifle out of its saddle boot. He said, "I hope your Winchester's the same caliber as mine. If this thing drags out very long, we might run low."

"I've got two boxes of .44-40s here. If you need some—"

"I'm all right for now." The Ranger was distributing cartridges from his saddlebags into his pockets. Longarm emptied one box of shells into a capacious coat pocket and put the other box back in the saddlebag. He pulled out a cheroot and lighted it.

Dodd said, "Well, I guess we're as ready as we'll ever be, and they still won't get here for a few minutes. You feel like telling me what this is in favor of?"

Wasting as few words as possible, Longarm explained the events leading up to the choice he'd been forced to make. "There wasn't much else I could see to do," he concluded. "This way gives me about the best shot to keep walking around."

Dodd rubbed a thumb along his jaw. "Can't say but what I'd have turned myself into a toll-horse, if I'd been in your fix."

"I'm sorry I got you wound up in it, though."

"Hell, don't worry about me. I can handle myself."

"Sure. But it ain't your fight."

"It wasn't, maybe, but it is now. And if there's going to be a fight, we'd better get up in back of those rocks before Sanchez and his outfit get too close."

They scrambled to the top of the little rise. The rock ridge that crowned the crest was high enough to give them good protection, and even from that small height they would have an almost perfect field of fire across the downslope. The *rurales* were within sight of the knoll, though still out of range. They'd been forced to slow their pace as their mounts grew tired, and were strung out in a straggling vee on both sides of the trail. Their pace had been slowed to a lope.

Dodd asked thoughtfully, "You don't hold much of a grudge against any of those fellows, do you, Long?"

"No. Except maybe Sanchez. Or that big one on the next-to-last horse on the right, the pinto. That's Zoribal, I'm pretty sure. He's the one started all the ruckus, an he's about as mean a son of a bitch as you'd want to run across."

"Hell, all *rurales* are sons of bitches in my book," Dodd spat. "But a man can't kill every son of a bitch that he runs into, now can he?"

"I been thinking about that, too. We'll go for the horses instead of the men, then."

"I'd say so. I don't see much point in killing, unless we get into a worse bind than I figure right now."

"I sorta like that better myself," Longarm agreed. "Not that I got any more liking than you have for a *rurale*."

"In a bind like this one, a dead horse is worth more to us than a dead *rurale*. That means Sanchez will have to leave some of his men behind, or some of the rest will have to carry double," Dodd pointed out.

"All the better for us. All I ever aimed to do was to keep 'em from mixing in between Mondragón and Mateo's friends."

"Oh, we ought not to have any trouble keeping 'em busy for a while. And without getting ourselves hurt, either."

"I make the range just about right, now," Longarm suggested. He lifted his rifle and sighted. "You pick out whoever else you want, Dodd, but leave Sanchez and Zoribal for me."

Longarm fired. Sanchez's horse lunged forward, dropping to the ground as its forelegs collapsed. Sanchez sailed over the animal's head and landed in the dirt. He lay still for a moment, then sat up. His angry commands reached Longarm and Dodd only faintly. A split second later, Dodd's rifle barked and another *rurale* horse went down, rolling its rider off.

To a man, the *rurales* were battle-wise. Most of them carried their rifles across their saddles. They started firing. Longarm and Dodd crouched behind the rock outcrop, levering fresh rounds into their Winchesters as a half-dozen slugs ricocheted above their heads.

"Not very good shooting," Dodd remarked dispassionately.

"Range is just a mite long for them old Mausers most of the *rurales* is toting," Longarm said, his voice equally calm.

He and Dodd broke cover to fire again. The *rurales* had gotten closer now, and the return shots began sounding almost as the two had triggered their rifles. Before they dropped behind the rocks again, they saw that another horse had fallen and one more was limping.

"Damn nag reared just when I let go," Dodd apologized as they ducked behind their protective bulwark.

"Well, you just as good as dropped it." Longarm took off his hat before peering over the outcrop. "I guess one more round, Tom. Then we oughta hightail while they're still milling around."

"Any time," Dodd replied.

"Now's as good as another."

They fired again and crippled two more *rurale* horses. Sanchez was calling his men back to where he'd been unhorsed, and the range had changed.

Longarm and Dodd slid down the back of the knoll and swung into their saddles. They kept the knoll between themselves and the *rurales* as long as possible. When they had to veer to avoid a slope too steep for their horses, they heard the shouting that arose when their pursuers sighted them.

Dodd looked back. "They'll be starting again right soon, they're just getting horses swapped around," he reported.

"Fine. We'll make ground on 'em, then. There's bound to be another place like that one we just left, not too far ahead."

They rode on, saving their horses as much as possible by avoiding the sudden steep slopes that appeared in front of them, skirting rocky stretches and keeping their pace at a trot instead of a lope or gallop. Only when the *rurales* began to gain on them did the two lawmen spur up and begin looking for another natural formation they could defend.

"Up ahead there," Longarm called, pointing to a grove of longleaf pines thick enough to provide cover.

"Too chancy!" Dodd replied. "We can't hold 'em off there! All they'd have to do is circle around us!"

"Hell, Tom, we can't have everything our way! Let's shelter behind them trees and give 'em a couple of quick shots, then ride on! They'll have to stop, if we make every shot count!"

"I guess it's still your show, Longarm. We'll do it your way!" Dodd looked back. "Maybe we'd better, anyhow. They sure are spurring! Just the horses carrying double are hanging back."

Longarm swiveled enough to get a clear look at the pursuing *rurales*. Sanchez was in the lead again. He'd evidently taken over a horse belonging to one of his men, for he was not sharing his saddle with another *rurale*. Longarm looked for Zoribal, and saw the giant *rurale* riding in the forefront of the shrunken group. He noticed that Zoribal's mount was a handsome chestnut stallion, and reminded himself to look for it when he and the Ranger stopped to fire.

They reined in when they reached the stand of pines and let their mounts pick a way between the tree boles. When they were deep enough in the grove to be screened from the road, Longarm told Dodd, "Let's stay in the saddle. We'll let 'em get close enough so's we've got sure shots, and then slant out and let off two quick rounds. If we drop four more of their horses, we'll damn near be able to hold our own with 'em, next time we stop."

Dodd asked, "Which way you want to head when we start out again? From what I saw in front of us, we've gone about as far upslope as we better. The horses are slowing down, but I guess you noticed that."

"We're still in better shape than they are. But maybe we better just level off. Don't climb, don't drop down. And keep looking for another rocky place where we can make our next stand."

Shielded by the brush, they watched for the *rurales*. When the pursuing horsemen came in sight, Longarm frowned. It was hard to be sure, watching from among

118

the trees, but there didn't seem to be any *rurales* sharing mounts, and it didn't look to him as though there were as many of Sanchez's men as there should be.

"How many men did you count in Sanchez's outfit?" he asked Dodd.

"Ten at the most. Where the hell did the rest go?"

"He's split his bunch up. Chances are they dropped the ones who didn't have horses and sent a half-dozen slanting ahead to cut us off."

"Then we better shoot fast and ride off faster!"

"They're near enough now," Longarm said. "Let's go!"

Rifles ready, Longarm and Dodd rode out of the protecting pines. They reined in, snapshotted at the horses nearest them and, without waiting to see the effect of their shots, wheeled their mounts and galloped off. Bullets whistled past them, but the *rurales*, taken by surprise again, were shooting wildly. Several of the slugs came uncomfortably close, and a few of them kicked up dust between the hooves of their straining horses, but none of the lead found a target.

"Like I said a while ago," Dodd called to Longarm, *rurales* can't shoot for sour owlshit!"

"As long as we keep far enough ahead to be outside the range of them worn-out Mausers," Longarm agreed.

They were riding parallel with the slope now, along its side, across a stretch of country that was mostly grass and knee-high underbrush. The only cover they saw was far above them, and their horses were beginning to tire. The *rurales* were not gaining, but Longarm and Dodd were unable to stretch their lead on their pursuers.

Longarm looked back and did a quick tally. He called to Dodd, "They might be shooting better'n we think! As close as I can count, there's only nine of 'em after us now!"

"There was twenty-two or twenty-three when we started out," Dodd shouted back. "We took out five horses that first place and one the next place. Damnit, that don't add up!"

"It does if Sanchez did what I'd do myself. I'll bet a bottle of Maryland rye against a chew of plug tobacco he's got the rest of them streaking on below where the land's level, trying to get ahead of us!"

"You could be right, by God! If that's so, we might be in a spot of trouble after while!"

Jaws set grimly, Longarm and Dodd forced their rapidly tiring horses to maintain their pace. The animals were beginning to lag now, and it did little good for the two lawmen to remember that the *rurales*' mounts were in as bad shape as their own. They dogged along on the path they'd set for themselves, going neither upslope nor down, trying to find the easiest going, looking back occasionally to see how their pursuers were holding up.

For another half-mile the grim, stalemated chase continued. Longarm could feel the flanks of the cavalry roan heaving now, and knew Dodd's mount must be in the same condition. A short distance further along, Dodd confirmed Longarm's guess.

"We better find a place we can stand 'em off from pretty soon," the Ranger shouted. "This nag of mine hasn't got much more go left in him!"

Longarm had been peering ahead. "Neither has mine, and we got more trouble coming at us fast!" Longarm pointed ahead. A dust cloud raised by the hooves of four riders rose not more than a half-mile in front of them. "Sanchez did it, all right! He split his men!"

Behind them, they heard shouts bursting from the throats of the *rurales*. They looked back to see the group led by Sanchez quirting their flagging mounts to a fresh effort. The *rurales* had seen the dust cloud, too, and were trying to close the gap to squeeze Longarm and Dodd between the two forces.

Longarm pointed upslope and wheeled his roan. Dodd followed suit. The going was tougher for the horses now, and they slowed measurably. When Longarm looked back, he could see that the men led by Sanchez were gaining. He glanced ahead. The distance between them and the oncoming *rurales* was narrowing fast. They were close enough for Longarm to recognize the giant figure of Zoribal riding in the lead.

Shots sounded behind them. The pursuing *rurales* were

firing as they galloped, aiming their rifles like pistols, letting go of their reins to work the bolts of their Mausers when they reloaded. All the slugs still fell short, but from the spurts they kicked up when they landed, the lawmen knew the time they had to find cover was growing shorter by the minute.

"Up there, just ahead!" Dodd shouted.

Longarm looked to see where his companion was pointing. A wind-felled tangle of trunks of the small longleaf pines lay a dozen yards up the slope. The tree trunks were little bigger around than the calf of a man's leg, but almost a dozen of the trees had toppled in a crisscross of boles and branches.

"It's not such a much for cover, but I reckon it'll have to do!" Longarm said. "It won't help the horses much, but they'll have the same chance we will!"

"We'll make it do!" Dodd told Longarm as the panting horses neared the cover. "'I hope yours will lay. Mine's trained to."

When they reined in their mounts behind the windfall, the *rurales* coming behind them were still out of easy range for their second-hand Mausers. The four men led by Zoribal were much closer.

Before dismounting, Longarm sent a shot crashing at them, and one of the horses stumbled. It did not go down, but continued to limp ahead. The shot and the limping horse distracted the attention of Zoribal's group and delayed them long enough to allow Dodd and Longarm to grab their horses' heads and wrestle them to the ground. Pulling their rifles out of their saddle scabbards, they threw themselves prone behind the thin cover offered by the tree trunks.

"I don't know about you, Tom," Longarm said grimly as they waited for the *rurales* to come into certain range, "but this time around, I ain't going to be aiming for no horses. I'll have a *rurale* in my sights now, every time I squeeze the trigger!"

Chapter 11

"They're in range now," Dodd said.

He sighted through the bushy twigs of the fallen pines. Longarm had raised his weapon seconds before Dodd spoke, and was holding the sights on Sanchez, waiting for the range to close. He and Dodd fired at almost the same instant. The *rurale* riding next to Sanchez dropped out of his saddle. The shot man's horse reared wildly and Sanchez wheeled his mount to avoid the animal's wildly flailing hooves.

Sanchez's sudden move spoiled Longarm's shot. The slug winged one of the other riders, who swayed in the saddle but did not fall. Dodd's next bullet took down a horse, but missed its rider.

Seeing one of his shrunken force fall and another wounded, Sanchez led the men downslope until they were out of range of the lawmen's Winchesters. Zoribal and his force of four joined Sanchez's group. There were now twelve *rurales* pitted against Longarm and Dodd.

"We've cut 'em down some," Longarm commented, scratching a match across his thumbnail to light the cheroot he'd clamped between his teeth earlier, but hadn't yet had a chance to light.

"Yeah. If they behave like most *rurale* outfits, they'll mill around awhile trying to make up their minds what to do, then they'll rush us. We'll knock off another two or three, and they'll turn tail."

Longarm nodded silently, remembering his earlier battle against a squad of *rurales* up north along the border. "They sure don't believe in rushing you, even when they got all the odds going their way."

Both men fell silent then, their attention concentrated on their besiegers. Sanchez and Zoribal had pulled their mounts a few yards away from the men and were talking together. Sanchez was making sweeping gestures with his arms, and the giant *rurale* nodded from time to time.

"They're framing something up," Longarm remarked.

"Looks that way. I guess we'll find out what it is soon enough," Dodd replied.

They did not have long to wait. Zoribal walked his mount back to his bunched troops, who grouped around him. Sanchez sat where he was, turning his horse to study the windfall where Longarm and Dodd were holed up. Then Zoribal and three of the *rurales* separated from the group. They rode parallel to the slope, in the direction from which they'd arrived. They were very careful to stay out of range of the Winchesters.

"That damn Sanchez is smarter'n I figured," Longarm grunted. "He's splitting his bunch. Them three with Zoribal are likely circling us. They'll cut upslope in a minute and work around in back of us."

Dodd rolled over to get a clear view of the terrain behind their position. "There sure ain't a hell of a lot of cover up that way," he told Longarm. "Think we better try moving?"

Longarm shook his head. "There's not much place to move to. If we go on ahead, we'll still be caught between them two bunches. And I don't recall seeing any spot we passed by that's any better'n this one."

Dodd nodded. "That's about how it looks to me. Well, everything else being equal, I guess we stay where we are."

Sanchez was moving his men now. The *rurales* were spreading out along the downslope in a half-circle, with Sanchez himself in the center. Zoribal and his three riders were just beginning to move up the valley wall to get behind Longarm and Dodd. The sun was at midmorning height now, in a clear, bright day.

Dodd turned from their studying of the shifting *rurales* and said to Longarm, "What we need right now's a couple of Billy Dixon shots."

Longarm frowned. "I thought I knew just about every kind of shooting there is, but you sprung a new one on me, Tom. What in hell's a Billy Dixon shot?"

"Oh, that's a sorta Texas saying. Six or eight years ago there was a fracas between some Comanches and buffalo hunters at a little trading post up in the Panhandle, called Adobe Walls. The Indians had jumped their reservation over in the Nation, looking for trouble, and they got the hunters holed up in the post. Billy Dixon took a shot with a lot of Arkansas elevation on it and knocked down one of the Comanche chiefs where he was sitting his horse on a bluff about a mile away."

"Kill him?"

"Damn right. Spooked the Indians, they figured their war medicine had gone sour. They turned tail."

"A mile sure is one hell of a long shot," Longarm said. "I wonder what kind of gun he was shooting?"

"Buffalo gun, I'd imagine. Must've been a .50 Sharps or something like it."

"Well, we got plenty of shells. You want to try a little Billy Dixon shooting?"

"I can't see we'd lose anything by it. We might just get lucky with a round or two."

"Well, I don't hold much with by-guess-or-by-God shooting, but let's give it a try."

Because the sights of their Winchesters were not adjusted for the extreme elevation they'd need in order to reach the distant *rurales*, Longarm and Dodd folded their legs under them and sat up, Indian-fashion, with their legs crossed in front of them. The new stance raised their heads above the tree trunks, but they knew very well that their rifles outranged the older European-made weapons of the *rurales*.

"Looks like we're all set," Longarm said. He and Dodd were holding their rifles with the muzzles elevated far higher than was usual with the flat-shooting guns. "Let 'em have it!"

They fired in unison, sending off shots as fast as they could lever fresh shells into the chambers. Aiming was out of the question. All that they could do was to try to sight at a target and then hold the sight line true while they elevated the muzzles and fired.

Puffs of dust rose at the feet of the spread-out *rurale* formation and, in some cases, behind the line of riders. A lucky shot took down a horse, and in a moment, a second slug knocked one of the *rurales* out of the saddle. The *rurales'* line wavered and then broke. The half-circle that Sanchez's men had been forming dissolved into a panic-stricken bunch of individual *rurales*, all whipping their tired horses into a semblance of a gallop as the *rurales* streamed down the slope, trying to get out of range of the rifles they'd thought could not reach them.

"Now's the time to take after 'em!" Longarm called.

He and Dodd yanked their mounts to their feet and swung into their saddles. They swept downslope, firing now as the *rurales* had earlier, holding their Winchesters like pistols and letting their reins fall slack when they reloaded.

Now that the *rurales'* formation had been broken, Sanchez was unable to regroup his force. The *rurales* were soon strung out in a scattered bunch of individual horsemen, each concerned only with his own safety. After the chase had gone on for a half-mile or so, Longarm and Dodd stopped shooting except for an occasional shell that they wasted on purpose to remind the *rurales* they were still being chased.

Absorbed in the chase, neither Longarm and Dodd nor the fleeing *rurales* paid much attention to their surroundings as they swept down the slope and started across the rolling, broken terrain north of La Escondida.

Shortly after the *rurales* reached the valley floor, they veered north and headed up a wide canyon that began to grow more and more shallow as they drew closer to its end. The canyon merged with the flatlands in a final steep rise, and the *rurales* disappeared over the top of the slope.

Longarm and Dodd were close behind Sanchez's fleeing men and did not slow their pace. They topped the canyon slope and found themselves facing a full squad of regular Mexican Army cavalry, with whom the *rurales* were now mingling.

125

Before they could pull up, they were within a dozen yards of the mixed group of *rurales* and cavalrymen. They pulled rein fast. By the time their horses slid to a stop, the cavalrymen had their carbines out, covering them.

"Detenga su tiro!" the gold-braided, medal-splashed officer in charge of the cavalry commanded his men. The cavalrymen obeyed the order not to fire, but kept their weapons leveled. Coldly, the commander gazed at Longarm and Dodd. "My men will not shoot as long as you make no move to use your guns," he said. "And the *rurales* will obey my command also. I am *Coronel* Felipe Delgado, aide to *Presidente* Díaz. Now, remain silent while I discover what this is about."

His eyes turned to Sanchez, and in a voice as chilly as he had used in addressing the Americans, he asked the *rurale*, "Will you favor me with an explanation, *Capitán* Sanchez? I have always thought the *rurales* ran toward a fight, not away from one."

Sanchez saluted hastly. *"Sí, mi Coronel. Estes ladrones—"*

"Basta!" the colonel snapped. *"Habla Inglés. Quiero que los gringos oyen que su dice."* To the Americans he said, his voice still icy, "I have told him to speak your language. I want you to hear what he says, so that you can add any explanations you care to when *Capitán* Sanchez finishes."

"Thanks, Colonel," Longarm said. "That's real thoughtful of you. Neither one of us talks your lingo very good."

Sanchez looked questioningly at the colonel, who nodded. The *rurale* captain began, "These men are criminals, *Coronel* Delgado. One of them escape from our *carcel* after he tie up the jailer and *golpeada* the sentry. We see them when they try to leave La Escondida and chase them. And then . . ." Sanchez stopped, searching for an explanation of how the pursued had suddenly become the pursuers.

"How does it happen that they were chasing you when you met us, *Capitán* Sanchez?" Delgado demanded. He looked accusingly at the *rurale*. "Two *Americanos*! Two! Chasing eight of you *rurales*! Explain this to me, if you can!"

Longarm had been studying Delgado during his exchange with Sanchez. The aide to Díaz was stocky, but burly rather than fat. He had the high cheekbones and dark skin that denoted a good portion of Indian ancestry, the type of man whom Díaz trusted more than he did the thin-faced, lighter-skinned *guachapines* of Spanish descent or those whose lineage was mingled with the blood of the French who had occupied Mexico before being driven out by Juarez. Delgado's high cheekbones pushed his small obsidian eyes up into narrow, constantly suspicious slits.

"Maybe I can straighten this out, Colonel Delgado," Longarm volunteered. "In the first place, me and my friend ain't crooks. I'm a deputy U.S. marshal. Long's my name. This man here's Tom Dodd, he's a Texas Ranger." Longarm pulled out his wallet; seeing him, Dodd did the same. Longarm added, "And here's our badges to prove it."

"You will still wait until I hear *Capitán* Sanchez finish his explanation," Delgado told Longarm, his voice severe. He turned back to Sanchez. "Well? I am waiting, Sanchez."

"It is happen this way, *Coronel*," Sanchez began haltingly. He was saved further explanation when Zoribal and his three men came over the top of the slope at full gallop and reined in barely fast enough to avoid colliding with the group.

"*Sangre de la Virgen!*" Delgado exclaimed. "More *rurales*, Sanchez? With all these men at your command, how could you fail to capture two Americans?"

Sanchez began pleadingly, "*Mi Coronel—*"

Delgado cut him off. "*Bustamente! Vamonos a La Escondida. Escucho a sus cuentos en el Palacia Federal!*" He wheeled his horse, showing Sanchez his back, and said to Longarm and Dodd, "We ride to the village. Put your rifles away. You will not need them now. When we get there, I will listen to your stories and see if I can decide who is telling me the truth."

A few sharp commands from Delgado formed the group into three files. The *rurales*, Longarm and Dodd—the Americans bringing up the rear—formed a center file between lines of the cavalry troopers.

Keeping his voice low. Dodd asked Longarm, "What the hell you think's going to happen now?"

"Not much way of knowing. That Delgado's nobody's fool. He'd couldn't be, and hold down a job as an aide to Díaz. I reckon the best thing you and me can do is to see what sorta tune Sanchez sings, and then play our own whatever way seems best."

"Looks to me like Delgado's made up his mind to take over."

"He'd have the weight to do it, Tom. Even if he was just a plain regular army officer, he'd be two cuts higher'n Sanchez."

"We'll just keep our fingers crossed, then."

"Yep. And be ready to draw if things start going bad."

During the remainder of the short ride to town, Longarm and Dodd had little else to say. Sanchez, riding at the head of the column behind Colonel Delgado, spurred up two or three times and tried to get Delgado to listen to him, but each time was rebuffed.

By the time the little procession reached the village, the sun was in mid-sky. Longarm's stomach was reminding him that it had been a long time ago, and almost in another world, since he'd had dinner at Julia Wheatly's. He told his hunger to stop reminding him what the time was, and concentrated on what lay ahead.

Instead of dismounting on the street in front of the *rurale* headquarters, Delgado led the riders around behind the building. There, enclosed by a high stake fence, were corrals and a *cocinilla*, an outdoor kitchen where two women were waiting beside bubbling pots. Delgado waved the cavalrymen and *rurales* to the food, but pointed a finger at Sanchez, Longarm, Dodd, and two of his own non-commissioned officers.

"*Adentro!*" he snapped.

Longarm and the Ranger got the idea, and joined the others as they went inside. The back door led through the *rurales*' quarters, rows of cots and walls lined with pegs on which they hung spare clothing.

They went into the office, and Longarm was surprised to see Mateo sitting in the chair usually occupied by a *rurale*

128

sentry. The jailer caught Longarm's eye and gave an almost imperceptible shrug, which told Longarm nothing as to how Flores and Zaragoza had fared in their effort to depose *el Patrón*. Delgado waved Mateo away, and the jailer shuffled off.

Delgado took the chair behind Sanchez's desk. "Now," he announced, "I will listen to your story, *Capitán* Sanchez. You will begin by telling me how you came to arrest this man—" he pointed to Longarm— "in the beginning. What crime did he commit? And you will speak in English, so that he can understand of what he is accused."

"This one calls himself an officer of the *gringo* government. He taunted one of my best men, *Sargente* Zoribal, to fight him last night, and by some—"

"A moment, Sanchez," Delgado broke in. "This fight. Where did it take place?"

Sanchez frowned angrily, but choked out the words, "In a cantina on the plaza, *Coronel*."

"I see. Go ahead, then."

"By trickery," Sanchez continued, "the *gringo* bested Zoribal and brought him here. I naturally arrested him, and placed him in the *carcel*. But he is treacherous indeed, this one! He somehow overcame the jailer—you saw Mateo a moment ago, Excellency, and saw that he is but an old and feeble man. Then he came up here and overcame my sentry and escaped."

"Your sentry," Delgado asked dryly. "Was he an old and feeble man, like your jailer?" Sanchez's face darkened, but he said nothing. Delgado looked at Longarm. "Well? How speaks the captain? Have you anything to say here?"

Longarm's mind had clicked when Sanchez mentioned his arrest. He said coolly "Well, part of what Sanchez said was right. Me and that Zoribal, we had a little fracas in a saloon, but it was Zoribal begun it. I had to take his gun and a knife off him. And Zoribal wasn't in no shape to go roaming the streets, Colonel. So I brought him here where he'd be safe. I give Sanchez the gun and knife I took off his man, you can ask him if that ain't how it happened."

"And *Capitán* Sanchez arrested you?" Delgado asked.

Longarm didn't answer the question directly. Instead, he

said, "Sanchez held Zoribal's gun on me, then had a couple of his boys grab me and throw me in a cell. Sure, I got out! I wasn't charged with no crime. I reckon you'd've done what I did, in my place."

Sanchez's face had been swelling and growing even darker while Longarm talked. The instant Delgado turned to him, he burst out, "Lies! *Gringo* lies!"

Longarm interrupted, "You can check up on whether or not I was arrested, Colonel Delgado. Look in Sanchez's records. If he did arrest me like he said, you oughta find my name in there, oughtn't you?"

"Give me the arrest records, Sanchez," Delgado ordered. "I will look at them myself to see which of you is lying."

Moving very reluctantly, Sanchez dug into the drawer of his desk and handed Delgado a tattered ledger. The colonel opened it and ran his eyes over the last page on which entries appeared. He looked up at Sanchez.

"I see no name of 'Long' listed here. Nor of any other *norteamericano*."

"Call Mateo, the *carcelero*!" Sanchez urged. "He will tell you the *gringo* was put in jail!"

"Your jailer would only lie, thinking he was helping you," Delgado said. "And what you have done is not in keeping with the law, Sanchez. If you have no record of an arrest, I can only conclude that you did not arrest this man, as you claim. And as you did not arrest him, you had no right to place him in jail."

"But, *Coronel*," Sanchez pleaded, "you yourself know that there are times when records of arrest are not written down at once!"

"I know no such thing!" Delgado snapped. "It is no wonder our *norteamericano* neighbors have a bad opinion of us! And *el Presidente* Díaz has ordered such irregularities to be stopped!"

When Sanchez heard Díaz's name, he grasped for the first time on what thin ice he was treading. He gulped and said, "I am sorry, *Coronel* Delgado. Perhaps I have made a mistake."

"Indeed you have, Sanchez. Now. This other man—" He pointed to Dodd. "Did you arrest him too?"

"No, *Coronel*."

"Then why were you pursuing them?" Delgado asked. "Because this man Long fought one of your *rurales* and got the better of him? Or did you have other reasons, reasons of your own, perhaps? Some old grudge which you have not mentioned?"

"I have admit my mistake, *Coronel*," Sanchez said with as much dignity as he could muster. He looked at Longarm. "You are free to go, if *el Coronel* agrees."

"He was never my prisoner," Delgado shrugged. "Nor was he yours, either, it appears."

Longarm asked, "You mean that both of us can go now, Colonel?"

"With my apologies and those of *el Presidente* Díaz, *señores*. And of *Capitán* Sanchez as well, I am sure."

Showing how much it hurt him, Sanchez nodded. "*Sí*. With mine, too, as *el Coronel* say."

"Now, that's right nice of you, Colonel Delgado," Longarm said. "I give you credit for getting things squared away. And since we've got no more business here, we'll bid you goodbye."

An angry voice grated from the doorway, "Not yet, *gringo cabrón*! There is business we have yet to settle!"

With the others, Longarm looked across the room. Zoribal stood in the door that led to the barracks. How long he'd been listening was impossible to guess. The giant *rurale* had his revolver in one hamlike hand. It was aimed at Longarm.

Zoribal grinned wolfishly as he said to Longarm, "Now we will finish what we did not finish last night!"

131

Chapter 12

"Zoribal!" Sanchez's voice was almost a shout as he started toward the big *rurale*.

Longarm stretched out an arm and stopped Sanchez. "Now, wait a damn minute! He wasn't talking to you, Sanchez. It was me he was talking to, so I aim to answer him."

Delgado asked Sanchez, "This is the man who fought in the cantina with the American?" When Sanchez nodded, the colonel said to Longarm, "We are waiting for your answer, *Señor* Long."

"Now, you know damn well, Colonel, there's not but one answer a man can give when another one calls him a son of a bitch and dares him to fight."

"Wait a minute—" Dodd began.

Longarm cut him off. "You keep out of it, Tom. This is unfinished business between me and Zoribal."

"*Sí,*" Zoribal said. "He is make me look a *tonto* two times, now." He faced Longarm again. "Well, *gringo*? We fight, you and me?"

"Looks that way," Longarm said coolly. "Whenever you're ready, Zoribal, I'll be pleased to accommodate you."

"Is no better time as now," the *rurale* replied.

"Maybe we better ask the man who appears to be in charge of things around here now." Longarm looked at Delgado. "Colonel, you just heard how it is between me and Zoribal. He's the one that wants to fight, not me."

"You refuse to take his challenge, then?" Delgado frowned.

Longarm shook his head. "Now, that ain't what I said. Except somebody ought to tell Zoribal he's biting off more'n he can chew. There ain't no way he can get that big clumsy hogleg of his out of the holster before I cut him down."

Zoribal snarled, *"Gringo cobarde!* You run from danger, now! But me, I got no afraid from you!"

"Oh, I ain't going to back off," Longarm told the *rurale.* He turned to Delgado. "Except I want you to see that everything's handled on the level. No backshooting by some of Zoribal's chums. Last time I faced a *rurale,* that's what happened, and two of 'em got killed instead of just one."

"You intend to go on with the *mano a mano,* then?" Delgado asked.

Longarm had his eyes fixed on Delgado's face. For a fleeting second he got a glimpse of the real man behind that impassive bronze mask. A flicker of pure animal pleasure flashed in the colonel's slitted obsidian eyes—the same pleasure, Longarm thought, that Delgado's Aztec ancestors must have shown at the prospect of a blood-letting.

"I don't walk away from unfinished business," Longarm replied. "If you guarantee me I'm only taking on Zoribal, and not Sanchez and the rest of his outfit, I'm ready right now."

"We will go, then." Delgado indicated the door in which Zoribal stood. "There is room for all behind the building. And you have my word, *señor,* that the fight will be a true *mano a mano,* between only the two of you."

Zoribal must have boasted to his companions about what he planned to do. The barracks was deserted, and the *rurales* and cavalrymen were all in the stake-fenced enclosure between the rear of the building and the stables.

As they went out into the open, Dodd lowered his voice and told Longarm, "You ain't asked me to, but I'm going to be keeping an eye on that Delgado. If he don't do what he says, I'll be ready."

"Thanks, Tom. But I think Delgado's going to let Zoribal have a crack at me without Sanchez butting in. Zoribal gets killed, he might figure that'll learn Sanchez a lesson."

"What if it's the other way around, Longarm?"

"You let me worry about that, which I ain't."

"Just the same, I'll be on the lookout."

Neither Longarm nor Dodd seemed aware that at some time that morning they'd stopped prickling at one another like bantam roosters and that something akin to friendship had developed between them.

Colonel Delgado's appearance hushed the excited talk that had filled the yard. The cavalrymen and *rurales* drifted into a division, one on the side of the yard in front of the stables, the others on that nearest the building. The area between the two groups was left clear to serve as the dueling ground.

Delgado asked Zoribal, *"Entiendes Inglés, Sargento?"*

"Sí, Coronel."

"Pues, hablo en Inglés," Delgado said. "You men will stand back to back in the center of the clear space. You will keep your hands at your sides. I will count to five, and at each count you will each take one step forward. On the fifth count, you will turn and draw your weapons and fire. Is this clear?"

"Claro, Coronel," Zoribal replied.

"Clear as day," Longarm said.

Delgado raised his voice. *"Ningun hombre se tira pistola ni fusil! Algún se hace, tiro yo mismo!"* He asked Longarm, "If you did not understand, I have warned the men that I will shoot anyone who tries to use a weapon. Does that satisfy you that the combat will be fair, *señor?"*

"Couldn't ask for more, Colonel. And I'm ready whenever Zoribal is."

"Take your places, then," Delgado said unemotionally.

Longarm and Zoribal walked to the center of the cleared area between the lines of the cavalrymen and the *rurales*. They did not speak or look at one another. When they stood back to back, the peaked crown of the *rurale's* sombrero towered nearly a foot above Longarm's flat-creased hat.

From the front of the *rurales'* straggling line, Delgado's voice came clearly as he began to count: "One! Two! Three! Four!"

At the count of four, Longarm tensed the muscles of his

right arm ever so slightly. Then, instinctively, he drew and whirled, ready to trigger his Colt, when the sound of a pistol shot blasted the quiet before the colonel gave the fifth count.

He saw Zoribal crumpling to the ground, the big Dragoon Colt falling from his lifeless hand. Delgado stood with his own pistol still extended. Longarm stopped his trigger finger just in time. He looked at the colonel.

"Bastardo peon!" Delgado growled. "He turned when I counted four!"

Longarm holstered his revolver as he walked slowly toward Delgado. When he reached Delgado, he said, "I'll give you this, Colonel. You kept your word." He extended his hand to Delgado.

Delgado ignored the proferred hand. Icily, he said, "I could not let an ignorant *peon* shame me and Mexico. You will go now, *norteamericano.* I do not want to look at you again."

Turning on his heel, the colonel stalked into the barracks. With his departure, a burst of excited talk swept over the yard as the men began to gather around Zoribal's body.

Dodd hurried up to Longarm. "Let's grab our horses and get the hell out of here."

"It can't be a minute too soon for me," Longarm replied. "I don't figure we're going to be what you might call popular around here."

"It would've been worse if you'd shot that *rurale,* instead of Delgado doing it," the Ranger pointed out.

"Sure. I'm glad I didn't have to kill Zoribal, though, Tom. I never did see a man packing a Dragoon who could get it out fast enough, when push comes to shove."

Mateo caught up with the two just as they were leading their horses out of the gate into the alley. In response to Longarm's questioning look, the old jailer shook his head.

"Nada," he said. "But it is too soon for me to have hear from Cristobal and Luís. *Pues, hay otra cosa* I must tell you, *Brazolargo,* a thing I hear from *los soldados* of *Coronel* Delgado."

"What's that?"

"You are friend of *la Señora* Wheatly, no?"

"I guess you could say I am. Why?

"And you are know *el Coronel Delgado es ayudante del Presidente Díaz*?" Longarm nodded and Mateo dropped his voice to a hoarse whisper. "Delgado is here to learn about the gold."

"You mean the mine Mrs. Wheatly's been trying to get going again?"

"*Sí. El capital* is not too far away from anyplace in Mexico to keep Díaz from smelling gold."

"What about the mine, Mateo? What's Díaz thinking about?"

Mateo shrugged. "*Quién sabe*? Who is know what *el Presidente* is think?"

"You guess Díaz is putting a watchdog here, afraid *el Patrón* might hold out on splitting his share of the mine with Díaz?"

"Who can know, *Brazolargo*?"

"Where does that leave your friends Flores and Zaragoza?" Longarm asked. "What's Delgado being here going to do to their scheme to get rid of Mondragón? Won't Delgado be on his side?"

Mateo shrugged. "*Quién sabe*? They do not know yet that Delgado is here, or why. I will send word to them, but what can they do?"

"Ain't much anybody can do right now, I guess," Longarm said thoughtfully. "Looks to me like it's just a case of wait and see."

Mateo nodded. "*Es sobre los brazos de Dios*."

"Get word to me if you hear anything, will you, Mateo?" Longarm asked. "Mrs. Wheatly's a nice lady. I'd hate to see her get crossways with Delgado."

"*Sí*. So soon as I have news, I will send you."

Dodd had been listening, frowning occasionally, while Longarm and Mateo talked. As they mounted their horses and walked them toward the street, he asked, "What in hell do you think you can do about Delgado and that gold mine, Longarm? If you start mixing in between Mrs. Wheatly and Díaz, you're going to find you've bit off a mouthful you can't swallow."

"Maybe not. But I can sure do a lot of chewing."

"I'm glad it's your mess instead of mine. I've got to get on with the job I was sent here to do."

From Dodd's tone, Longarm concluded that their temporary truce, an alliance of professionals in a strange country, was over. He said, "Sure. And I ain't forgetting I owe you for helping me out today. Well, you go ahead with your work, then, Tom. I'll be going to call on Mrs. Wheatly and sort of hint at what she's got to be watching for."

At the corner of the plaza they separated. Dodd rode in one direction, toward his hotel, and Longarm rode in the other, heading for Julia Wheatly's.

Julia was sitting in the patio, sipping from a tall glass, when he rode in. She smiled and waved, the wave turning into an invitation to join her. The stable boy came running up to take the cavalry roan. Longarm dismounted and walked over to where Julia was sitting.

"Good Lord, Longarm!" she exclaimed when she saw his grimy face and the condition of his clothes. "You look like you've just come home from the wars! Where in the world have you been? I was looking for you to come and have lunch with me."

"I got sort of sidetracked last night," Longarm explained as he sat down. Her mention of food had suddenly brought back his ravenous hunger. "Now you mention it, Julia, I didn't have time to stop for a bite at noon. And I guess I missed breakfast, too."

"You're starving, then! I'll call Estella and have her fix you something. And your clothes! We'll have to take care of them, too, but that can wait until you've eaten. I'll go get Estella. It won't take a minute."

Julia disappeared into the house. Longarm walked across the patio to the stable, where he found the boy unsaddling the roan. He dug out his bottle of Maryland rye and a handful of cheroots and walked back to the table. He thumped the bottom of the bottle on the heel of his hand to spring the cork out to where he could take it between his teeth and pull it the rest of the way. Taking a healthy swallow, he put the bottle on the table and lighted up. When Julia returned, he was leaning back, wreathed in a cloud of fragrant smoke.

"Estella will bring you some food right away," she said. "I see you've already served yourself a drink."

"If you've got a glass handy, you're welcome to join me," Longarm said.

"Pour a drop or two into my lemonade. Just enough to flavor it. Then tell me where on earth you've been and what you've been doing."

While Julia sipped her drink and Longarm alternated small swallows of the rye with puffs at his cheroot, he sketched what had happened. He stopped after he told her of the aborted shootout with Zoribal. The news that Mateo had given him still needed some digesting before he passed it on to her.

Estella brought Longarm's lunch, which consisted of *albondigas*—balls of finely chopped meat spiced with ground chili peppers and coriander, cooked in a tomato-like sauce heavy with diced onion and slivers of garlic, with fried eggs—accompanied by paper-thin *tortillas de harina*. He ate hugely, in spite of his preference for plain fried steak and potatoes, and topped off the meal with a tot of whiskey.

Lighting a fresh cheroot, he leaned back in his chair and told Julia, "Now I feel like I could start all over again."

"I'll tell Estella to bring you some more. There's plenty in the kitchen."

"I was only funning you, Julia. I had plenty."

He looked at her across the table. She was wearing a *china poblano* blouse of fine-spun white cotton with a U-cut neckline that was open almost to the ends of her shoulders and dipped low enough in front to show the beginning of the cleavage between her breasts. A full skirt, its fullness emphasized by several underskirts, was gathered by a drawstring at the waist. A pair of native *huaraches* completed her costume.

Longarm said, "You look awful pretty today. I just wish I felt as good as you look."

"You'll feel better after you've had a bath and get some

138

fresh clothes on. That must've been a wild ride you and Mr. Dodd had this morning. To say nothing of what happened later."

"I do feel right grubby. Only I felt more hungry than dirty, a few minutes ago."

"We'll take care of that right away. Estella's heating water for your bath, and she'll give your clothes to the *lavandera* to wash while you're bathing. They'll dry fast, in this warm sunshine. You can wrap up in a bedsheet if they're not dry when you finish your bath."

"Now, you don't have to do all that for me. I can fix it up at the place I'm staying to get my clothes looked after."

"Nonsense. Why should you do that, when I've got all these servants just sitting around idle half the time? Come on, we'll go in and see how your bath is doing."

Longarm followed Julia into the house. She led him through the main *sala* and down a hallway to a large room —her bedroom, Longarm realized—furnished with only a wide bed, a bureau, a dressing table, and two chairs. Just as they entered, Estella came through a door at the opposite side of the room, carrying a large pail.

"'Sta listo el baño, señora," she said.

"Bueno," Julia replied. "Quedarse un momento, Estella; tome los vestidos del señor a la lavandera." Estella nodded, and Julia told Longarm, "Go in the bathroom and hand your clothes out. I'll have the *lavandera* wash everything but your coat and vest."

"Whatever you say," Longarm replied.

He went into the bathroom. A built-in tub made of tiles occupied one wall of the room; along the other stood a wide, padded lounge. A washstand beside the tub held towels, a washbowl and a pitcher, and, Longarm was sure, a slops jar concealed in the compartment below it.

Longarm took off his gunbelt and hung it carefully from the corner of the stand, worked his feet out of his boots, and shed his clothes. He handed the soiled garments through the door and stepped into the tub. The water was lukewarm, neither too hot nor too cool to fit the warmth of the late afternoon.

Cupping the warm water in his hands, Longarm lifted

them above his head and let the water cascade over his face and down his shoulders, feeling the surface grime melt away. There was soap in a saucer on the rim of the tub. He was just dipping the soap in the water when the door opened and Julia came in.

Somewhat hesitantly, she said, "I thought you might like for me to soap your back for you."

"I can't think of a thing I'd like better. But there's not any need for you to stop with my back. It'd feel good to me if you was to soap me all over."

"I'll have to get in the tub with you to do that, Long-arm."

"I thought maybe you would. That's why I said what I did. It's a big tub. There's plenty of room for both of us."

Julia was already slipping her blouse down over her shoulders. She pulled the knot of the drawstring at her waist and slid blouse, underblouse, skirts and petticoats over her softly rounded stomach and flaring hips. Lifting her feet out of the *huaraches*, she stood beside the tub looking down at Longarm.

He looked up at Julia. She was a rounded column of pink flesh, long thighs tapering up from her trim calves to a sparse black pubic vee. Her hips and stomach arced into the curve of her waist, and above them her full breasts swelled, their tan-tinted rosettes already pebbling and their tips beginning to pucker and thrust outward.

Longarm felt his groin twitching. He reached up a hand, and she took it and stepped down into the tub, then lowered herself to stretch out beside him. Her body entering the water raised its level until they lay together weightless, almost floating.

As their lips came together and opened to allow their tongues to meet, Longarm felt Julia's hand brush down his side to grasp him and enclose him. When they could hold the kiss no longer, he lifted her body, a light weight in the buoying water, and started to caress her breasts with his lips and tongue.

Julia took Longarm's wrist with her free hand and guided his fingers between her thighs. He fingered her gently, her legs parting to allow him to reach her better.

140

Julia gasped as Longarm touched her pulsing clitoris. She tightened her grip around him, and slid her hand gently back and forth to bring him to an erection faster.

Longarm was still not quite hard, but he knew that Julia was waiting impatiently. He stopped caressing her with his fingers and took her hand with his, lifted it, and let her tuck the tip of his hardening shaft inside her. The warmth of her inner lips, hotter than the water in which they lay half-suspended, began to finish what her hand had started.

Even while his erection was still growing, Longarm was sliding slowly inside her. Julia accepted his penetration with throaty murmurs of delight. She curved her back and slid her thighs languorously up his sides. Longarm did not hurry. He stopped the slow thrusting of his hips to kiss her, and Julia wrapped her arms around him, pressed her breasts hard against the wet brown hair on his chest, and began twisting her torso to rub her nipples against its roughness.

"What a sensation!" she sighed. "I love it when I can feel you swelling up to fill me, Longarm."

"You make a man want to swell up."

"Let's just stay in the tub the rest of the day," she suggested. "At least until the water gets cold."

"I'll stay as long as you want me to. Or as long as I can."

"Make it last a long time. We were in a hurry, the other day. Not that I didn't enjoy it, but I've been without a man for such a long time that I kept coming before I wanted to."

"We won't hurry till you say so," Longarm promised.

He began a measured stroking, withdrawing until he almost slipped from her hot wetness, then returning slowly to full penetration. Julia rotated her hips with equal languor and, when he ended deep inside her at the end of each slow thrust, tightened her knees around his waist to hold him pressed against her. Longarm was content to let her set the pace until he felt the muscles of her thighs begin to grow taut. He speeded the tempo of his stroking.

"Go faster if you want to, now. I'm going to float off,"

141

she whispered to him between their tongue-twining kisses. "But don't you stop, even when I do."

Longarm increased the timing of his deep lunges. Julia's head was lolling back now, her taut lips outlining her open mouth as she began to gasp and tremble. Longarm thrust harder and she twisted in his embrace as her back arched spring-tight and she cried out while shaking and trembling each time he pounded into her. Then her entire body shook in a long convulsion and she lay limply in his arms.

Longarm was far from ready. He slowed down, timing his long thrusts carefully. Slowly, Julia revived from her massive orgasm. Longarm continued to drive into her, faster now as he began to build. He held himself back until Julia began whimpering again, until he felt her muscles tighten and tremble, then he moved as fast as he could in the hampering, cooling water.

"Whenever you're ready!" she gasped. "Oh, Longarm, hurry, hurry! I'm just beginning to—oh, now, Longarm, now!"

Longarm thrust again and then again, and let himself go and pulled Julia to him tightly while they shook together, the water rippling over their quivering bodies until their breathing slowed and their muscles relaxed and they lay still.

Chapter 13

When the water reminded them of time's passing by growing cooler, Julia laughed and said, "I never did soap your back."

"Why, you can do that anytime. We enjoyed what we were doing a lot more than we would just a soaping."

"I'll soap it for you now," she offered. "Not just your back, either. Kneel down in the tub, and I'll soap you all over."

Longarm got on his knees. The air was just a bit cooler on his wet torso than the water on his calves. When Julia stood up, the water level in the tub dropped to the middle of Longarm's thighs. Julia leaned down to cradle his flaccid flesh in a brief caress before she picked up the bar of soap and began to rub it across his shoulders and down his back and over his chest. Each time her fingers encountered one of Longarm's scars, she exclaimed with surprise.

"How can one man carry this many scars and still be as powerful and healthy as you are?" she asked when she finally finished soaping him.

"Maybe it's luck. Maybe I just ain't got enough sense to know when I'm beat. They don't bother me a bit anymore, though."

"At least the most important part of you isn't scarred," she smiled.

While they talked, Julia had filmed his chest and the rippling muscles of his belly with the soap, and now she lay the bar aside after rubbing it well over her hands. She dropped to one knee beside Longarm and began soaping his crotch. Her hands, warm and slippery, lifted his pouch and massaged it gently, cradling it in her cupped fingers.

She began working in his pubic hair, sliding the length of his flaccid flesh with her soft, silk-smooth fingers. When Longarm began to grow hard under the massaging of her slippery hands, she gave a chuckle of delight.

"You're wonderful, Longarm! It's only been a few minutes since you were in me for almost an hour, and now you're getting hard again." She looked at him questioningly. "Is it too soon for you? Because feeling you swell up in my hands is doing things to me."

"It's not too soon. Rinse off this soap you've slathered me with, and I'll prove it to you."

Julia cupped her hands and brought palmsful of the cooling water up to his shoulders, smoothed the rivulets down his torso, until the soapy film was gone. Longarm reached for her to embrace her. She pulled away.

"Not in the tub, this time. The water's too cold now. Let's go in my room and get in bed."

"I'm still soaking wet and you are, too," Longarm objected. "If we don't want to get your mattress all wet, we'll have to dry off."

Julia ran her fingers caressingly along his jutting erection. "I don't want to wait that long! You don't either, from the way you look. Come on, we'll use the bench over there."

She was out of the tub first, leaving a trail of wet footprints on the tile floor as she pattered across to the low, padded bench. By the time Longarm followed her, Julia was kneeling on the bench, her buttocks high. One of her hands was stretched back between her spread thighs. Longarm stepped up to her, and Julia grabbed him and positioned him and Longarm drove into her. Buried full length, he pressed firmly against her soft buttocks and held himself still for a minute.

Julia lowered her shoulders to the bench and rested her head on her forearms. "Now, drive hard!" she urged him. "Quick and deep!"

He spread his feet, grabbed Julia's hips, burying his calloused hands deep in her soft flesh, and thrust with full force until a whimper of mixed pain and pleasure burst from Julia's lips.

"Faster!" she gasped. "Faster!"

Leaning backward, Longarm pounded, pistonlike, into her. Julia was panting now, her hips twisting in his grasping hands. Her urgency was bringing Longarm along quickly. He did not try to hold back. There was no need, for Julia's body was already heaving frantically in a prolonged climax that lasted until Longarm reached his own and jetted in furious, shaking jerks until he was drained and becoming flaccid even though he was still buried deeply in her.

Julia sighed. She moved her hips and Longarm released her and sat down on the bench at her feet. Julia stretched out, her legs resting on his thighs. Twilight had crept into the room unnoticed, and in the soft light she smiled at him contentedly.

"It's better every time," she said. "And I didn't think that was possible." She swung her legs off the bench and sat up. "I'm so pleasantly tired. Would you like to take a nap with me, Longarm? You must be exhausted, after the day you've had."

"I can't think of anything I'd enjoy more, right now."

Longarm stood up and stretched. He didn't relish the job he was facing. Sooner or later, he was going to have to give Julia the unpleasant news about Delgado's interest in her mine, but he thought that a delay of an hour or so wouldn't make all that much difference. And Julia might not get so upset if she was rested when he broke the news. The mood into which they'd both fallen was too pleasant to shatter at the moment.

He took his gunbelt and followed her into the bedroom. His coat and vest were hanging over the back of a chair, neatly brushed. His shirt and underwear lay folded on the chair's seat. Longarm fished out a cheroot and lighted it while he hung his gunbelt on the bedstead, arranging the holster so the butt of the Colt would be within ready reach.

Julia stretched out on the bed and watched Longarm curiously while he was making his preparations. She asked him, "Are you always this careful when you take a nap?"

"Pretty generally. In my line of work, a man's got to be."

He looked at Julia, and saw her eyelids drooping. Stubbing out his cigar, he lay down with her. She snuggled up to him and turned her face up for a kiss. Longarm kissed her gently. Julia laid her head on his muscular shoulder with a contented sigh. Sleep claimed them both almost instantly.

A soft rapping at the door roused Longarm from sleep. He rolled to his feet beside the bed and stood there, ready to reach for his Colt.

Julia woke more slowly. She sat up in bed and called, "Yes?"

"*Señora?*"

"*Sí, Estella. Que pase?*" Julia replied.

"*Es un hombre quiere hablar con el señor,*" the maid said.

"*Momento,*" Julia answered. She said to Longarm, "There's a man who wants to talk to you. What shall I tell Estella?"

"It's all right." Longarm was already starting to dress. "Only two people know I was coming here." Raising his voice, he asked "*Qué se llama el hombre?*"

"*Digame su nombre es Mateo,*" the maid answered.

"That's the jailer from the *rurale* headquarters," Longarm told Julia. "Maybe he's heard how his people are doing at the Mondragón place." He hesitated a moment, then said, "But I guess I better tell you now, Julia. There's a chance he might have some news you won't like. I didn't say anything before, but you better come along while I talk to him. Tell your maid we'll be right along. I'll fill in the gaps while you get dressed."

"Bad news?" Julia frowned.

"Might be, might not be. I don't rightly know myself, yet."

Julia rose from the bed, calling to the maid, "*Diga el hombre quedarse, Estella. Venemos prontito.*"

"*Segura, señora.*"

As she went into the bathroom to get her clothes, Julia asked, "What kind of bad news are you expecting, Longarm? And why didn't you say something before?"

146

"Because I didn't know, Julia. And still don't. It might not have anything to do with you at all, but that Colonel Delgado I told you about might've come here to nosey around your mine."

"Why? I know that Edgar did everything Mexican law required to make his ownership legal. And the attorney he hired in Monterrey filed a copy of his will when the mine passed on to me. I can't see any reason—"

Longarm interrupted her. "Now don't go borrowing trouble. All I know is that Mateo heard Delgado's men mention your mine. But Delgado might be here on some business with Mondragón, and his men just heard him say something about the mine and got to talking among themselves."

Julia was standing in front of the dressing table now, arranging her hair. She was frowning. Finally she said, "Well, let's go and find out whether it's good news or bad."

There was no one in the *sala* when they got there. Julia called, "Estella?" and the maid came to the door. "*Adónde 'sta el hombre?*" Julia asked.

"*Afuera.*" Estella's nose wrinkled. "*Es peon, señora.*"

"*Pues, llevarse aquí.*" Julia told her. She smiled at Longarm when the maid flounced out. "Estella has the Mexican sense of propriety. Poor people don't belong in the parlor."

Mateo came in, clutching to his chest a straw hat with a ragged brim. After acknowledging Julia's presence with a bow, he said to Longarm, "Cristobal and Luis have send me message, *Brazolargo*. They have take *el Patrón y su esposa* prisoner. All the *peones de la hacienda* have join them. Even the *pistoleros* have help them."

"What're they figuring on doing now?" Longarm asked.

Mateo gave one of his expressive shrugs. "They think maybe there is paper *el Patrón* must sign to give them land. If they have paper saying they own land, then he must pay them for work and for crops, no?"

"That's the way it'd be where I come from," Longarm agreed. "I guess it'd be the same here."

"*Pues*, they are work on that now. But *el capitán y el coronel*, they know what is happen at *la hacienda* now."

"What're they going to do? Go help Mondragón?"

147

"No, *Brazolargo*. Not now. *El Capitán* want to go right away, but *Coronel* Delgado, he say to wait."

"Why? Seems to me he'd be as anxious to help Mondragón as Sanchez is."

Mateo shook his head. "I am hear what they say when they talk about this thing, *Capitán* Sanchez and *Coronel* Delgado. The *coronel* is say what you and me we talk about before, the mine of the *señora*." Mateo inclined his head in Julia's direction.

"Apaserado de la mina, qué dicen?" Julia asked Mateo.

Mateo looked questioningly at Longarm, who nodded. The jailer said, "Delgado is say *el Presidente* is hear the mine is one that will soon be *muy rico*. This is why Delgado has come with his men to La Escondida. If it is true about the gold being found in rich veins, then Delgado is to . . ." Mateo stopped, struggled for the unfamiliar word.

Julia asked, *"Decomisar?"* For Longarm, she translated, "Confiscate."

"Sí," Mateo agreed. "To take it for Díaz himself."

"He can't do that!" Longarm exclaimed. He looked at Julia, and asked, "Didn't you tell me a minute ago that your husband went through all the legal flummery with the government before he started looking for that new vein?"

Mateo interrupted. *"Brazolargo,"* he said sadly, "Díaz *is* the government. What he want to do, he is do and no one is to stop him."

"He's right about that," Julia told Longarm. "If Díaz wants my mine, he'll find a way to get it, legal or not."

"Señora Wheatly is speak true, *Brazolargo,"* Mateo confirmed. "If *el Presidente* is want the gold, he is take it." He shook his head. "He is maybe not only take the gold, he is *probablemente* tell Delgado that he must *disembrazar* who is have it now."

Julia nodded, and her voice was unsteady when she turned to Longarm and said, "Díaz is a pirate, you know, and they have a saying that dead men tell no tales."

"You mean he'd tell Delgado to get rid of you?"

148

Julie had recovered her composure by now. "It wouldn't be the first time something like that happened."

"What about Mondragón?" Longarm asked. "Ain't the mine on his land?"

"But if the people have taken over the Mondragón *hacienda*, then Díaz will find it easier than ever," Julia said. "He won't be dealing with an aristocrat, he'll be putting down a revolt of the *peons*."

"*De verdad*," Mateo said soberly. "*El Patrón* is have only what Díaz give him. And I say again, *Brazolargo*, Díaz have no *lealtad* for those who help him yesterday."

"Like Mondragón," Longarm commented. "Well, Mateo, I guess you'll let us know if there's any more news from your friends, if they get Mondragón to give in."

"*Sí, Brazolargo*. I will find the way to get you the message. Better I go back now to the Palacio Federal. It might be something happen there you want to know about."

With a courtly bow to Julia, Mateo left. For a moment, Julia and Longarm stood looking at one another. Her face was so creased with worry that Longarm took her in his arms to comfort her.

"Damn it, Julia! If I'd thought I'd be hurting you by helping Mateo's friends, I'd have butted out of this mess before I ever got into it!" he said.

"It's not your fault," Julia assured him. "Delgado was on his way here even before the *peons* revolted. Díaz was ready to take the mine while he thought Mondragón was still the *hacendado*."

Longarm said angrily, "There's got to be a way to clean this mess up!"

Julia replied grimly, "Short of getting rid of Díaz, I don't see what it would be."

"We'll sit down and hash it over," Longarm told her. "Maybe one of us can figure something out." He reached for a cheroot, and realized that he'd left them in the bedroom when he hurried down to talk with Mateo. He said, "You sit down, I'll be back as soon as I go get my cigars."

He was just coming back into the *sala* when a slow thudding of hooves reached them from the patio, followed by a brief, indistinguishable murmur of conversation.

149

"That sounds like Sam coming back from the mine," Julia said. "Maybe he'll have some idea about what we can do. He's spent a lot more time on mining operations here in Mexico than I have."

Sam Ferris came in. His face was streaked with grime, his flannel shirt bore big stains where dirt had dried on sweat, but he was smiling broadly. He said, "Mrs. Wheatly, it looks like we've hit it! We've finally got down to that big vein Edgar always said was there!"

"Are you sure?" she asked. In spite of the threat she was facing, the dream of gold still drew her. "As big as Edgar thought it'd be?"

"A lot bigger than I thought when we first saw the color of it yesterday."

"Well, I'm real glad to hear about your luck," Longarm said. "Now, what we better do is figure out how Mrs. Wheatly's going to keep what you found."

Ferris frowned. "What's that mean?"

Longarm looked questioningly at Julia. She nodded for him to go ahead and tell Ferris what had been happening. In as few words as possible, Longarm explained the situation they now faced.

"It's what we've always been afraid of," Julia added when Longarm had finished. "We've talked about it before, but now it looks like it's about to happen."

Ferris shook his head, discouragement and anger mingling on his face. "If Díaz and his bunch move in on you, there's not a Chinaman's chance you'll ever get a penny out of the mine."

"That's what Edgar always said," she observed grimly. "He'd depended on *el Patrón* to keep Díaz at a distance, but now we can't look to him for any help."

"Looks like I'm to blame for part of the mess you're in," Longarm told her thoughtfully. "And I'm right sorry about it. From what Mateo said, though, Mondragón wouldn't've been able to do much for you against Díaz."

"Oh, you're not to blame, Mr. Long," Julia said, carefully maintaining a semblance of formality for Ferris's benefit. "From what that jailer told us, Díaz was going to

150

take the mine over whether I had it or whether *el Patrón* had taken it away from me."

"All the same, I figure part of it's my fault," Longarm replied. "And when I make a mess of some kind, I always like to be the one to clean it up."

"It looks to me like the only way you can clean it up now is to go to Mexico City and get rid of Díaz," Ferris said bitterly. "He's the one we've got to deal with, Díaz or his man Delgado."

"Be practical, Sam," Julia told him. "There's no way in the world for us to influence Díaz; he might as well be on the moon."

"You're right about that, Mrs. Wheatly," Longarm agreed. "Delgado ain't his own man. And even if we argued him over to our side—which we ain't got a chance of doing, with no telegraph line between here and Mexico City—he couldn't get new orders from Díaz."

Julia frowned. "I don't see what we can do about Delgado."

"That's the way it looks to me, too," Sam Ferris nodded. "As soon as he finds out we've made another good vein, he's bound to move in and take over the mine. And from what Mr. Long's told us, he's got his own man to do the assay work, so there's no chance we can pull any wool over his eyes just by telling him we still haven't hit anything."

"I hate to give up without a fight, though," Julia said, "after all the work and waiting."

"Oh, we ain't going to give up," Longarm assured her.

"It sounds easy when you say it, Long," Ferris shot back. "But I don't see that anything but a miracle can save us now."

"Well, I don't set much store by miracles, and it don't look like frettin's going to help," Longarm smiled. "It just happens I got part of a bottle of rye in my saddlebag, out in the stable. If you'll excuse me, I'll go fetch it."

"I guess we could all use a drink," Julia said. "And some food. You must be starved, Sam. While Mr. Long goes after his bottle, I'll get drinks for us and tell Estella to put dinner on the table. We'll forget about the mine while we eat. You might just be right, Mr. Long. Maybe we're so upset right now that none of us can see the forest for the trees."

In spite of their efforts at optimism, dinner was a subdued meal. Even the *mole de pavo* that had been simmering on the *parrilla* since early morning in its subtle sauce of peppers, *cominos*, tomatoes, cloves, cinnamon, and bitter chocolate failed to inspire more than passing interest. They carefully avoided mentioning the mine, Delgado, Mondragón, or anything that might remind them of the problems they faced.

Longarm had sipped sparingly at his whiskey before dinner, and after they'd moved to the *sala* with their coffee cups, he had a second swallow. Both Julia and Sam Ferris looked at him as he set the bottle down.

"Well," Ferris said challengingly, "did that famous whiskey of yours water your brain any, Long?"

"Maybe it did, maybe it didn't, Sam. I got the glimmerings of a notion, but I don't know whether it'll work or not. You been in a lot of mines, I guess."

"A few. Enough to know my way around in one."

"Met up with any highgraders?"

"I've heard tell of some."

"You ever meet up with a *low*grader?" Longarm asked.

Ferris looked at him with astonishment. "I never even heard of lowgrading!"

Longarm grinned. "Well, when you come right down to it, neither have I. It's something I just made up. But it stands to reason that if you can salt a mine to make it look richer than it really is, with gold dust you've got from someplace else, you ought to be able to salt one backwards."

A puzzled frown had been forming on Julia's face while she listened. She said, "I was married to Edgar long enough to learn that highgrading means somebody's salted a poor mine with rich ore to make the mine look better than it is. But I'm like Sam. I never did hear of salting a mine backwards."

"There's a first time for everything, I guess," Longarm told her. "Now, a highgrader generally salts a mine that he's figuring to unload on some poor devil who don't know what's going on. Well, what we got to do here, Mrs. Wheatly, is to make your mine look worse than it is. And if that ain't lowgrading, I don't know what else you'd call it."

"I think I see now what you're getting at," Ferris said slowly. "If Delgado has his assayer run samples, and the tests don't show how rich the vein we've hit really is, then Díaz won't be interested any longer."

"You got the idea," Longarm nodded.

"It sounds like it'd work," Julia smiled. Then her face grew serious. "But if it's never been done before, how do we know whether or not we can do it?"

"Well, I can't give you an answer to that quite yet, Julia," Longarm replied. "But between me and Sam, if there's a way to do it, we're going to find out. And then we're going to do it!"

Chapter 14

"You sound like you really mean business, Long," Ferris frowned.

"Sure, I mean business! Damn it, Sam, we can't fight Delgado. He's got a troop of Mexican cavalry regulars to back his play. The only thing we can do is outfox him."

"How do you think we're going to get by with the kind of job you're talking about?"

"We might not," Longarm admitted. "But if we don't, we ain't lost more'n a few hours of work. And I ain't heard you come up with a better idea."

"He's right, Sam," Julia said. "I'll admit, I don't really know what Mr. Long's thinking about, but doing *something* certainly seems like a better idea than just sitting here and waiting for Delgado to confiscate the mine."

"Well . . ." Ferris sounded undecided. Then he grinned and said, "It sounds to me like a crazy scheme, but I'm with you."

"Fair enough," Longarm told Ferris. "Because you're the one I figure to make it work, Sam. You ever salt a mine before?"

"No. I've heard about salted mines, but I've never seen one. And I sure never have tried to salt one."

"Well, I run into a highgrading gang on a case I had a while back," Longarm said. "It don't seem to me like it's much of a trick to do the job. All we've got to do is cover up the face of the new diggings you've been making with some dirt that's got a bunch of low-grade ore mixed into it. At least, that's how I recall it's done."

"That's about as much as I know about it, too," Ferris said. "And if we're going to fool an assayer into thinking we've hit a dud vein instead of a good one, we're going to have to do a pretty fair job, I'd say."

"Of course you are," Julia agreed. "And I can see one big problem you've got before you can start. Where are you going to get the low-grade ore you'll need?"

"Why, out of the old vein," Longarm replied. "You're bound to have some out there."

Ferris shook his head. "I'm afraid not. When we quit work on that old vein, it was completely played out. And every bit of ore that we'd taken out has been sent to the smelter up in Monterrey."

"You don't think we could go out and dig up a little bit of dirt from that old vein and put it on the face of the new one?" Longarm asked thoughtfully.

Ferris shook his head. "Not a chance in a million, if that assayer Delgado's brought with him knows his stuff."

"We can't risk him not knowing it," Julia put in quickly. "I'm sure Díaz wouldn't send an incompetent assayer all the way from Mexico City."

Longarm nodded. "You got a point there." He turned to Ferris. "Well, Sam? You're the miner. How do we go about pulling the wool over Díaz's men's eyes?"

"I'm going to have to think about that a minute, Long. Give me a little time."

"Sure. Only don't take too much time. I figure Delgado's going to be out at that mine bright and early in the morning. If we don't do our job by then, it'll be too late."

Longarm lighted a cheroot and reached for the rye bottle. He watched Ferris's face as the mine superintendent frowned in concentration. Julia was watching Ferris, too. Her brows were drawn together thoughtfully.

"Do we really have to use ore?" she asked. "Wouldn't any kind of dirt with some bits of gold in it do just as well?"

"No. It's got to be ore," Ferris said. "Gold's not pure when it comes out of the ground. It's all mixed up with dirt and salts and things like that until it's smelted."

"What do you mean when you say 'things like that,' Sam?" Longarm asked Ferris.

"Oh, traces of salts and maybe other metals. The ore

155

out of this mine's always had traces of lead and copper in it, along with the gold."

"You think this assayer with Delgado knows what he's looking for?"

"Not unless he's seen assays from here before. But if he didn't find some traces of other metals common to this part of the country, he might get suspicious," Ferris replied.

Longarm sipped from the rye bottle again to help him think. Then he said, "Sam, tell me just exactly what this assayer's going to do when he tests the ore for Delgado."

"Well, he's going to start with about a half-shovelful of dirt from the face. He'll spread it out in an assay pan and bake it in the little furnace we've got out there for assay work. Then he'll pour some acid on it and give the acid a little time to work. After that, he'll dump the dirt in a miner's pan and swirl it with water to wash the loose dirt away. Then he'll test the sludge that's left with two or three acid solutions. The color the sludge turns will tell him what metals are left."

Longarm whistled expressively. "That's quite some order. And he'll be looking for something besides gold, will he?"

"If he knows his business, he will. He'll expect to find lead and copper, maybe a trace of a few earth acids. But they'd be there, anyhow, of course."

"Well, that ought not be so hard for us to fix up." He turned to Julia. "Did your husband have a shotgun?"

"Yes. An old one. He never did use it much."

"There's shells for it, I guess?"

"I don't think there're any loaded. But there's some bags of shot and a cannister or two of powder. And a lot of shell cases and primers. I don't know much about guns, Longarm, but I heard Edgar talk about his guns with other men."

"Well, you get all the shotgun truck you can find down here. And all the *centavo* pieces you've got in your household money." He dug into his pocket, pulled out a handful of coins, and fingered through them until he found a two-and-a-half dollar gold piece, then tossed it on the table. "I helped get you in this mess, so I'll furnish the gold."

"What're you planning, Long?" Ferris asked.

"We're going to give Delgado's assayer something to keep him busy for a while. Sam, you better see if that little stove out in the patio's got a fire going in it. Start one, if it ain't. Use charcoal, if Julia's got any."

"Of course there's charcoal," Julia said. "The cook uses it when she's roasting or baking."

"That's fine. We'll just get busy here and see what kind of mess we can cook up."

As they stood up, Ferris said doubtingly, "I hope you know what you're doing, Long."

"So do I, Sam. But if you want the truth of the matter, I got to admit I ain't real sure."

Getting together all the materials took less than a half-hour. By that time, Julia had unpacked the shotgun, together with its brass shell cases and sacks of powder, shot, primers, and loading tools; Ferris had a deep bed of charcoal glowing red in the little *parrilla*, the grill-like oven that stood in the patio; and Longarm had scraped the gold coin into a tiny heap of thin shavings and was now working with his pocketknife on the copper *centavo* pieces.

Ferris watched him trying to scrape the copper as he had the gold piece. "You'll need a file to work on those," he said. "But I don't see why you'd bother with them. Just toss a few of those primers in the pan when we start baking the mess."

Longarm looked at at the miner. "You figured out what I got in mind, I see."

"It was pretty obvious."

"You think it'll work?"

"Well, you called the shot a while ago, Long," Ferris replied, "when you said we'd have to outfox Delgado. This scheme of yours is about the only way I can see to do it."

"Glad to hear you say that. You'd know better'n I do what it's going to take to mix up this salting mess."

"We can't lose anything by trying," Ferris said with a grim smile. "And when it comes to mixing up the salt, I've got a few ideas myself. But those copper pennies won't scrape the way the gold piece did. Most mints add a little tin to the copper before they mint it. Makes a harder metal."

"You said toss in a few primers. Will they do the job?"

"I think so. Shotgun primers are pretty good-sized, and they're almost pure copper. And the fulminate in them will add some salts that an assayer'd expect."

"That's all we need, then, I guess. Let's start our salt cooking. We still got a lot of work to do before the night's over."

Longarm, Julia and Ferris gathered around the *parrilla*. Longarm had found a deep cast-iron baking pan among the kitchen utensils, and after Ferris lined the bottom of the pan with a layer of dirt scooped up from the street outside the patio wall, he spread on top of it a mixture of the gold shavings, lead shotgun pellets, and a half-dozen copper primers.

"I'm betting that as the metal melts, it'll sink down and mix with the dirt," he explained. "Then all we'll have to do is spread some of it here and there over the face of the new vein."

"I certainly hope you're right," Julia sighed. "I'd hate to lose the mine. It's about all I've got, now."

"Don't worry, Mrs. Wheatly." Longarm spoke with much more assurance than he really felt. "If there's a way to get Delgado to tell Díaz the mine's worked out, this is it."

To the three watching the mixture in the big pan, it seemed that hours passed, and still the scraps of metal showed no signs of melting. The tiny thin slivers of gold twinkled in the lamplight, the lead pellets glowed dully, and the copper nose-creases of the primers gave off a dull pumpkin-colored sheen.

"Isn't anything ever going to happen?" Julia asked nervously.

Ferris shook his head. "I'm afraid that fire's not hot enough. We use coke in our little assay furnace at the mine."

"We can make this one hotten up a little bit," Longarm said. He took off his hat and began fanning the coals with slow, even sweeps across the opening of the *parrilla*.

Almost at once, the effects of the fanning began to show. The burning charcoal's hue changed from red to orange and then to yellow. Longarm continued his gentle fanning. One of the primers in the pan fizzed in a shower of popping sparks, then another went off, and a third. The lead shotgun pellets slowly turned from gray to silver, then one by one they fluxed out of shape and vanished. The gold was next to disappear, and shortly after it, the cases of the primers sagged and dissolved and merged with the dirt on which they'd lain.

"By God, we did it!" Ferris said. His voice was just a bit lower than a shout.

"Sure looks like it," Longarm agreed. He dug out a cheroot and lighted it, then pulled out his bandanna and wiped the sweat off his face before putting his hat back on his head.

"For a while, I didn't think we were going to, though," Julia sighed. She picked up the short poker leaning on the side of the *parrilla* and stirred the dirt in the pan. The crusted mass broke up into lumps and granules where the molten metals had run together and amalgamated. The lumps were irregular and crusted with dirt.

Looking at Sam, she asked, "Do you think that's going to fool Delgado's assayer?"

"I'd like to guarantee it would, but I'm not all that certain," Ferris replied.

"All we can do is go out and put the stuff where that Mexican assayer can find it, and hope what we mixed up is right," Longarm said. He went on thoughtfully, "We'll have to cover that new vein with a foot or so of dirt, Sam. Make it look like it's where you and your men knocked off for the day."

"It'll mean some shovel work," Ferris said thoughtfully. "We'll just toss a little bit of it in every shovelful. Then we'll pack the dirt good, so they'll have to dig it out. Assayers don't need much to run a sample, just a half-shovelful of dirt. They screen it to get out the lumps of ore, and crush the ore in an iron pestle to get the test samples."

"These chunks are going to have to look like they been

there all the time," Longarm frowned. "Sam, I got me an idea. Bring that pan in where I got light to work by. We'll fix that face to look like it ain't never been touched."

In the *sala*, Longarm spread the brass shotgun shell cases and the loading tools on the table. He primed a half-dozen of the cases and measured a light charge of powder into them, then filled them with the metal chunks and granules from the pan and pressed a thin cardboard wad into their tops. Julia and Ferris watched while Longarm's hands worked deftly with the loading tools. When he'd finished, he lined the six shells up on the table and looked at them with satisfaction.

"Now, all we'll have to do is shovel some dirt over the face of the new vein and pack it tight," he said. "Then stand off and shoot the salt into the dirt."

"I only hope that fools Delgado's assayer," Julia sighed. "If it doesn't, we've wasted a lot of work."

"If this scheme don't do the job, we'll come up with a new one," Longarm promised her. He turned to Ferris. "Sam, let's get saddled up and ride out. It'll take us a while to get to the mine, and we want everything to look good out there. You and me, we've got a lot of work ahead yet."

"What do you mean, you and Sam?" Julia demanded. "You don't think I'm going to be left out of this, do you? I'm going too!"

"Now, Mrs. Wheatly, remember what Edgar always used to say—" Ferris began.

Julia cut in, "Edgar and I didn't agree on some things, Sam. One of them was that a gold mine is no place for a woman."

"This ain't just a sightseeing trip," Longarm reminded her. "All the mines I ever seen was dirty, and some of 'em was downright dangerous."

"I'm going, just the same," she insisted.

"We'll go right by the *obreros*' shacks," Sam said. "I'll rouse them and they can do the heavy shoveling."

"No," Longarm said quickly. "You'd best give up that idea, Sam. They'd be sure to talk about it if you rousted 'em out to do a job like this. Delgado'd be sure to hear."

Julia nodded. "He's right, Sam. You can't use the

160

obreros tonight. It'd be too risky. I'm sure I'll find some way to help you."

Longarm recognized determination when he saw it. When Sam opened his mouth to argue with Julia, he held up his hand. "She's right, Sam. We might be glad to have a little help before the night's over."

"Thank you for being on my side, Mr. Long," Julia said. "Just give me a chance to slip into my riding habit. You men can get the horses saddled while I'm changing."

Before Longarm and Ferris had quite finished saddling the horses, Julia joined them. She'd changed into riding habit and boots, and carried saddlebags.

"I thought we'd need some food, if this job lasts any length of time. It's not much, just same *chorizos* and *tortillas* and a bottle of wine, but it'll keep us from starving. And I'm ready to go, whenever you are."

La Escondida was completely dark and all its inhabitants asleep when they rode out and started through the wide valley. The Wheatly mine was on the western slope, about eight miles from the town. Horses and *carretas* and burros had beaten a fair road along the valley floor, between the cultivated fields, and the going was easy in the bright silver moonlight. Then, when they turned off to start the last two miles upslope to the mine, the good road ended and their trail became deep ruts cut by the wheels of the ore wagons that had used it during the mine's earlier, productive period.

In the brilliant moonlight on the rising ground ahead of them, they saw the black portal of the mine yawning ahead of them a hundred yards before they reached it. The shaft opened on a vertical cut made in the upward-sloping terrain. A score of feet distant from the rectangle of the portal, a tiny spring gushed out of a rocky cleft and trickled into a streamlet that zigzagged down to the valley floor.

Beyond the spring, a long ramshackle shed had been erected to house the equipment used by the workers. Small ore carts stood on a narrow set of rails that ended a dozen yards from the portal.

"We'll put the horses in the shed," Sam said. "There's

plenty of room. Not that anybody's apt to come prowling around before we get our work finished."

Longarm had been studying the moon's angle. "Don't be too sure. We're not more'n two or three hours away from daylight."

"Oh, we'll be through before then, I hope," Julia said, "if we all turn to and work hard."

Ferris lighted lanterns and took a pick and three shovels from the stools that were leaning against the wall, while Longarm tethered the horses to stanchions on the opposite side of the shed. Longarm and Julia each took a shovel and lantern, and Longarm cradled the shotgun under one arm as well. They started out. The lanterns were dimmer than the moonlight had been during their short walk to the portal, but once its gaping black mouth had swallowed them, the lanterns suddenly seemed brighter.

Ferris led the way along the shaft. The going was rough underfoot, with the tracks on which the ore carts ran occupying the center of the shaft, and the sides cluttered with clods that had fallen from the carts or just been pushed aside when the tracks had been laid. The tracks led to a Y, and into one of the tunnels that ran off the junction.

"That's the old shaft," Ferris told Longarm, indicating the trackless tunnel. "I had the men move the tracks as soon as we began getting signs of color. The old shaft dead-ends about two hundred yards from the Y. The new one's only about sixty feet into the ground right now."

In the new shaft, the ground underfoot was even rougher, and the rough timbers that shored the ceiling were only inches above Longarm's head. He and Julia silently followed Ferris to the face where the vein was being worked. Ferris put down the pick and shovel he'd been carrying and hung his lantern on a nail driven into the shoring.

Longarm and Julia found other hooks on which to hang their lanterns. She said to Ferris, "You're the miner, Sam. Tell us what to do."

"I'd say to start out, we'd better cover the new vein. Lucky I didn't have the *obreros* move the gangue before they quit work today. We won't have a lot of extra dirt

162

to replace." Seeing Longarm's blank look, Ferris explained, "The gangue's the dirt around the vein, the part that doesn't have enough ore to work right now. They cart it out to give them more room at the face."

Longarm studied the wall of earth that ended the shaft. An irregular opening, perhaps four feet deep and a little more than a yard in its irregular diameter, extended beyond the face.

"That's the vein, that hole in the wall, there?" he asked.

"Yes. The dirt around it's what we call gangue. Waste. All we've got to do is plug the vein itself for a couple of feet, then we'll salt the fresh dirt and leave enough of an opening in the face so the assayer will take his samples from what he thinks is the actual vein," Ferris said.

Julia was digging into the wall of the shaft, a short distance from the face, by the time Ferris had finished his explanation. Longarm and Ferris took their shovels and joined her, Ferris stopping now and then to scrape the piled dirt high upon the face of the vein and pack it with his fists. After he'd compacted a layer of soil a foot thick over the new vein, he motioned for Longarm and Julia to stop.

"We'd better start salting here," he said.

Longarm picked up the shotgun, a handsome Tatham double-barreled twelve-gauge, with gold scrollwork on the frame. He put the selector on the full-choke barrel and slid in a shell. Then, while the others stood back and held their hands over their ears, he fired the charge into the fresh dirt that Ferris had packed over the vein. The shotgun's detonation rang thunderously in the confined space. The irregular pellets that had come from their laboriously prepared work over the *parrilla* drilled into the compacted earth. They crowded up to inspect the broken soil. Ferris took down one of the lanterns to enable them to see better in the smoky, sulfurous gloom.

"I don't know what you think, but it looks damn good to me," he said, grinning. "Scattered, just like ore would be in a vein of this kind."

"Well, if it passes with you, I'd guess it'll fool Delgado's assayer," Longarm said.

Julia nodded. "You'd know better than we would, Sam. If you think it's all right, let's put another layer up."

They worked silently and quickly after that, adding a second layer and, as soon as Longarm had peppered it with the salting pellets, a third. They were well along on the fourth layer, the mine shaft silent except for the muted scraping of their shovels on the dirt sides of the shaft, when a distant but sharp tinkling of metal on metal sounded from the shaft behind them. All three froze instantly.

"Sounded like harness rigging to me," Longarm frowned. He took out his watch and glanced at it. "Damn! We been too busy to watch the time. It's past daylight now. That might be Delgado!"

"Oh, no!" Julia gasped. "Not when we've worked so hard!"

"Sam, you gather everything up and get it down the other shaft," Longarm snapped. "Douse all but one of the lanterns. Then you and Julia stay away from the opening till I get back. I'm going to have a look-see."

Longarm moved carefully toward the portal. It was dark in the shaft, and he had to feel his way along the wall. He saw a glimmer of light ahead and crept cautiously forward until he could peer outside.

Colonel Delgado stood a little aside from the three horses and the pack mule that two of his troopers were tethering. One of the men wore the stripes of a sergeant on his sleeve. A yard distant from Delgado stood a man in civilian clothes; Longarm recognized him from his earlier encounter with Delgado's force as the assayer sent by Díaz from Mexico City.

"*Prestesale, Manuel!*" Delgado commanded. "*Poderemos aquí todo el día si no accelerarse!*"

Longarm watched until the sergeant had tethered the mule and begun to work at the straps of the leather *albardas* the mule bore on its back. By then, he'd seen enough. He hurried back through the shaft, feeling his way again through the gap of darkness between the portal and the Y. A faint glimmer of lantern light guided him into the unused shaft. Julia and Ferris looked anxiously at

Longarm as he entered. They did not have to ask questions. The questions were on their faces.

Longarm nodded. "It's Delgado. Him and two men out of his outfit and that assayer Díaz sent along. And that means we're going to have to stay put and keep quiet until the assayer's finished and they leave. Because if Delgado catches us in here, he'll know damned well we been up to something, and he won't spare us a bit until he finds out what it was!"

Chapter 15

"Can we fight our way out?" Sam asked.

Longarm shook his head. "Two on one ain't big odds, and if it was just you and me, it'd be worth trying. But seeing as Mrs. Wheatly's with us, I ain't of a mind to risk it."

"I'll fight right along with you!" Julia exclaimed. "And hold my end of the fighting up, too!"

"I bet you just would," Longarm told her with a smile. "But I still hold to what I said. The smart thing for us to do is sit tight, right where we are."

"How long will it take the assayer to run the tests?" she asked Ferris.

"Oh, an hour, I'd guess. Depends on how fast he works."

"I suppose we can stand it that long, then," she agreed somewhat reluctantly.

"We better settle down, while we can still burn the lantern," Longarm said. "They was still unloading the mule they brought along, getting the assayer's gear out, I'd imagine. But it won't be long before they'll be coming into the shaft."

Although the bare, clod-strewn dirt floor of the old shaft offered them very little choice, they looked around in search of spots that seemed to offer a promise of some minimal comfort. In the end, they settled for positions along one wall, within whispering distance of each other. They sat down, smoothing away the bumpy spots beneath them as best they could, and Longarm blew out the lantern. Then they waited.

Darkness seems to stretch time to infinity, and each of them felt that an eternity passed before they heard the shuffling of steps approaching and saw the gleam of the lanterns that Delgado's party carried. The lantern light increased until the trio in the old shaft could see each other in a dim, ghostly fashion.

For a few moments the light grew brighter, and they got a fleeting glimpse of Delgado carrying a lantern, its rays striking glints from the brass buttons of his uniform jacket and the insignia on his cap. He was followed by the assayer, carrying a small satchel in one hand, then the sergeant, who carried the bulkier items of the assayer's equipment as well as a second lantern. Then the Mexicans entered the new shaft and the light abruptly dimmed to a feeble glow that showed the end of the shaft in outline, but shed no light up the old tunnel.

Sound traveled better than light. They heard Delgado say, *"Bueno, Manuel, ponese el equipo al suelo. Aquí."* There was a clatter of metal, the noise of the sergeant placing the assayer's gear on the floor of the tunnel, and Delgado's voice sounded again. *"Ahorita, Bernal, empeza su chamba."*

"Se necesito agua, Coronel," the assayer said.

"Manuel!" Delgado snapped. *"Tome un farol y llevarse agua, pronto!"*

Ferris whispered, "Sounds to me like he's getting right down to work. I guess Delgado don't like to waste time."

Longarm had been as interested as his companions in interpreting the sounds that came from the new shaft. His command of Spanish was sketchier than theirs, though, and he wasn't sure he'd understood everything.

"Got the assay gear laid out, and sending the trooper for water, ain't he?" he whispered to Julia.

"Yes." She stopped talking when the light of the lantern carried by Delgado's man brightened the main shaft. They could see the cavalryman as he walked past the opening of the Y in the tunnel, the lantern in one hand, a bucket in the other. When the soldier had disappeared, Julia asked Ferris, "How long will the tests take, Sam?"

"Ought not take very long, once he gets his equipment set up. Like I told you a while back, there's not much to

167

a spot assay like he's going to make. A half-hour, more or less."

"Well, I'll be glad to see him finish. I hope that stuff we put in there is good enough to fool him," she whispered.

"If it ain't, it won't be because we didn't try our best," Longarm said.

They fell silent again as the light of the soldier's lantern showed at the opening of the shaft. They watched him pass, water sloshing from the bucket he carried, and then the light faded to the dim glow they'd seen before.

Unidentifiable sounds of movement and activity reached their ears from the new shaft during the period of waiting that followed, but no conversation. Waiting, even under the best of conditions, is a nerve-stretching affair; waiting in almost total darkness becomes an abomination. All three of them jumped when Delgado's harsh voice broke the stretched-out silence.

"*Cómo se va, Bernal?*"

"*Bueno, Coronel.*"

"*Cuanto acabase?*"

"*Poco a poco. Momentito.*"

Again the trio listened. The noises were even less distinguishable than before, mere whispers of sound in the dark silence of the mine. They could identify voices by now, though, and recognized Bernal's light nasal tones when the assayer spoke.

"*Hay terminado, Coronel.*"

"*Y qué tal?*"

"*Pues, no hay mucho oro en este ejemplo.*"

"*Cómo? Es imposible!*" There was disbelief in Delgado's voice.

"*Imposible que si o no,*" Bernal replied, "*es verdad que no hay mucho oro aquí.*"

"*Porqué no?*" Delgado asked. "*Explicame, Bernal!*"

"*Bueno.*" The assayer sounded resigned, as though he was accustomed to blasting dreams of riches. "*Mira, Coronel. Aquí, aquí, aquí, estas tachas son oro. Oro rico, si, pero poquito. Aquí y aquí son cobre, y esto residuo es nada de valor. Es solamente plomo.*"

"No se paga para descubre cobre y plomo!" Delgado snarled. *"Es oro que quiere el Presidente Díaz!"*

"No me culpa, Coronel!" Bernal protested. *"Es imposible descubrir que no hay 'sta aquí."*

"Válgame Dios!" Delgado exclaimed. *"El Presidente sera colerico!"*

"Mal suerte," Bernal replied.

In the old shaft, the listening trio could almost see the shrug they heard in the assayer's voice.

Delgado's voice was angry when he spoke after a brief silence. *"Su ejemplo esta errado! Hace otro, inmediatamente!"*

"Si mandame, Coronel," Bernal replied coldly. *"Pero sera inutil."*

"No desputir, Bernal!" Delgado growled. *"Hace ejemplo otra vez!"*

Again there was silence from the new shaft, broken only by the same small rattlings and scrapings the Americans had heard before, as the assayer carried out a second set of tests.

"Delgado sure ain't a man to take no for an answer, is he?" Longarm's whisper was broken by his chuckling. "Well, we got about all the answer we need to that mess we cooked up. It sure as hell fooled that assayer."

"I'm proud of both of you," Julia whispered back. "It's beginning to look like you've saved my mine for me. And I don't know how I can ever thank you enough."

"We don't look for thanks," Longarm said.

"Not for a minute," Ferris affirmed. "Beating that damned Delgado and his boss is all the thanks I want."

Their conversation was cut short when Bernal's voice reached them from the other shaft.

"He sido el ejemplo, Coronel."

"'Cómo parece?" Delgado asked.

"Mismo como el otro. Justo como dijo."

"Cagado!" Delgado exclaimed. There was a long pause, then he went on, *"Llevarse el equipo, Manuel. Cuando se hace, vaminos."*

"Bueno, mi Coronel," the sergeant replied. *"Tan pronto como es posible."*

In the abandoned shaft, Longarm and his group relaxed as the sounds of the cavalryman assembling the assayer's gear were heard. They did not notice the light at the Y brighten, and were completely unprepared to see Delgado appear in the opening, a lantern held high, staring at them.

Blinded by the sudden light, cramped in his squatting position against the shaft's wall, Longarm was slow in drawing. His shot thudded into the side of the shaft beyond the Y as Delgado dodged behind the sharp point where the two shafts branched.

"Damn it!" Longarm swore. "He caught me when I couldn't see or move!"

"I'd guess you'll get another chance at him, now that he's seen us," Ferris said dryly. "He's already mad, and finding us down here's just going to rile him a little bit more."

All three of them were on their feet now, facing the mouth of the Y. Julia had grabbed the shotgun from the wall against which Ferris had leaned it when they retreated from the salted vein. Ferris had drawn his revolver a few minutes after Longarm's shot, but had not fired. In the other shaft they could hear Delgado's voice giving orders, but he was speaking in a half-whisper, making it impossible to hear what he was saying.

"You think they're getting ready to rush us?" Ferris asked in a whisper.

"Not hardly," Longarm replied. "There's only the two of 'em, unless you count that Bernal, and I misdoubt he's carrying a gun. Delgado don't strike me as being the kind of man who'll jump into a fight unless he's got the odds on his side."

"What will they do, then?" Julia asked.

"Starve us out, most likely. Oh, I don't mean starve, but we're going to get mighty thirsty even in a cool place like this before very long."

"We've got the wine," she reminded him.

"Sure. But that ain't the same as water. All Delgado's got to do is keep guard at the opening, and pretty soon we'll have to give up or die."

"And if we give up?" Ferris asked. "What happens to us?"

"Hard to say. I guess that'd depend on how mad Delgado is." Longarm didn't bother to mention that the chances were good that Delgado would release Ferris and Julia while holding him. "About the only good thing we got going for us is that they can't shoot at us—or hit us, anyhow—unless they come right on in here. The way that shaft curves, they can't do much shooting from the main shaft."

"What do we do, then?" Julia asked.

"Wait," Longarm told her. "Just wait and see what kind of play Delgado decides to make. Then we'll try to figure out what we'd best do."

They waited in the dark silence. Delgado's low-voiced instructions had stopped, but now unidentifiable sounds came from the new shaft. Then the strange noises became recognizable as the sound of feet hurrying along the main shaft toward the portal.

"Quick, Julia! The shotgun!" Longarm commanded.

Julia fired. The orange-red blast of the slow-burning black powder lighted the shaft ahead for a tiny fraction of a second. Longarm got a glimpse of fleeting figures in the main shaft, and thought the one in the rear faltered as the salting mixture peppered the walls. Then it was dark once more, and he couldn't be completely sure of what he'd seen.

"They got away!" Julia said, as the shuffling noise of the footsteps faded to silence. "I tried to fire the other barrel, but I guess it wasn't loaded."

"No. I just put a shell in the full-choke barrel when we was salting the vein," Longarm said. "But you did fine. Too bad you didn't have another crack at 'em."

"But they got away, damn it!" Ferris snorted angrily. "And we're still shut up in here. Sitting ducks!"

"Smart ducks don't set and wait for somebody to make targets of 'em," Longarm told him. "You and Julia stay put, Sam. Before they get organized, I'm going to meander down that shaft and see if I can find out anything."

"Maybe we'd better go, too," Ferris suggested. "Then we'd be right there if there's a chance to break out."

Longarm shook his head. "There won't be. Delgado didn't get to be a colonel on Díaz's staff by being stupid. We're bottled up. But bottles can be busted if you hit 'em hard enough. Now just settle down till I get back."

Longarm began feeling his way down the mine shaft. He moved slowly, pausing every few steps to listen for any faint noises or hint of someone stirring ahead—anything that might give him warning of an ambush. He didn't really expect Delgado to post a man inside the mine. There'd be no advantage in placing a sentry in a position where he couldn't see someone advancing, and where he'd be trading shots without aiming.

He worked along the wall, stretching his left hand out to touch it every few steps to avoid getting his feet caught in the rails of the narrow track that ran down the center of the shaft, keeping his gunhand free. He saw the first dim hint of light ahead, and at the same time heard voices outside the portal. He stopped to listen, but could not hear what was being said. He edged forward cautiously, but stopped again when a grating of metal on metal sounded at the mouth of the shaft. Then he heard Delgado's voice.

"Bueno! Ahora, pujarle el carro, Torres. Pujarle, hombre! Ponese en marcha!"

Longarm frowned, trying to figure out what Delgado was telling his man to push forward. He got the answer quickly. One of the small ore carts that he'd noticed standing outside the mine when they arrived was rolling slowly through the portal. It blocked the light for a moment; then, as its outlines became clear in silhouette against the outside light, he could see the shoulders of a man bending behind the cart, pushing it into the shaft on its track.

That damn Delgado's got plenty of savvy, old son, Longarm told himself as the ore cart creaked and squeaked closer to him. *He gets that cart in the middle of the shaft, then we got to squeeze past it to get out. And that really sets us up for what Sam said we was, sitting ducks.*

As the cart continued to get closer, Longarm began retreating, and when the cart was past the area where daylight filtering in from the portal dimmed to darkness, he gave Delgado another point for smartness.

A lantern had been placed in the cart, and its glow lighted the shaft for several yards ahead of the cart and behind it, creating a zone of light through which anyone trying to leave the mine must enter and, once in the lighted area, become an easy target. Protected as it was by the cart's high metal walls, the lantern would be impossible to shoot out.

"Basta, Torres!" Delgado called from the Portal. *"Dejarse ahí el carro! Volve aquí! Bernal, cubiertese!"*

Blinking to peer beyond the lighted area, Longarm saw the soldier who'd been pushing the cart start at a zig-zagging run out of the shaft. Silhouetted in the brighter light at the edge of the portal, the barrel of a rifle and the rimmed outline of a man's body showed on one side of the opening. The unmistakable silhouette of Delgado's peaked cavalry cap popped into sight on the other side.

It was chancy shooting at that range in the uncertain light, but Longarm sent a snapshot at Delgado's cap. His target was at best an inch wide, the range extreme. The slug kicked dirt from the rim of the portal, and Delgado dodged back to cover before Longarm could fire again.

"Long!" Delgado called. "It is you, no?"

Longarm debated for a moment whether or not to answer, but decided he might as well. He replied, "It's me, Delgado. What's on your mind?"

"I warned you to stay out of my way," Delgado answered. "Now I find you and your friends setting up an ambush for me! I am not a one like Sanchez! When you get in my way, I step on you like I would on a *cucaracha!*"

"You just come stepping any time you feel like it, Delgado!" Longarm invited. "I'm ready whenever you are!"

"I am no fool, either, Long!" the colonel called. "And I am in no hurry. You and your accomplices will need water soon. Then is when I will take you in charge, and all of you will go back with me to the capital as my prisoners, to answer for your crimes against the people of Mexico!"

Longarm didn't find that idea appealing. He'd seen Mexican "justice" dispensed by the *rurales* on his last trip. It was gunshot justice, with the judge also acting as prosecutor and jury, and often as executioner. He imagined that the same kind of justice would be handed him by a Díaz-controlled kangaroo court in Mexico City.

"That's the first I've heard about me committing any crimes, Delgado," he said. "But I guess that don't matter much, the way you handle things down here. So if you aim to put me on trial, you'd better come get me, because I damn sure don't mean to walk out of here with my hands up."

"We will see what we will see!" Delgado snapped. Then his voice rose and he called, *"Tome el gringo, Manuel!"*

A voice spoke from behind Longarm, so close that it seemed right in his ear, and the cold muzzle of a pistol touched the nape of his neck. *"Llevase sus brazos, gringo! No hace un moción más."*

Still holding his Colt, Longarm slowly raised his hands above his head.

"Tengo el gringo, Coronel," the man holding the pistol on Longarm called to Delgado.

"Bueno, Manuel!" Delgado replied. Then he asked, *"Tiene su pistola?"*

"Inmediatamente, Coronel!" Manuel called back. Lowering his voice, he commanded, *"Dame su pistola, hombre!"*

Longarm let his revolver drop to the ground.

Manuel raised his voice to report, *"Ya tengo, Coronel!"*

"Pues, marchase ahí!" Delgado commanded.

Longarm felt the soldier's pistol shove into his neck. He needed no other command, but started walking toward the portal.

Delgado greeted him with a cold smile. "So. I do not need to go in to get you, Long. I have left my good sergeant to do that for me."

Longarm looked around. Delgado was standing directly in front of him. On the other side of the mine portal, the soldier who'd pushed the ore cart stood with his carbine trained on Longarm's head. Bernal, the assayer, stood at a little distance away, close to the horses. Manuel, the sergeant, held his position at Longarm's back, his revolver raised. Longarm noted that his Colt was in the sergeant's wide cavalry belt.

"Looks like you outsmarted me this time, Delgado," Longarm said, hoping his voice carried the proper note of frustration. "You mind if I let my arms down now? They're getting a mite cramped, lifted up this way."

Delgado nodded. He said, "Why should I fear a rattlesnake when its fangs are drawn?"

"Yes, sir, I'd say you got me, all right. Question in my mind is, what're you aiming to do with me? You know I carry a badge from the U.S. government."

"Every day in Mexico, men disappear, Long," Delgado said with a low chuckle. "I am sure *el Presidente* Díaz will send our country's official regrets to your government when you do not return from whatever mission brought you here."

"Now wait a minute—" Longarm began.

Delgado cut him short. "No. You have too much to answer for, Long. Do you think I don't know you have aided a group of *peons* in an uprising against one of *Presidente* Díaz's good friends, the *hacendado* Ramón Mondragón?"

"Hell, Delgado, you was ready to get rid of Mondragón for Díaz, before you found out this mine here ain't worth anything."

"If you know that, Long, you know too much to be allowed to live." Delgado studied the mine portal for a moment. "I suppose this is as good a place and time as any. Who would think of looking for a grave in a worthless mine?"

"You mean you're going to shoot me down without a trial?" Longarm demanded.

"Why waste a court's time on a matter of this kind? They would only find you guilty."

"That's sorta hard lines," Longarm said.

"Mal suerte," Delgado shrugged. "The dice fall badly for one at times."

Longarm drew a deep breath. He looked over his

shoulder at the mine portal and saw that the sergeant, absorbed in listening to his commander sentencing the *gringo* to death, had let his pistol fall to his side.

"If I'm going to be shot, I guess I'm entitled to a last smoke," Longarm suggested.

Delgado nodded. "It is a custom of our country. Smoke your last *cigarro*, Long."

Longarm brought his hand up to his vest pocket as though to take out a cigar. His fingers slid along his watch chain and snaked out the ugly little derringer clipped to its other end. Delgado saw the gun too late. He clawed for his revolver, but the heavy slug from the derringer plowed into his chin and came out the back of his head, taking off his cap in a spatter of blood.

Before Delgado could fall, Longarm had grasped his slumping body and pulled it to him, whirling to interpose it between himself and the sergeant. The soldier's slug thudded into Delgado's back. Longarm's second shot cut down the sergeant.

Longarm gambled that the other soldier wouldn't stop to realize that the derringer held only two shells. He trained the little snub-nosed weapon on the man and commanded, *"Salise el fusil, hombre!"*

His command was not really needed. The soldier had opened his hands to let his carbine drop the instant he saw the derringer's muzzle staring at him. The assayer had not moved as the action in front of him exploded. He still stood by the horses, his jaw dropping in surprise. He saw the soldier raise his hands, and lifted his own.

From the portal, Sam Ferris said, "Damned if that wasn't the quickest turnaround I ever hope to see!"

Longarm took his eyes off the two Mexicans long enough to glance at Ferris. Julia stood beside Sam in the portal, her eyes still wide open with shock. She started to run to Longarm's side, but he shook his head and she stopped.

"Let's finish this business first, Julia," Longarm said. "Sam, you pick up that soldier's gun and see if the other fellow's got a pistol. I don't much think he has, the way

176

he was acting, but let's make sure. Then we'll figure out how to wind up this thing we got on our hands here."

"Are you sure you're all right?" Julia asked him.

"Sure. Everything worked out just like I figured it to."

Ferris came up, carrying the carbine and pistol he'd taken from the cavalryman. He asked incredulously, "You mean you planned all this?"

"Why, sure, Sam. Didn't you catch on?"

"I guess not. We came out of the old shaft when we heard the first shots, figuring you'd stirred up some kind of hornet's nest, but by the time we got up to the front, that soldier you just dropped had his gun stuck in your neck. I was afraid to shoot him; there was too much danger he'd kill you before he died. After that—" Ferris shrugged— "everything happened so fast, it was over before I could do anything."

"How could you plan all this?" Julia asked. "You didn't know that it'd all work out the way it did!"

"Well, now," Longarm explained, "I knew Delgado'd left that man of his back of me when he had to have the assayer cover the other soldier after he pushed in that ore cart. So, once I knew where everybody was, it wasn't such a much to put a scheme together."

"What're we going to do about these two?" Ferris asked, pointing to the soldier and Bernal. "They'll spread the word of what's happened out here. We'll still be in a mess when Delgado's troopers hear you killed their colonel."

"Oh, I got an idea about that, too," Longarm said. He motioned for Bernal to join them, and the assayer moved slowly toward the group.

"*Habla Inglés?*" Longarm asked him.

"*Sí, señor. Un poco.* A little bit, I speak," Bernal replied.

"Now here's what you're going to do," Longarm told him harshly. "You're going to take charge of Delgado's cavalry outfit when we get back to town. You're going to tell them soldiers that Manuel shot the colonel and Delgado killed him before he died. You make up some kind of fuss they had. You understand?" Seeing Bernal's bewildered look, he told Julia, "You talk their language. Tell him what I said."

Swiftly, the Spanish flowing easily from her lips, Julia translated. When she stopped speaking, Bernal nodded eagerly.

"*Sí*. I will do what you tell me, *señor*. I want no more trouble over this useless mine."

"Good," Longarm said. "And you tell them soldiers that before he died, Delgado said they was to scoot back to Mexico City just as fast as their nags will get 'em there."

Julia took over again and relayed Longarm's words to the assayer. Bernal nodded again, "*Sí, señor*. That is where I want to go, *tan pronto como es posible, el capital!*"

Ferris asked, "You think he'll do it?"

Longarm nodded slowly. "If I'm any judge of men, he will. But just to make sure, Julia, you tell him if he don't, I'll track him down if it takes a hundred years, and shoot him on sight!"

Her voice stern, Julia relayed Longarm's threat. Bernal seemed to shrink. "*Por la vestida de la Virgen, señor*, I swear I will do just as you are tell me!"

Longarm nodded. "I think he will, too. Now let's get this mess cleaned up and ride back to town. I left my bottle of rye at your house, Julia, and after a little dust-up like we just had, a drink sure does a lot to soothe me."

Chapter 16

Longarm and Julia stood beside the road south, a short distance from the plaza, watching the cavalry troop depart. Bernal rode at the head; in the center of the column the canvas-wrapped bodies of Delgado and Manuel were draped over their horses. When the last rider was out of sight and the dust was settling down, Julia turned to Longarm with a relieved sigh.

"I'm so glad to see them out of town! I'm just beginning to realize how close I came to losing the mine, and how much I owe you for saving it," she said.

"You don't owe me a thing, Julia. All I was doing was cleaning up a mess I'd made myself."

"I'm grateful to you, just the same."

"Don't start counting chickens yet, Julia. There's still a batch of eggs on the nest being hatched."

"Oh! *El Patrón*! I'd forgotten about the *peons* taking over the *hacienda*!"

"Well, let's don't worry about that right now. Old Mateo's supposed to let us know if anything happens out there. But I ain't about to butt into what's none of my business."

"Just what *is* your business here, Longarm?" Julia asked as they turned away from the road and started toward La Escondida.

"About what you'd expect. I'm looking for a man the government wants."

"A criminal?"

"You'd call him that, I reckon."

"And you think he's here?"

179

"So far, I ain't real sure. That's what I aim to find out, now we're rid of Delgado and his bunch."

"You're not planning on doing it before dinner, are you? Because I thought it'd be nice if we had another party, not anything grand, just all the other Americans, to celebrate getting rid of Delgado."

"Why, I'd enjoy that. It's sort of short notice, though, ain't it?"

"Oh, no. There's plenty of time. When Sam left to go back out to the mine, he said he'd get away early, just as soon as he had the *obreros* clear away the dirt we put over the new vein, so they can start work without waiting, tomorrow."

They'd reached the corner of the plaza now. Longarm said, "Tell you what. I'll walk you home and pick up my saddlebags, then you go ahead and get your party started and I'll go to the hotel and sort of reorganize myself."

Julia didn't try to hide her disappointment when she said, "I was hoping you'd stay with me awhile."

"After the party tonight, Julia. We'll have a longer time then."

"Yes. That's even better," she agreed, smiling.

As tired as he was, Longarm planned to visit both of the town's cantinas before returning to his hotel. The siesta hour was getting close, and he'd seen how La Escondida closed down for its duration. He had a hunch that Terrance Barns might be in one of the saloons having a pre-siesta drink. After the way Sam Ferris had behaved during the fight at the mine that morning, Longarm had come to the point of changing his mind about the identity of the man he was seeking.

Ferris had covered his failure to jump into the fight, but as far as Longarm was concerned, the mine superintendent's story was as full of holes as a sieve. Judging by his failure to join Longarm in the fight's early stages, and his apparent indifference to the outcome, Ferris just might have been hoping Delgado would win. Even though he was pretty sure to see Terrance Barns at Julia's party that evening, Longarm wanted to talk with Barns alone once more before making up his mind which of the two men might be Clayton Maddox.

Barns was not in the cantina where Longarm's trouble with Zoribal had started; in the other there were two of La Escondida's *pulque* drinkers at one table, and Tom Dodd was sitting by himself at another. Dodd waved an invitation, and Longarm went over to join the Texas Ranger.

"I was hoping I'd run into you, Tom," Longarm said as he sat down. "Got an invitation for you from Mrs. Wheatly to come have supper at her house tonight."

"Any special reason?"

"Oh, sort of a blowout for everybody from home."

"Celebrating what you helped her do today?"

"Why, I didn't do anything much."

"From the tales I've been hearing around town, you've had yourself quite a day," Dodd said. He indicated the whiskey bottle on the table. "Have one with me."

Though he'd rather have had rye, Longarm knew this was the best he'd do in the local saloons. "Thanks, Tom. Don't mind if I do. A man's entitled after his day's work's finished."

"Especially if his day's work was buffaloing and then stampeding a troop of Díaz's cavalry."

"I didn't do it all by myself." Longarm sipped the whiskey and found it was like all bourbon, too sweet for his taste. "I had help, remember."

"Not a hell of a lot, if what's being talked is true."

"Well, I can't say nothing to that, seeing the gossip ain't caught up with me yet. And I reckon it's like all town talk—about half of it's true."

"Tell me the right of it, then. I'd like to know what it had to do with the job that brought you here."

"If you're nosying around for something that'll help you do your own job, you can rest easy, Tom. What happened today was just part of a mess I got into, one I didn't ask for."

"You can be right close-mouthed when you've a mind, Longarm."

"I take that as a compliment. Back where I was born,

in West-by-god-Virginia, the folks have got a saying that a man who talks too much grows blisters on his tongue."

"Not much danger of that happening to you," Dodd smiled. "Well, you can't fault me for trying."

"Oh, I don't." Longarm finished his drink and stood up. "Next round's on me, when we get together again. And don't forget Mrs. Wheatly's party tonight."

"You can just bet I'll be there. Maybe I'll find out what really went on out at her gold mine today."

Longarm picked up his saddlebags and went up to his room. After he'd washed away the taste of the bourbon with a sip of Maryland rye and a cheroot, he took out his Colt and derringer and cleaned them. Midway through the job, he began to grow sleepy. When the weapons were finally cared for, freshly loaded and restored to their places, he pulled aside the edge of his window shade and looked out on the plaza. It was deserted under the beating sun. Longarm washed the gun oil off his hands, wrestled his boots off, and lay down to join the rest of the town in a prolonged afternoon nap.

As deep as he was in dreamless sleep, Longarm was wide awake and on his feet before the first soft scratching on his door died away.

"Who is it?" he called.

A light voice, that of a child or a woman, answered, *"Brazolargo?"*

"Who are you?" Longarm repeated.

"Ernesto, señor. Nieto de Mateo Esquival."

Mateo's name brought Longarm to the door. He opened it; a boy ten or twelve years old stood there. His black hair was tousled, his face dirt-streaked. He wore a junior-size version of the baggy white trousers and loose jacket that seemed to be the standard garb of males in La Escondida.

"You're Mateo's boy?" Longarm said.

"No, señor. No soy su hijo. Mateo es mi abuelo."

"Your grandpa, eh? Well, what do you want, Ernesto?"

"Mi abuelo diga que es peligro a la hacienda, Señor Brazolargo. El Capitán Sanchez—"

"Wait a minute," Longarm interrupted the boy. "You

182

better come in so's I can close the door." With the boy inside and the door safely shut, Longarm asked, "Listen, sonny, can you talk English?"

"No, señor. Pero entiendo un poquito."

"Well, I ain't so good at your language, either, but I can catch a little bit of it. Now tell me real slow. *Muy despacio.* What's wrong at the *hacienda?"*

Longarm wasn't sure how much the boy understood, but the youngster did make an effort to talk slower and more distinctly. *"Los rurales,"* he said. *"Vienen a la hacienda sobreponer nuestros amigos."*

"Sanchez is going to fight your grandpa's friends?"

"Sí, señor."

"Por qué?" Longarm asked.

"Porque el Capitán Sanchez quiere enganarse lo mismo el hacendado."

Longarm struggled through his inadequate Spanish until he thought he'd arrived at a translation of what Ernesto had said, but couldn't really believe he'd gotten it right. He asked the boy, *"Sanchez quiere ser el Patrón?"*

"Sí, señor. Este es que quiere."

Longarm shook his head. "I better go talk to Mateo about this."

"No, no, Brazolargo!" Ernesto exclaimed. *"Mi abuelo dígame que usted no va al Palacio Federal! Es muy peligroso!"*

"Dangerous for me to go to headquarters?" Longarm asked. When the boy nodded, he asked, *"Por qué?"*

"A causa de Zoribal."

"Well, that'd figure," Longarm said, more to himself than to Ernesto. "I guess the *rurales* is like any other bunch; you kill one of 'em, the rest come down on you."

Sitting down on the bed, Longarm began pulling on his boots. He still wasn't sure he'd understood Ernesto correctly, and he needed more information than he could get, struggling along in a language in which he wasn't fluent. He could think of only one person he'd trust to translate for him.

"Qué pasa, Brazolargo?" Ernesto asked him.

"You come along with me," Longarm replied, standing

up and buckling on his gunbelt. He spent a moment adjusting it before putting on his vest, coat and hat. Then he went to the door and motioned for Ernesto to follow him. "We're going to go see somebody. *Vamos!*"

Unquestioningly, Ernesto followed Longarm through La Escondida's siesta-deserted streets to Julia Wheatly's house. Longarm felt enough at home there by now to go through the deserted patio and enter the house without knocking. Julia was in her bedroom, and the door was open. Longarm called her softly to awaken her.

"Longarm?" she asked, sitting up in the bed, her eyes still sleep-heavy. "Is something the matter?"

"That's what I'm trying to find out. This boy's Mateo's grandson, and he don't talk my lingo any better'n I do his. I figured I better make sure about what he said before I go off half-cocked."

Her face drew into a puzzled frown. "What's he told you?"

"From what I could get, Sanchez has decided to set himself up as *el Patrón,* now that the *peons* have bounced Mondragón out. Thing is, I ain't real sure that's what the boy's been telling me."

Julia questioned Ernesto in rapid-fire Spanish, too fast for Longarm to follow. Finally, she looked at him and nodded. "You got his message right, Longarm. That's Sanchez's plan. Mateo's worried about his friends out at the *hacienda.* He doesn't dare leave the jail, and he's asking you to go warn the *peons* so Sanchez won't take them by surprise."

"How'd he come to pick on me?" Longarm asked.

"Ernesto said you're the only one his grandfather could think of. Sanchez has the village people so cowed that they won't lift a finger against him." Julia looked worriedly at Longarm. "That could affect me, too, couldn't it? If Sanchez does put himself in as *el Patrón,* he'd treat me like Delgado was planning to, if only to gain Díaz's support."

Thoughtfully, Longarm twisted the tips of his mustache. "I reckon he would, Julia. It'd be the only way he could buy the job. And I sure wouldn't like to see that happen."

184

"I'm not asking you to do any more on my account," Julia said quickly.

"You don't need to ask. I owe you and Mateo both. When's Sanchez going to move?"

Julia relayed the question to Ernesto. The boy replied, *"Sobre la siesta, señora, esta tarde."*

"After the siesta hour, this evening," she repeated.

"I got plenty of time, then." Longarm stood up and put on his hat. "And the longer they got at the *hacienda* to get ready for Sanchez, the easier it's going to be to stand him off."

Longarm wasted no time in his ride to the *hacienda*. The fields bordering the road to the Mondragón estate were deserted, in sharp contrast to his earlier view of them, when they'd been busy with workers. A ghostly, desolate feeling hung over the area. He reached the last stretch of road leading to the box canyon at just about the time he calculated Sanchez would be leaving La Escondida.

Which don't give you too much time to get this outfit organized, old son, he told himself as the imposing building came into sight. *I just hope there's enough of 'em who can handle guns to give 'em a decent chance to cut them* rurales *down to size.*

Inside, as Longarm walked down the wide central hallway, looking for Flores and Zaragoza, black eyes followed his every step. The *hacienda* was a mass of confusion. The new occupants had taken over the huge building, with families sharing a room apiece. Carpets had been rolled back to allow cooking fires to be built on the stone floors. He saw makeshift beds in almost every corner of each room.

Longarm discovered that the largest room, the main ballroom or dining room, had been converted into a headquarters for the *campesinos*. Flores and Zaragoza were sitting at an ornate French Empire table, in deep discussion with several of the other men.

"Brazolargo!" Flores greeted Longarm. "You are welcome to our new *edificio communidad*. It is very fine place, no?"

185

"Looks real good," Longarm agreed. "Except I got to tell you you're going to have to do some fighting to hang on to it."

"Cómo así?" Flores frowned. "We have *el Patrón* safe, lock up in his room with *su esposa.* And you have whip the *caballería* Díaz is send, they go now back to *el capital,* no?"

"That's where they was heading the last time I saw 'em," Longarm agreed. "But now Sanchez has got ideas about setting himself up in Mondragón's place."

"Válgame Dios!" Zaragoza exclaimed. "To beat the *pistoleros* of *el Patrón,* that was easy. But how are we to fight *los rurales?"*

"Well, I'd say you're going to have to, unless you want Sanchez taking over. You got some guns, ain't you? Mondragón must've kept a few around a fancy place like this."

Zaragoza shook his head. *"No tan mucho.* Three rifles, two *escopetas,* some *pistolas."*

"How about ammunition?"

"Solamente un poco," Zaragoza shrugged.

"And we are *campesinos, Brazolargo,"* Flores pointed out. "We do not know so good how to shoot."

"You got one thing in your favor, Zaragoza. This place is built like it was intended for a fort. The *rurales* are going to be out in the open," Longarm pointed out. Then he added, "If you aim to fight 'em, that is."

"Oh, we will fight, *Brazolargo,"* Cristobal Flores said quickly. "We have won so much and held it for so little time, we will fight to keep what we have!"

Longarm nodded. "Good. If you feel that way about it, then I'll give you a hand."

As they'd talked, either Zaragoza or Flores had been translating for the benefit of the others, few of whom had any English. Now the big room was filled with a buzz of voices. Other men joined the original group as word spread through the building, and wives and children were packed in the doorways, listening. When Longarm announced his decision to help, a few ragged cheers rose from the crowd.

186

"Tell us what we must do, *Brazolargo*," Flores said. "We will do our best!"

"That's all a man can be expected to do," Longarm said. "Now, then. What we better do first is get the three best shots in your bunch to handle the three rifles you got." He frowned. "Didn't them *pistoleros* of Mondragón's join up with you?"

"Emiliano and Humberto, *sí*," Flores nodded.

"Then they ought to get two out of the three rifles. Who else you got who can shoot straight?"

Zaragoza and Flores exchanged questioning looks. Finally, Flores shook his head. "*Ninguno, Brazolargo.* Who of us could afford a gun, even if *el Patrón* would have given us permission to own one?"

"Then what about Mondragón?" Longarm asked.

"*El Patrón?*" Zaragoza gasped.

"Sure. Why not? He loses, either way the fight goes. And I suspicion he'd sooner see you folks win it than the *rurales*. You'd be likelier to give him a decent shake than Sanchez would. And he'd be a better shot than anybody else in your outfit."

Flores and Zaragoza began arguing in their own language. Longarm could not follow their rapid speech; he didn't know which of them was for enlisting Mondragón's help and which was against it. Several of the men closest to the table joined the discussion, and at last they reached an agreement.

"*Bueno,*" Flores said. "We are agree to ask *el Patrón,* if you will go with us when we do."

"Suits me," Longarm agreed. "And we better get on with it, because Sanchez and his bunch is likely halfway here by now."

He followed Flores and Zaragoza upstairs, where one of the men stood guard over a door. Flores knocked.

"*Quién es?*"

Longarm recognized the light voice and arrogant tone as belonging to Ramón Mondragón.

"*Abierta la puerta, por favor. Es necesario que hablamos con usted,*" Flores replied.

There was no reply from the room, but in a moment the

187

door opened. Mondragón's face was set coldly until he saw Longarm, then he smiled and shrugged.

"*Señor* Long. I hope you bring me the news that these people have come to their senses—though why you should be involved in this matter escapes me," Mondragón said.

"I got mixed up in more things here in La Escondida than I like to be," Longarm said. "Had a scrape with your *rurales,* and another one with Colonel Delgado that your President Díaz sent out from Mexico City to put you off your land. And—"

"A moment, *señor!*" Mondragón interrupted. "I know nothing about these things you speak of! The *rurales,* yes, I can understand. They give my country a bad name. I have little love for them, myself. But that *Presidente* Díaz should—"

"*Señor* Mondragón," Longarm broke in, "I ain't got time to go into all of that business right now. Just take my word I'm telling you the truth."

"But I am bewildered!" Mondragón gasped. "That *el Presidente* Díaz should wish to—"

"He did," Longarm cut Mondragón off. "There'll be time to go into all of it later on. Right now, everybody in this place has got trouble. Sanchez and his *rurales* are riding out here to take over your *hacienda* and everything that goes with it."

"*Bastardo! Perro!*" Mondragón burst out. "He has—"

"Shut up, Mondragón!" Longarm snapped. "All that can wait for a while. I get the idea you don't doubt what I just said about Sanchez, though."

"I would put no evil beyond him," Mondragón replied. "But, as you are in a hurry, go on, *señor.* Tell me why you are here."

"These folks are going to try to fight Sanchez off," Longarm said. "They got three rifles and I got one, and they got two shotguns. I guess none of 'em has done any shooting before, but I imagine you have. Will you handle one of the rifles and fight with 'em against Sanchez's bunch?"

"Why should I?" Mondragón asked coldly. "They are

my enemies as much as the *rurales*. Why do you think I should help them?"

"Because if they win, you'll walk out of here alive, you and Mrs. Mondragón. If they lose, Sanchez'll likely stand you up against a wall. And I leave it to you to figure out what'll happen to that pretty little wife of yours."

Corazón Mondragón appeared for the first time; she came around the edge of the door Mondragón was holding ajar and stood beside her husband. Her hair was unbound, her face drawn and pale. In the simple, unornamented dress she wore, she looked more than ever like a young girl just out of her teens.

"For once, we have something in common, Ramón," she told her husband. "But I would not allow the *rurales* to take me alive. I do not propose to become one of their sluts. Go, Ramón. Fight beside the people, as *Señor* Long asks you to do."

"Volve a su bordadura, Corazón," Mondragón said coldly. *"Es un hecho para hombres."*

"Despues, sé hombre!" she snapped. *"Si no se combate al lado de los campesinos, irá yo mismo!"*

"Callate, mujer!" Mondragón commanded.

Longarm understood only part of their angry exchange, but he had no time to waste on domestic bickering. He said, "You and your wife can settle your affairs later, Mondragón. I need your answer right this minute."

With a final angry look at his wife, Mondragón said, "Your reasoning is logical, *Señor* Long. I will fight with you against the *rurales*." Then, to Flores and Cristobal, he added, *"Sera precio, pero mas tarde colocurse."*

Anger swept over the faces of both men, and Zaragoza was about to reply to the deposed *hacendado,* when a shout from the lower floor stopped him. Longarm did not recognize the voice, but he did understand what the man said.

"Cristobal! Luís! Acelerese! Vienen los rurales!"

Chapter 17

While Flores and Zaragoza hurried toward the stairs, Longarm brushed past Mondragón and Corazón and headed for a window. The second-story elevation gave him a good view of the approach to the *hacienda*. The *rurales* had just ridden into the mouth of the box canyon. They were still more than a mile away, at the foot of the gentle rise on which the mansion stood. He estimated that he had fifteen or twenty minutes to organize the defenses.

Sanchez was waving an arm command to his men, and as Longarm watched, the riders spurred their mounts to a gallop. He counted quickly. After the *rurales*' brush with Longarm and Dodd, their strength had been reduced to twenty-one men.

Turning to Mondragón, he said, "You know this building better'n I do. Is there a way in or out besides the doors and windows?"

After a noticeable hesitation, the *hacendado* replied, "A tunnel leads from the cellar to the small hill behind the stables. It is a precaution—"

"Sure," Longarm broke in. "I don't suppose it'd be noticed from outside?"

"It is hidden both in the cellar and at the hill."

"That's fine. All we got to worry about's the doors and windows, then." Longarm said. "I guess this corner room's as good a place as any for you to shoot out of. I'll leave it to you to see that Mrs. Mondragón's safe. Put her down on the floor, or under the bed, or someplace like that."

"Of course. I will attend to it. And where will I get my rifle, *Señor* Long?"

190

"I'll send you one up. And shells. Now I got to go get the other windows covered."

At the foot of the stairs, Longarm skidded to a halt just in time to avoid running into his cavalry roan. One of the *campesinos*, whether on his own initiative or following instructions from Flores or Zaragoza, had led the animal into the house through the wide front door, and hitched it to the stair-rail. Longarm paused long enough to lift his Winchester out of its saddle boot and slip a fresh supply of cheroots in his pocket before going on down the hall.

In the big downstairs ballroom, Longarm found that Zaragoza and Flores had almost completed the job of sending the women and children to the bedrooms, with instructions to lie on the floor. The two rifles had been given to the *pistoleros*, and Longarm had them take the third rifle to Mondragón when they went upstairs to their positions in the windows of the rooms that covered the *hacienda*'s other three corners.

Flores and Zaragoza were given the two shotguns. The half-dozen pistols were handed out to men the leaders recommended as being reliable; these men were given positions in the downstairs windows with instructions to hold their fire until the *rurales* were so close that their shirt buttons could be seen clearly.

For himself, Longarm reserved a roving assignment. He planned to move from room to room, taking his place where he was needed most.

Outside, the yells of the *rurales* could now be heard. Longarm stepped to the nearest window and glanced out. Sanchez's band was within reasonable but not certain rifle range. Longarm was just raising his Winchester to let off a warning shot when the *rurale* leader flung his arm up to bring the group to a halt. They reined in, a straggling U-shaped line, with the captain inside the arms of the U. Sanchez pulled a strip of almost-white cloth from his pocket and knotted it around his rifle barrel, then rode slowly forward.

His voice bitter, Flores said to Longarm, "Sanchez is take us to be fools. Now he is play the old *rurale* trick.

They offer surrender and safety, then shoot after their victim is give up his weapons."

Zaragoza added, "We are not surrender, of course, even if we do not know what he is plan. We have learn not to trust the *rurales.*"

Longarm nodded. He'd learned that lesson at Los Perros.

"*Por supuesto,* we must talk to him," Flores said. He looked at Zaragoza. "*Quién ya, Luís? Tu o mi?*"

Zaragoza shrugged. "*Qué más da!*"

"*Pues, voy,*" Flores said.

He left the room and started down the hall. Longarm, after a moment's thought, followed a few steps behind him.

Flores leaned his shotgun in the corner at the end of the hall, swung open the wide front door, and went out to the top step of the *hacienda*'s entrance. Sanchez walked his horse a dozen yards closer to the building. Longarm stayed inside the shadow of the entryway, out of sight.

"*Qué quieres, Sanchez?*" Flores called when the *rurale* reined in. "*No hay nada de hablamos.*"

"*Hay mucho, Cristobal!*" Sanchez replied. "*Mira, hombre! Soy el patrón nuevo del país! Llevada acabo, Mondragón! Ahora, tu y sus amigos obedece mís ordenes, en el nombre de la Republica de Mexico!*"

"*Cagado!*" Flores snorted derisively. "*Tu no es hacendado, tu es peon lo mismo como nosotros!*"

"*Oigame, Cristobal!*" Sanchez shouted angrily. "*No me enoje! Despiderse la hacienda, volve a sus casas y la campaña, a su trabajo!*"

"*Y no vaminos?*" Flores asked. "*Qué tal despues?*"

"*Despues, castigate!*" Sanchez replied threateningly.

"*Chingale!*" Flores snorted. "*Quedaremos en la hacienda!*"

"*Pues, matarles!*"

"*Come cagado, Sanchez!*" Flores retorted. "*No hay más que dice!*"

Standing in the deep shade of the hallway, Longarm had been able to follow the exchange between Flores and the *rurale* enough to understand Sanchez's announcement that he'd assumed the role of *el Patrón*, and his orders to the *campesinos* to go back to their homes and take up their jobs in the fields. He'd caught the spirit, if not the precise meaning, of Cristobal's defiance and taunts, including his final response to Sanchez's threat of death. He had listened to the speakers, but while listening, he'd been watching Sanchez's men.

One of the *rurales* at the end of the semicircle closest to the *hacienda* had drawn Longarm's particular attention. While the other *rurales* still carried their rifles in saddle scabbards or by slings across their backs, this one held his rifle across the horn of his saddle. As Sanchez wheeled his horse and started to rejoin his men after his final threat to Cristobal, Longarm caught a flash of movement out of the corner of his eye when the man at the end of the formation raised his weapon.

By the time Longarm could lift his Winchester, the *rurale* had his rifle shouldered, but Longarm sighted faster. The Winchester roared and the *rurale*'s dying reflex triggered his own rifle after the muzzle began rising in the air as he toppled from his horse. Longarm switched his rifle sights to cover Sanchez, but the *rurale* leader was bent low in his saddle, streaking away from the building. Most of the other *rurales* had their guns in their hands by now, but Sanchez's erratic zigzags kept him between most of them and the *hacienda*. Those on the open ends of the semicircle fired, and bullets rang against the mansion's thick stone walls. Longarm grabbed Flores, pulled him inside, and slammed the door.

"I thank you for my life, *Brazolargo*," Flores said gravely. "It is a thing I will not forget."

"Well, hell, I couldn't just watch 'em use you for target practice," he told Flores. He fished out a cheroot from his pocket and lighted it, then added, "Anyhow, you sure called the turn on Sanchez."

Now they could hear the yelling of the *rurales*, the thudding of their horses' hooves as they charged the *hacienda*, and the *splat* of lead slugs on the stone walls.

"Sanchez es un mentirador! Hijo de perro!" Flores re-

plied. Then, as riflefire began from inside the building, both he and Longarm hurried to a window.

It was obvious that Sanchez had ordered his men to stay at extreme range, for they were darting back and forth in a wide loop around the mansion, shooting wildly. Most of them held the reins in one hand, their rifles in the other, and fired the guns as though they were pistols.

For every ten shots the *rurales* let off, one shot answered from the men in the upper story of the *hacienda*. One of the *rurales* was sagging forward over his horse's neck. Another had been unhorsed; his mount was lying on its side, and the *rurale* was tugging at the reins, trying to get the beast back on its hooves. Sanchez was nowhere to be seen, though Longarm looked for him. The *rurales* kept up their futile fusillade for a few minutes, then pulled away, out of range. They huddled in a compact group beside the road that led out of the canyon.

"What you think they do now, *Brazolargo*?" Flores asked.

"Oh, they'll hit at us again after while. Sanchez has got a look at how we're fixed here, now. He knows we ain't got many guns, and I'd say the first thing he'll do is go for the men that are using 'em."

"But we are in strong position, no?" asked Zaragoza, who'd joined them in time to hear Flores' question and Longarm's reply.

"Four rifles and two shotguns and a handful of pistols ain't much against twenty," Longarm replied soberly.

"But we are inside, behind stout walls," Zaragoza said.

"That helps," Longarm agreed. "Let's just set tight and see what happens. What bothers me is that it's getting on for dark real fast. We got maybe another two or three hours, and then the plate tilts their way."

"We will not give up, *Brazolargo*," Flores said firmly. "We have many men, we will keep good watch tonight, and they can see to aim no better than we can."

"You got a point," Longarm agreed. "Why don't you go on and tally off men to stand sentry-go after it gets dark. I'll sort of mosey around and see what I can do to shore things up a little."

Longarm was on the second story, in a room with one of the *pistoleros*, when the *rurales* launched their next attack.

This time there was no wild riding and wilder shooting. Sanchez divided his men into groups of three, each group reining in at a different corner of the *hacienda* and concentrating its fire on the marksmen on the upper floor. Pinned down by a constant hail of bullets crashing through the windows, the riflemen inside could do little. They spent their time crouching behind the walls beside the windows, or on the floor under the sills, while slugs sang through the windows and scored the ceiling plaster, then lodged in the inner walls.

Meanwhile, the remainder of the *rurales* staged an attack on the big front door. Spurring their horses up the stone steps, they battered at the thick panels with their rifle butts. The sturdy door quivered, but its crossbar held. Zaragoza finally ended the effort by leaning far out of a window and peppering the attackers with a shotgun blast. The tiny birdshot of the gun's load stung the attackers into retreat, but brought none of them down.

Longarm spent his time on the upper floor, running from one window to the next, trying for a clean shot at Sanchez, but the *rurale* captain always seemed to be somewhere else. When Sanchez finally called off his men, and the *rurales* regrouped well out of rifle range, Longarm went back to the lower floor to talk with Flores and Zaragoza.

"We are drive them off again, *Brazolargo*," Zaragoza said with a cheerful smile. "Maybe soon they see they cannot win and give up, no?"

"No, Luís," Longarm answered. He lighted a cheroot before continuing thoughtfully, "There ain't a way in the world we're going to get Sanchez to give up. He's got a chance to be a big man. He won't buckle under."

"*Brazolargo* is right, Luís," Flores agreed. "We are have too few guns to fight them good. And what will we do when there are no more bullets, eh?"

A fresh thudding of hooves broke up their discussion as the *rurales* launched still another attack on the *hacienda*.

This time they came in a compact group, their target the spread of windows on the lower floor where only two of the defenders' rifles could be brought to bear. The riders reached the walls of the house, only one of them brought down by the firing from the upper windows.

From their saddles, they could almost reach the windows, and two of the *rurales* managed to raise themselves to the sills before Flores and Zaragoza rushed in with their shotguns to pepper them. Even at close range, the birdshot did not kill or even wound seriously, but the *rurales* began milling in a disorganized way, and their retreat was assured.

Longarm had gone back to the upper floor to reinforce the two men, Mondragón and the *pistolero*, Humberto, in the corner rooms. The *hacendado* was leaning far out of the window, trying to aim at the riders almost directly below. Longarm saw him jerk as the bullet from a *rurale* rifle tore through his chest. Mondragón was sagging, almost falling, and Longarm leaned out to pull him back inside.

Looking down, Longarm found himself staring into Sanchez's face. The *rurale* captain raised his revolver and fired at Longarm. His hands full, Longarm did the only thing possible. He pulled Mondragón's limp form up as Sanchez triggered his weapon. The slug plowed into the *hacendado*'s shoulder, glanced off bone, and fell harmlessly onto Longarm's chest. Before Sanchez could fire again, Longarm had dropped to the floor, carrying Mondragón with him.

Corazón crawled from beneath the bed and, still on hands and knees, reached the wall where Longarm and Mondragón lay. From below, Longarm heard the shotguns booming and, in a moment, the drumming of hooves on the baked soil as Flores and Zaragoza on the floor below sent the *rurales* into retreat. The gunfire died away. Longarm stood up and looked out the window.

A dead horse and a dead *rurale* lay on the ground beside the house. This time, Longarm noticed, the *rurales* did not go back to their earlier position beside the road. They dashed away from the house to the canyon wall, where they drew rein in a patch of shade created by the setting sun dropping behind the canyon's rim. They were still out of reach of the lone rifleman who was still sniping at them from the *hacienda's* corner window. Even this last defender quit shooting as Longarm gazed outside.

When he saw that the skirmish had ended, Longarm turned back and looked down. Corazón was sitting on the floor, cradling her husband's head in her lap. Mondragón's eyes were open, his breathing shallow. Blood from the superficial shoulder wound inflicted by Sanchez's shot was spreading across the *hacendado's* shirt and mingling with that from the first shot, which had entered his chest.

Corazón looked up at Longarm. "He will die," she said flatly.

"Maybe not. Here." Longarm picked up Mondragón and laid him on the bed. Corazón followed. Longarm said, "Tear a sheet up and make some bandages. I've seen men get well after worse bullet holes."

Corazón pulled at the corner of a bedsheet, but stopped when Mondragón stirred and said, "*Señor* Long is wrong, Corazón. I will not recover. But before I die, I will say this to you. Let the *peons* have the estate. You will have enough; you know where my money is, in Monterrey and in *los Estados Unidos.*"

"Hush, Ramón," Corazón said. "I will care for you."

"Why bother? I have not been such a good husband, that you should languish over me. But you were never a very good wife, were you?"

Mondragón's body shook. He gasped and his eyes rolled upward. The sarcastic smile that had formed on his lips with his last words to his wife froze on his face as he died.

Corazón stood looking at her husband's body for a moment, then leaned forward and pulled the bedspread over his face and torso. "He spoke the truth, you know, *Señor* Long. Death brings truths to light, I suppose. When I failed to give him a child, the son he wanted, his love died, though I think from the first he had as little love for me as I felt for him."

"Just the same, I'm sorry," Longarm told her.

She shrugged. *"Por supuesto.* It is not pleasant to look

197

at the reality of life." She paused thoughtfully. "I will do what he wished, of course, and give this estate to the *campesinos.* I have never been happy here."

"There's plenty of time to think about that later," Longarm said. "Right now, we got to figure out a way to get rid of Sanchez and his outfit, because if we don't, you won't have no estate to hand to nobody."

"Yes, of course." Corazón looked around the room. "I am a good shot; for some time my only amusement was firing at a target. Shall I take Ramón's place?"

Longarm's eyes went to the window. His Winchester lay below the opening, but the rifle Mondragón had been using was not there. "His gun must've dropped when he got shot," Longarm said. "And with as few rifles as we got, I better go get it back before the *rurales* hit at us again. I'll see what Flores and Zaragoza say about you taking your husband's place up here, Mrs. Mondragón."

"Please. With Ramón dead, I will not use his name. Call me Corazón, if you will, *Señor* Long."

"I got a sort of nickname my friends call me. If I'm going to call you by your first name, I guess you better call me Longarm."

"Of course." She nodded gravely, her dark eyes fixed on his gunmetal-blue ones. "I have heard the *campesinos* call you so, *Brazolargo.*"

Longarm nodded. He said, "I better go see if I can get the rifle back from outside. I got a hunch we're going to need it, after dark. I'll see that somebody brings it up here."

Flores and Zaragoza, surrounded by a small group of the men, were in the big dining hall. They were all grinning happily after the third retreat they'd forced on the *rurales.* His news of Mondragón's death caused little stir. To most of them, *el Patrón* had been a distant figure, to be obeyed, perhaps hated, but never familiar to them as a person. Longarm did not tell them of Mondragón's dying wish; that news he felt should be left to Corazón to break.

"We can't afford to lose that rifle Mondragón was using," he concluded. "So if a couple of you men feel like giving me a hand, I'll go get it back."

A half-dozen of them followed Longarm into the room where the *rurales* had almost succeeded in entering. There was no glass in the windowpanes. Longarm leaned out cautiously to look. The rifle lay below the window, a few paces away from the dead *rurale,* whose rifle also lay beside him.

"I'll drop out this window," Longarm told Zaragoza, "and toss the rifle up to you. If I got time, I'll get that other one, too. Then I'll jump and put my arms up, and two of you catch me and boost me back inside before the *rurales* can shoot me."

"Seguro," Zaragoza nodded. "And I will be ready with the *escopeta* if the *rurales* start back when they are see you."

Longarm lowered himself out of the window and dropped the yard or so between his boot soles and the ground. He picked up the rifle Mondragón had dropped and tossed it up to waiting hands, then two long steps took him to the side of the dead *rurale,* where the other rifle lay. He had to lift the *rurale*'s limp body to free the man's ammunition-loaded bandolier, and while he was still working to pull the ammunition belt free, the *rurales* spotted him.

Sanchez recognized Longarm at once. *"Es el gringo!"* he shouted angrily. *"Cargale instamente! Matale! Matale!"*

None of the *rurales* had dismounted, and they reacted instantly to Sanchez's command. A half-dozen dug spurs into their horses and galloped toward the *hacienda.* Longarm freed the bandolier, picked up the rifle, and dashed for the window. He threw the gun and cartridge belt up to the window and leaped. Hands were waiting, and they grasped his arms and hauled him inside just as the *rurales'* bullets started spattering on the wall.

Longarm landed prone on the floor. He raised himself and looked over the windowsill. The *rurales* had stopped firing when he disappeared inside, and were returning to the spot where Sanchez sat on his horse. It was easy to see, even at a distance, that Sanchez was furiously angry. His arms were waving wildly, and he pointed now at one of his men, now at another, as though putting on them the blame for their failure to shoot Longarm.

Sanchez's angry diatribe continued for several minutes. Then his waving arms dropped. He twisted in his saddle and groped in his saddlebags. At the same time, one of the *rurales* dismounted and began scaling the sloping canyon wall. A small longleaf pine stood on the rim. The *rurale* grasped one of its lower branches and twisted and bent it until he tore it from the tree. He slid down the slope on his heels and handed the branch to Sanchez.

"You got any idea what he's doing?" Longarm asked Flores, who stood beside him at the window. "What's he want with that piece of tree limb?"

"I have the fear of what he does," Flores replied soberly. "I hope to be wrong, but we shall find out soon."

Longarm restrained his curiosity. Sanchez had wheeled his horse and his back was now turned toward the watchers in the *hacienda*. In a few moments he turned his horse again and rode toward the *hacienda*. One of the *rurales* followed him a yard or two behind. At the edge of the shadows, Sanchez reined in, and so did the man behind him.

"Damned if he ain't made himself a little flag," Longarm said, a half-smile lifting his mustache.

"No, *Brazolargo*," Flores said, his voice troubled. "It is not a little flag, I am fear."

Sanchez spurred his horse a few steps forward, into the slanting sunlight. He lifted the branch and waved it. The flag he'd made was coal black, and beside it the shadow veiling the valley rim seemed bright in the sun's dying glow. Sanchez gestured to the *rurale* behind him without looking at the man. The *rurale* produced a little concertina; in his big hands the little octagonal instrument looked like a child's toy. He pulled the bellows apart and began to play.

What poured from the concertina was music such as Longarm had never heard before. It was a shrieking cacophony of evil, a message from the Devil himself, the wailing of souls of the damned undergoing Hell's tortures.

At any other time, music from such a toylike instrument would have been amusing. This was not.

Longarm looked at Flores and Zaragoza, intending to ask them what the music was. When he saw their faces, he decided not to. They were staring transfixed at Sanchez and the musician. The music did not last long, two minutes at the most. Sanchez waited for a moment after the last strains died before he spoke.

"*Mira y oigame!*" he shouted. "*Conoces que significa este bandera y se oige el Degüello! Sentides es muerte! Muerte a todos en este país! Algún a todos in este hacienda, y sobre todos los gringos adonde en la villa! En nombre de la Republica de Mexico! No hay cuarto de ningún de este minuto!*"

His long pronouncement completed, Sanchez dismounted long enough to jab the end of the pine branch into the dirt. Then he swung into the saddle and walked his horse back slowly to where his men were waiting.

There was complete silence in the *hacienda* after the *rurale* planted the black flag. All eyes were on the drooping strip of cloth that sagged motionless in the still air, draped around its improvised staff. Longarm finally broke the brooding silence.

"What was all that about?" he asked Flores. "I don't know your language good enough to follow what Sanchez was spouting off about."

Flores' voice seemed to come from deep within his chest. "He is play the *Degüello, Brazolargo.*"

Longarm shook his head. "Don't recall that I've ever heard that word. What's it mean?"

"Death," Luís Zaragoza explained when Flores did not reply immediately. "*El Degüello es la musica de la muerte, del fuego. Es la musica del asesino.* Sanchez is tell us is to be no mercy to any here. Men, women, children, *todos se muerten.*"

"Strikes me as a hell of a thing to say. Plum damned uncivilized. You think he means it?"

"Do not make mistake, *Brazolargo,*" Flores said. "Sanchez is mean what he tell us. But not us alone. He is rule

201

death to everybody in our valley and all your countrymen in La Escondida."

"Now wait a minute!" Longarm exclaimed. "He can't do that!"

"It is our country's law and custom," Flores replied. "*Sí, Brazolargo*, he can do it. When any of Mexico's forces show the black flag, the death flag, in such a fight as this, if he win the battle, all those who are with the losers, they die."

"And he will kill all, too," Zaragoza said bitterly. "For me, myself, I do not mind to die. But my wife, my children, my sons, them I want to live!"

"And if he wipes us up here, he'll go into town and kill all the Americans there? He can do that, too, and nobody in the government'd say anything against him?"

"It is our law and custom," Flores repeated.

"We'll just have to whip the son of a bitch, then!" Longarm snapped. The barbarity of the custom angered him as he'd seldom been angered before.

"Is easy to say." Zaragoza's voice was sad, almost plaintive. "But how we are to win? Three rifles, two *escopetas*, a few pistols. And but little ammunition. You tell me how we do this thing, *Brazolargo*!"

"I don't know yet. But there's got to be a way." Longarm pulled out a cheroot and flicked a match into flame with his thumbnail. "I ain't thought about it yet. But give me a little bit of time to see what I can figure out. I sure don't figure it's my time to die. Especially not on account of some low, mangy cur like Sanchez."

Chapter 18

For several minutes no one spoke, but watched the *rurales* who were in the shade along the valley's west wall. Sanchez's men were busy with their weapons, checking rifle magazines and revolver cylinders, filling empty loops in bandoliers and pistol belts with fresh cartridges. Sanchez stood off at a short distance from the others. He kept glancing at the sky, and when he was not looking at the fading light, he turned his eyes to the black flag that hung ominously on its improvised shaft.

Longarm was very aware of the suddenly sagging morale of the *campesinos*. Everywhere he looked, faces were long and mouths drawn down, eyes shadowed with foreboding and turned inward to contemplate the idea of death. He walked away from the others, and went and sat alone on the stairs. He lighted a cheroot and gave himself over to thinking.

Old son, you being here is part of why Sanchez hung out that black flag, he told himself. *He didn't get real riled up, not right deep-down mad, till he saw you jump out of that window. Right then the shit started to fly, and it looks like he's bound to see that it spatters all over everybody. Now, you're to blame for a lot of this in the first place, helping these folks, which you done just to get yourself out of a jam. So it's up to you to step back and take a look at this mess you made and figure out a way to clean it up.*

He sat there, thinking deeply, until his cheroot was a stub, its coal threatening to singe his mustache. Then he walked up the stairs to the bedroom where Corazón Mondragón sat, looking out through the glassless window.

"I heard the *Degüello* played," she said. "I'm sure the

203

campesinos have told you what it means. It's an ugly thing to think about, isn't it?"

"Not if there's a way of getting out from under it," Longarm said. "Which we ain't going to do if we keep trying to stand them *rurales* off. We're going to run out of ammunition, it's about to fall dark, and I don't see as we got any choice but to turn tail and run."

"Run where? Starting from where? We're prisoners in the *hacienda*, as long as the *rurales* are out there."

"Maybe not, Corazón. You heard what your husband said about that tunnel in the cellar?"

"Of course. It was no secret to me."

"You know how to find the opening? And where it goes to, and how to get out of it at the other end?"

"Why, certainly, Longarm. But the tunnel doesn't go anywhere, really. Just to a little hump on the ground behind the stables. It doesn't lead outside the canyon here."

"Maybe that's far enough," Longarm said thoughtfully. "I got the beginnings of a scheme, but I better do a little more studying on it before I spring it on anybody."

"Longarm," Corazón said hesitantly, "I'm not being selfish, but even with the tunnel, how can I get free of Sanchez? I don't want to let those *rurales* take me, and I won't let them take me alive."

Longarm nodded. "I know what kind of fix you're in, even if you didn't say what's really in your mind.

"What do you mean?"

"Well, now, you're not only a real beautiful woman, the kind of woman like the *rurales* don't get their hands on very often . . ." he began.

Corazón smiled, dropped her eyes, and interrupted him with a murmured, "Thank you, Longarm."

Longarm continued as though she hadn't spoken. "There's more to it than that, though, Corazón. You're Mondragón's wife—widow, I guess I ought to say, if the word don't bother you. Sanchez and his men would kill you sure, as soon as they'd had their pleasure out of you, because when you're gone, there ain't a soul who's got a real claim to being the new boss of the valley."

She nodded. "Yes. That is really what I'm thinking, too,

in addition to the other thing. Unless I can get out of the valley, the tunnel will do me no good."

Longarm studied Corazón's face, trying to decide whether it reflected the beauty of pure Castillian ancestry, or of the mixed French-Spanish type which was called *gachupine*. It was a beauty of contrasts: full, dark red lips and deep brown eyes set in a background of pure ivory skin and framed by floating black hair. He imagined what Corazón would look like after the *rurales* had enjoyed her for a few days in a protracted session of mass rape.

"How easy do you scare?" he asked her abruptly.

"I'm not nervous at all, Longarm. Why?"

He answered her with another question. "You ride a horse pretty good, I guess?"

"I began learning when I was five years old. Why are you asking me these questions?"

"I'll beg off telling you why, for now. But you'll find out soon enough."

Longarm looked out the window. Twilight had arrived; the sky over the canyon rim was still tinged with a strip of red, the sky overhead shading from azure to purple. The *rurales* had started a fire and were gathered around it, cooking their supper.

"You better put on something heavier than that dress you got on," he told Corazón abruptly. "Night's setting in, and it won't keep you warm enough."

She looked at him and smiled. "You're a strange man, Longarm. I have an idea you never make a remark like that unless you have a reason. I won't ask you what it is until you're ready to tell me. And I'll change into something warmer. Boots, perhaps, and a riding habit."

"You do that," he said. "I'll be back after while, and we'll talk some more."

Longarm went downstairs into an atmosphere of gloom. Most of the *campesinos* had gone to their rooms, after seeing the *rurales* beginning to cook supper. Those he saw as he passed the open doors, and those he met in the hallways, wore somber faces that were unmistakable even in the dimness that was stealing into the *hacienda*. Cristobal Flores and Luís Zaragoza were sitting in the big dining hall. Their shotguns lay on the polished top of the table in front of them.

"You have thought, *Brazolargo*?" Flores asked.

"A little bit. Enough to see how we can get out of here alive, if you can get your people to leave."

Zaragoza said, "In Mexico, we dream, *Brazolargo*, but from the truth we do not turn away. I tell you so you know that for this *hacienda* we have dream and fight, but we know we cannot stay, if Sanchez attacks us with all his men and their guns, and in the darkness through which we cannot see."

"You're pretty sure you can get your folks to leave, then?"

"If you can show us how," Flores replied.

"There's a tunnel down in the cellar of this place," Longarm told them. "It don't go very far, just beyond the stables in back of the house, but I don't reckon Sanchez would know about it."

Flores nodded. "Most such *haciendas* have a hidden way out. The *patróns* know very well that we *campesinos* rise to fight for our freedom at times." Flores paused and frowned. "But such a short tunnel as you say this one is would do us little good. We would be in the open if we went through it."

"Not if the *rurales* are chasing after me," Longarm said.

"How do you propose to bring this about?" Zaragoza asked.

"My horse is out there in the hall at the foot of the stairs. Or did you forget about it?"

Both Flores and Zaragoza stared at Longarm with open mouths. Finally, Zaragoza asked, "You are to make yourself a rabbit, to run in front of the *rurales*?"

Flores said wonderingly, "You, a *norteamericano*, would do this thing for us, *Brazolargo*?"

"I got you into this mess, in a way. I aim to get you out of it."

"They will chase you and kill you, the *rurales*," Zaragoza warned.

"I don't figure they will. The moon won't be up till late.

I got a right good chance to give 'em the slip in the dark."

"No, *Brazolargo*." Flores shook his head. "It is too much to ask you."

"You ain't asking me. I just volunteered. Somebody's got to draw 'em off so your people can get away. It ain't just for your folks, anyhow. From what you told me about that *Degüello* business, Sanchez aims to go into La Escondida after he's finished out here, and kill all the Americans in town, mostly because he's mad at me. Now, I don't aim to see him do that, any more'n I aim for him to kill you people."

"It is a true thing, that Sanchez say this after the *Degüello* play," Zaragoza admitted. "And he will do it, too, if we do not leave now."

"Luís and I, we have talk of this," Flores explained. "In *la hacienda*, Sanchez can reach us too easy. In our homes, the fields, we can find places to hide until he is forget."

"That's about how I look at it," Longarm agreed. "So I guess all we got to do is figure out when we start." Then, as though it had just occurred to him: "Oh, I'll be taking Mrs. Mondragón along. And she says she's got something to tell you before we ride out."

Zaragoza and Flores exchanged looks, and Flores said, "If the leaving is to be soon, we should talk with her now, no?"

"I guess it'd be a good idea," Longarm agreed. "And as soon as you get through talking to her, you better tell your people they'll be leaving. There's a few more bits and pieces you and me have got to patch together, too, before we'll be ready."

Longarm's bits and pieces took an hour to patch together after Flores and Zaragoza finished their brief talk with Corazón Mondragón. Word of her promise to give the *hacienda* and valley lands to the *campesinos* spread rapidly, and most of those who made their way to the cellar when the hour of departure arrived looked less gloomy than they had earlier.

There was hope that they might escape the doom announced by the *Degüello*. The raucous laughter and singing

207

that reached the *hacienda* told Longarm that each of Sanchez's men had carried at least one bottle of liquor in his saddlebags.

Longarm had counted the *rurales*, and his tally showed eighteen of them left. Though the darkness kept him from being sure, as best he could determine, they were so confident that they had the box canyon sealed that they had posted no sentries.

Zaragoza and the *pistoleros* were the first to go through the tunnel that Corazón opened for them. The others huddled in the cellar until Flores gave them the signal to enter the black, cavernous opening, which had been concealed behind a wine rack that stood against the stone wall.

Flores was the last to go in. He looked at Longarm and Corazón for a long minute before extending a hand to each of them. *"Vaya con Dios, amigos,"* he said. "I will not try to thank you now, but perhaps we will meet again at a better time."

"Sure we will," Longarm told him. "And I'll bet you folks will do good here, when things settle down."

Flores disappeared into the tunnel, and Longarm swung the wine rack back against the wall. "Well," he said to Corazón, "I guess we better go back upstairs. It ought not to be too long now before the fireworks commence."

"Isn't it time you told me what we're going to do?" she asked. "I'll follow you, of course, but it would help if I knew what to expect. It might keep me from making a mistake later."

"Sure. I been a mite too busy to let you know before now. We're going to ride out of that front door, as soon as the shooting starts. That'll be when Zaragoza and your *pistolero*, the one called Humberto, gets up to the rim of the canyon. When the *rurales* go up the canyon to start shooting back, your other man's going to spook their horses, so we'll pick up a nag for you to ride on into town."

"What about the *campesinos* in the tunnel?"

"Oh, they'll stay there until the *rurales* go chasing after their horses. Then they'll go on home. After that, it's going to be up to them to figure out a way to hold onto what you've given 'em here."

Corazón nodded. "A shrewd plan, Longarm. I suppose we'll go on into La Escondida and warn your countrymen?"

"Something like that. What we do afterwards is going to depend on how Sanchez behaves. He's a little bit what you folks here call *loco en la cabeza*. Maybe he'll cool down, maybe not. We'll just have to wait and see."

While they were talking, Longarm and Corazón had mounted the cellar stairs and walked down the long hall to the foot of the main staircase. Longarm removed the bars from the wide entrance door and untied the reins of the cavalry roan. He maneuvered the animal to face the door, and had just turned to complete his instructions to Corazón when the first shots sounded.

"That'll be Zaragoza," he remarked casually, as though he were telling her the time of day. "We better go take a look out of the window, see what them *rurales* are doing."

When they reached the window of the corner room and looked out at the *rurales*' position, Sanchez's men were already streaming away from the fire. Longarm could see the *rurales* in silhouette against the blaze until darkness swallowed them. Then, when the *rurales* began responding to the shots from the canyon rim, the muzzle-blasts of their rifles showed the progress they were making.

A shadowy figure came out of the darkness beyond the fire's glow and pulled a burning branch from the blaze. The man stepped over to the tethered horses and quickly cut the lariat to which their reins had been tied. Then he began running back and forth in front of the animals, waving the flaming torch in their eyes.

In a moment the animals began to shy and rear, and their shrill neighs could be heard between the shots being exchanged by the *rurales* and Zaragoza and his companion on the rim. Suddenly the horses pulled their reins free and streamed away from the fire.

Longarm turned to Corazón. "We better start. You sure you feel all right, now that it's time?"

"I feel freer and better than I have for years," she smiled. "I'm ready whenever you say the word."

Longarm swung the entrance door open and mounted

209

up, then stretched a hand to Corazón, to help her swing up to the cruppers. He dug his heels into the roan's flank. The horse's hooves scraped metallically on the stone floor until it found its footing, then it moved swiftly through the door and out into the darkness, down the steps to the ground, and took the road out of the canyon.

Several of the horses that had bolted from the fire had slowed and stopped in the bottleneck of the canyon's entrance. Longarm reined in, walked the roan up to one of them, and leaned forward to grab its reins and pass them to Corazón. She swung from the roan to the *rurale* mount and settled into the saddle. Longarm's eyes were adjusting to the darkness by now, and he saw her smiling when she nodded that she was ready. They rode on out of the canyon, the shots still being swapped between the *rurales* and the *campesinos* fading in the distance. Longarm set their pace at an easy lope that ate up the miles. Soon the shots could no longer be heard.

"Does everything you plan work out so smoothly?" Corazón asked as they rode toward town.

"Not by a long shot. I sure as hell didn't figure to get into a fracas like we did back there."

"Even small revolutions create confusion," Corazón sighed. "I have been aware of revolutions all my life, Longarm. My grandfather fought with Zuloaga and Allende, my father with Lerdo and Iglesias. Ramón was on the side of Díaz, as was his father before him, but Ramón always swore this was only to hold onto their family's properties. Small affairs like this one do not disturb me."

"I must say, you're taking it like a real lady. Which you are, of course. It seems to me like you'd be right upset, after everything that's happened. Losing your husband and all this land and that fine *hacienda*."

"My father arranged my marriage to Ramón. Ramón arranged my life after we were married. I am free now of both the marriage and the *hacienda*. Do you wonder that I feel reborn?"

Longarm could find no reply to this, so he did not try to answer. In silence, they rode on toward the town through the quiet, moonless night.

• • •

La Escondida was almost totally asleep when they reached it. The houses that bordered the road were dark and still, but when they got to the plaza there were lights streaming from the *posada* and the two cantinas. Longarm led them directly to Julia Wheatly's house; it, too, was still lighted. Sam Ferris came out when they clattered into the patio.

"You got here just in time," he said to Longarm. "The party was just about to break up, and all of us have been wondering why you didn't show up." Belatedly, he recognized Corazón and made a half-bow. "Mrs. Mondragón." There was both recognition and a question in his voice.

As he swung out of the saddle and turned to give Corazón a hand down, Longarm said, "Glad I got here in time, Sam. We got a lot of things to talk about."

Ferris frowned. "Trouble at the mine?"

"There's trouble all over, tonight," Longarm said succinctly. "You'll hear about it fast enough."

In the *sala*, the guests who'd been at dinner were getting ready to leave. Longarm stopped them. "You better sit back and get ready to listen to some real bad news."

"What's happened now, for heaven's sake?" Julia asked. She'd greeted Corazón Mondragón cordially enough, but now her eyes went from Longarm to Corazón and back, as though she suspected that Corazón was somehow the reason for Longarm's blunt announcement.

"Sanchez and the *rurales* are on a rampage." He did not take time to go into details; that could be done later. He asked Julia, "Did you tell everybody about Delgado, and what he'd come here for?"

"Yes. And about the fight at the mine, and how you handled Delgado and his men."

"Well, I guess it was Delgado being here that give Sanchez the idea he could set himself up as the new *patrón*," Longarm went on. "Anyhow, him and his crew pulled in at the Mondragón place, ready to take it over. Thing is, the plain folks who'd been kowtowing to a *patrón* all these years had got fed up—"

"Julia told us about that, too," Terrance Barns interrupted. "I got the idea that you had a hand in helping them, from what she said."

"It ain't my way to lie, Barns," Longarm told him. "I did, and I'll be first in line to admit I ought to've stayed out of things. But I didn't, and by the time I saw I was wrong, it was too late to do much about it."

"Get back to Sanchez," Ferris suggested. "Unless it's all tied together. We're not worried about the *campesinos*, we can get along with them."

"Of course we can," George Blanton said. "Why, they're a nice, gentle bunch of everyday folks, when you get to know them."

"Hush, George," Dora Blanton told her husband. "Let Mr. Long finish his story."

"Now, I can't waste a lot of time dotting *i*'s and crossing *t*'s," Longarm went on. "The upshot was, after Sanchez got there, a fight started between him and the folks who'd already took over from the Mondragóns."

"A real fight?" Bobby Blanton interrupted excitedly. "With shooting and everything? Whillikers! I wish I'd been there!"

"You keep quiet, too, Bobby," Dora admonished. "You're as bad as your father!"

Julia turned to Corazón and asked her, "Where were you and your husband all this time, my dear?"

"We'd been taken prisoner by the *campesinos* when they came out and demanded that Ramón sign an agreement to pay them for the work they do in the fields and around the *hacienda*," Corazón replied. "And later, after the fighting started, Ramón was killed by the *rurales*."

"It seems to me what's happening is like another Mexican revolution," Tom Dodd said thoughtfully.

Carozón answered the Ranger before Longarm could speak. "I suppose you could call it that. But you should know that the *campesinos* are natural enemies to us *hacendados*."

"You folks better save your chitchat till later, and let me get on with what I got to tell you," Longarm said impatiently. "We might not have too much time left."

"Time for what?" Ferris demanded.

212

"Time to save our skins, if Sanchez goes on with what he's begun," Longarm retorted. Silence followed his blunt announcement. He went on, "Any of you ever hear of a tune called the *Degüello*?"

"Sure," Dodd replied. "That's the Mexican tune that they play when they're getting ready for a massacre. If I remember my history, Santa Ana had it played at the Alamo. I don't recall whether they used it at Goliad or not. Means they're going to wipe out everybody who's fighting against 'em. No mercy and no quarter for anybody, including women and children." He looked at Corazón. "That right, Mrs. Mondragón?"

She nodded. "It's close enough. One of my country's relics of old barbarous customs."

"What about the *Degüello*?" Barns asked. "Did Sanchez have it played at the Mondragón place?"

"Loud enough to raise your skin in goosebumps," Longarm replied. "And my hunch is that he aims to do it."

"But how does that affect us?" Julia asked nervously, as though she already knew the answer.

"Sanchez included all of us when he made a little speech after the music," Longarm told her. Then he overrode the buzz of talk that followed. "Now just calm down a minute! There's a few things that maybe some of you don't know about. First off, I got crossways of Sanchez up north of here a while back. I guess you might say I got crossways of all the *rurales*, too."

"We've heard about the trouble you had with the big *rurale*," Blanton said. "Gossip travels fast in La Escondida, Mr. Long. But I thought Colonel Delgado shot him?"

"He did. But then Tom Dodd and me had a brush with Sanchez and his outfit the other day. I guess between him and me, we got Sanchez so riled up that he went a little bit loco."

"So he plans to take it out on all of us?" Ferris asked.

Longarm nodded. "That's about the size of it, Sam. He might have got the idea, after Delgado and him talked, that Julia's mine is worth taking, too, and getting rid of you and her'd be the easiest way for him to do it."

Julia said thoughtfully, "It looks to me as though we're

all involved in this. I don't think any of us is safe from the *rurales* right at the moment."

"That's what I been trying to get around to," Longarm said. "Sanchez has put himself out on a limb, swearing he was going to kill everybody in the valley. Now he can't afford not to go through with it."

"Aren't you exaggerating a bit, Mr. Long?" Blanton asked. "After all, we haven't done Sanchez any harm. Surely, he'd—"

"If I were you, I wouldn't put Sanchez to the test," Corazón interrupted. "I know how men such as the *rurales* behave."

"If I didn't think I was right, Blanton, I wouldn't be standing here now." Longarm put all the sincerity he could summon into his voice. "But I reckon the best thing for everybody in this room right now to do is to hightail it away from La Escondida just as fast as we can move."

"But where would we go?" Dora asked. "This is the only home we have, Mr. Long. Why, we'd be—"

"I don't figure we got to go very far, Mrs. Blanton," Longarm interrupted. "Our best bet's Monterrey. That's only about seventy miles, and there's an American consul there, and regular Mexican troops that can handle the *rurales*."

"What about the mine?" Julia asked. "I don't want to leave it unless—"

"Your mine ain't going to run away, Julia," Longarm told her. "I misdoubt Sanchez is going to think much about it for a spell, anyhow."

"There's two other Americans in La Escondida," Barns said with a frown. "Should we ask them to join us?"

"If they're sober enough to travel, and feel like coming along, sure," Longarm replied.

"Well," Julia sighed, "I guess there's no help for it. Perhaps we'd better take Mr. Long's advice." She faced Longarm. "You're going, too, aren't you?"

"Why, sure. I wouldn't've come here, otherwise."

"Long's right," Dodd said. "The only way to be safe and get everything straightened out is to get the American

214

consul and the Mexican authorities in Monterrey to bring Sanchez under control. Then it'll be safe to come back."

"Does everybody agree, then?" Julia asked.

"What about horses?" Blanton asked.

"There are enough for everyone in the Mondragón stables here in town," Corazón said. "And saddles and other gear."

"All right," Barns said with a shrug. "If we're all going, I'd better join in."

"Yes. We will, too," Blanton agreed.

"I'll go wherever you say, Julia," Ferris offered. "With you folks, or stay here and be sure the mine's safe."

"Don't try to be a hero, Sam," Julia said. "You're coming along, of course. Now, I suggest we get a good night's rest, and pack the things we absolutely have to have, and—"

"No, Julia," Longarm broke in. "There's no time for that. I figure we've got maybe eight or ten hours' start on the *rurales*, if we leave here right now. It'll take them that long to round up their horses and prowl through the *hacienda* and sober up. But it's a two-day ride to Monterrey, and them *rurales* can move fast when they're riled up."

"You mean we can't—"

"I mean we better grab what we can, and that includes some grub, and get saddled up and go! And not waste any time doing it. Not if we all expect to get to Monterrey alive."

Chapter 19

Even the two cantinas and the *posada* on the plaza had
turned out their lights and closed their doors by the time
the Americans were ready to start. There had been horses
to fetch from the Mondragón town house, supplies to as-
semble and pack in panniers, last-minute trips between
houses and horses to retrieve some treasured possession
overlooked in the flurry of hasty packing. Midnight had
long been gone before Longarm led the group along silent,
dark, and deserted streets, and the little procession started
north.

Behind Longarm, Sam Ferris rode on the sturdy Morgan
that was his favorite working mount. Julia Wheatly was
next in line, then the Blanton family. All three of them
were mounted on local horses of indeterminate breeding.
Bobby carried his prized Winchester across his saddle horn,
ignoring the scabbard that was attached to the skirts.

Corazón rode behind Bobby, on a barb that showed the
ancestry of the Arabian steeds brought over from the
Spanish homeland by the *conquistadors*, and it was she
who led the two packhorses that the Mondragón town
stables had also provided. Terrance Barns forked a gelding
that matched in its lineage the barb that Corazón rode.
He and Tom Dodd on his quarter-Morgan formed the rearguard.

Longarm studied the sky as the string of horses and
their silent riders moved along the upward-sloping trail.
The moon had risen before they started, and was high in
the sky by the time they passed the deserted *rurale* sentry
post north of La Escondida. It was a three-quarters moon,
and already past its zenith.

Longarm was calculating times. He was sure the *rurales* would hurry their departure from the *hacienda*, once they discovered it was deserted. They'd then have to round up their spooked horses before returning to town. They'd lose another hour visiting the homes of the Americans, and looking for them in the most likely hiding places.

Once Sanchez had decided to put his men on the trail, they'd have to stop at the Palacio Federal to replenish their ammunition and ready themselves for travel. But that Sanchez would indeed lead his men in pursuit, Longarm had no doubt at all.

With all luck, he encouraged himself, *Sanchez and his crew won't even get away from town much before daybreak. If we can make any sort of time, we might stretch our lead on the murdering bastards to a full day. But it's a long ways to Monterrey, two good days of steady riding. And if them* rurales *are like the other ones, they'll kill their nags trying to catch up. But easy does it. Folks like the Blantons and Julia are going to need to stop and rest now and again. They ain't used to hard riding, like me and Tom.*

He and Dodd had talked briefly for a few minutes while the others, were scurrying around, packing. It had been, Longarm recalled, chuckling to himself, like a couple of banty roosters clucking a challenge to one another before squaring off to use their spurs.

"Looks like we're going to be on the same side again for a while," Dodd had said noncommittally.

"Looks that way," Longarm had agreed.

"So far, its been pretty much a standoff between us," the Ranger went on.

"So far."

"It'll be the same thing, as long as all of us are going."

"That's how I see it, too."

"I guess you gave up on the only two that won't be along."

"You mean them two saloon bums?" Longarm had asked.

During the brief time they'd had between deciding to leave La Escondida and the period devoted to preparation, the Americans had discussed inviting the two drunks to join them. It had been George Blanton's idea, but he hadn't pressed for their inclusion in the party after the others had agreed unanimously that the pair had become so imbedded in the local landscape that Sanchez would ignore them. It was understood tacitly that Longarm, Julia, and Corazón were the ones in the greatest danger.

"Yep. I took one look at that pair and decided neither one could be anything but what they look like and act like."

"I saw it pretty much the same way, Tom."

Dodd waited almost a full minute before he asked, "You made up your mind yet?"

Longarm didn't need to be told what the Ranger was asking about. He replied, "Well, I got an idea or two. But I'm still being what you might call open-minded."

"I've been thinking over what you said the other day." Dodd kept his voice carefully casual. "About murder being a bigger charge than whatever you federals want Maddox for."

"I'd imagine you could have him when we got through asking him a few questions," Longarm had said, matching Dodd in the offhanded way he spoke. "I'd have to put the proposition up to Billy Vail, of course. Can't say how he'd feel about it."

"I got a pretty good idea how Captain Hawkins'd feel. I don't think he'd cotton much to it."

"Well, it was just an idea, Tom. Might be it wouldn't work out, at that."

They'd ended the conversation then, each of them understanding clearly what neither had said, that after reaching Monterrey, the truce they'd declared wordlessly would end. There, they knew they'd inevitably move into a showdown to decide which one would return Clayton Maddox to the states.

In spite of himself, Longarm yawned. The night was wearing on, and he'd been a long time without sleep. He'd snatched a quick bite at Julia's while the others were getting ready, but he'd been moving virtually without pause since Cristobal Flores' grandson had roused him from his siesta the previous afternoon. He figured they'd covered perhaps eight miles since leaving La Escondida. Another mile or so ahead, he decided, the first good spot he saw, he'd call a halt.

Everyone in the party was glad enough to take a break, but Julia was the only one who asked him for an explanation."

"I don't understand why we're stopping to rest so soon," she said. "We were in such a tearing hurry to get away, now we're losing valuable time to take a rest none of us needs."

"Maybe we don't." Longarm tried to camouflage the reason for his decision. "The horses do, though. Mine's been rode hard today. Tom's on the only animal that's been working regular. The rest of 'em are soft as butter in July. They got to be gentled along for a while."

"It sure wouldn't help us if one of them went lame," Dodd said, supporting Longarm.

"I hadn't thought of that," Julia nodded. "Though I'll admit, I'm about as soft as my horse is. I'll be glad to rest a little while myself."

"We better all rest," Longarm told them. "If you packed your gear right, you can take your blanket roll off without it bothering anything else. Stretch out and nap. We're still a long ways ahead of the *rurales*, the way I figure it."

Longarm didn't take his own advice about the blanket. He folded his coat up for a pillow and stretched out on the bare ground. Several of the others did the same thing. Timing his mind to rouse him in a couple of hours, he went to sleep.

When he woke up, the moon had set, but the skyline was not yet showing in the east. He roused the sleepers— Dodd and Ferris had elected themselves sentries—and within a few minutes they were again on the trail. He called another halt in midmorning, and this time they broke out food: tortillas, cold refried beans, goat cheese in small, round loaves, and *chorizos* almost as hard as iron, but considerably spicier.

Spirits had begun to perk up by the time they mounted to go on. The sun was midway between rising and noon, not yet too hot at that altitude to be uncomfortable. For the next several miles, as the road leveled out along the spinal column of the Sierra Madre Oriente, the group looked almost cheerful.

On both sides of them, the mountains slanted down into sparsely wooded valleys, their sides dotted with feathery acacias, thin *ocote* pines, and low-crowned, spreading oak trees. The road they were traversing wound along the crests. It was not a formal, graded road, but rather a trail that had been leveled and widened through years of use by the horses and mules and occasional burro-pulled *carretas* of travelers who followed a deer trail or one of the runs of the piebald mountain sheep that were the mountains' principal large animal life.

Riding at the head of the little column, Longarm glanced back occasionally. He did not worry too much about the rear, as long as Tom Dodd stayed in the rearguard position.

There had been little conversation among the members of the party since the trip started. Strung out as they were, with a yard or so between each horse as they rode along in single file, talking was simply too difficult. Occasionally, Sam Ferris had dropped back to have a word with Julia, and Bobby Blanton had chattered to his parents almost constantly until they grew tired of answering.

From his trip south such a short time earlier, Longarm remembered each of the few spots along the road where there was water and shade. By midafternoon, when the travelers and their horses began to tire in spite of regular halts, he decided it was time to stop for the night at the next suitable place.

He carried a vivid mental picture of the spot he had in mind. It was a hollow a few yards off the trail, where a spur ran out from the main range and created a fairly level area large enough to accommodate the group. A small spring-fed pond provided water, and two large sprawling oaks shielded the place from easy observation by anyone stopping to scan the vicinity from either of the heights that rose above the little saddle. And any traveler approaching from either direction would be spotted at once on the rim of the saddle by a watcher in the hollow.

Longarm led the way off the road to the pond. "We'll stop here for the night," he announced. "All of us could use a hot meal, and the animals can stand some rest, too."

"You want me to go out and shoot a deer for supper?" Bobby asked. He was cradling his new Winchester in his arms.

"Not this time, Bobby," Longarm replied, suppressing a smile. "We better get along with the grub we're carrying."

Bobby looked disappointed, but accepted Longarm's decision. Longarm returned to the job of unsaddling the cavalry roan. He was still wrestling with a balky cinch buckle when Sam Ferris came up.

"I guess you've got your reasons for stopping this early," he remarked. "But we could've made a few more miles today, it seems to me."

"I guess we could, Sam. Except the women are getting mighty tired. And I want to get us fed a good hot supper and have our fires smothered out before it gets dark."

"You still think the *rurales* are going to come after us?"

"I'd be surprised if they didn't. Mostly on account of Julia and me. But if you'd been out there at the Mondragón place yesterday, you'd've seen how Sanchez was. He's got the itch to be a big man, and anybody sick with that kind of fever don't get over it easy."

"We'll keep watches, I reckon?" Ferris asked.

"Certain sure. Soon as we eat, we'll set down and work out who's going to stand sentry and how long."

Dora Blanton came up while they were talking. "I've sent George and Bobby out to look for firewood. There should be enough close by for us to heat some beans and meat for supper."

"Anything hot's going to taste good to me right now," Longarm told her.

Mrs. Blanton looked around at the hollow and the pond. "Do you think we can make the rest of the way to Monterrey tomorrow?" she asked.

Longarm shook his head. "We can't push all that fast. If we start out at daylight tomorrow, though, we ought to make it to within an easy half-day's ride to Monterrey before the day ends."

"We can't get there too soon to suit me," she sighed, turning back to join Julia and Corazón at the spot they'd chosen for the supper fire.

Longarm finished unsaddling and spread his blanket roll. By then, Blanton and Bobby had returned with a few sticks of wood, and a fire was burning. Dora and Julia had skillets out and were getting ready to heat the food that Corazón was taking from the panniers of the packhorses. Longarm assembled the men at a little distance from the fire.

"I been figuring all along that we got a pretty fair lead on the *rurales*," he told them. "Of course, they might know some shortcuts we don't, but their animals have got to rest, the same as ours, and they couldn't have left La Escondida much before noon today."

"Which means they'd be catching up sometime tomorrow morning, if you figure right," Dodd said thoughtfully.

"About then," Longarm agreed. "Two or three hours after daybreak, if I'm right. Which still don't mean we don't need to keep watch tonight."

"It's sensible," Dodd said. "I'd say a man on each side of camp, somewhere along the road."

"That's about what I had in mind," Longarm agreed. He looked at the others. "I don't guess it makes much difference who draws which watch?"

"Not to me," Dodd said promptly.

"Or me," Ferris agreed.

George Blanton and Barns shook their heads.

Longarm went on, "Well, if it's all the same, then, why don't you two men—" he indicated Barns and Blanton— "stand first watch. Tom, maybe you and Sam will take the middle trick, and I'll keep lookout then till daylight."

There was a general murmur of agreement, after which Dodd asked, "I guess we better figure on me and Sam shaking out of our bedrolls about midnight? And then you'll come on between four and five o'clock?"

"Something like that." Longarm looked at them in turn,

found no disagreement, and said, "If it's all settled up, let's go eat some supper. My belly thinks my throat's been cut."

Supper was eaten quickly and, for the most part, silently. Fatigue was beginning to show in the faces of all except Longarm and Dodd, both of them veterans of hard rides and little sleep. With the fire extinguished, all but the first two watchers sought their bedrolls.

Longarm lay awake, smoking his last cheroot of the day after a nightcap from the bottle in his saddlebags. He waited until he saw the first two sentries leave for their posts, Blanton to the south, Barns to the north. Then he lay awake another hour before rising quietly and walking along the road toward Barns's post. Moving with the quiet steps of a stalking hunter, he stopped a dozen yards from Barns and sat down Indian-style on the hard ground.

Barns was a nervous sentry. He walked along the road a few steps, crossed it, returned to his starting point, sat down for a few minutes, then rose and recrossed the road and took a few steps in the direction of the camp before changing his mind and returning to his original position. When he stood up again and began pacing along the road in the opposite direction, Longarm let him get within each earshot before speaking.

"Barns," he said quietly.

Barns's hand went to his gun butt, and when he spoke, his voice was throatily nervous. "Long?"

"That's right." Longarm stood up and walked the few paces that separated them. The moon had still not risen, and Barns's face was no more than a pale blur in the darkness.

"Checking up on us?" he asked.

"No. Just not sleepy. Thought we might finish that talk we begun in the saloon the other night."

"I don't know that there's a hell of a lot to say. You've been up the trail and back, and your eyes are in pretty good shape."

"You'd hit that bottle of—what was the stuff?"

"*Habanero.*"

"Sure. Well, you'd hit it at a pretty good clip. Don't reckon you had time to get one to bring along, did you?"

223

"I'm off it, Long. Not that I don't miss it, but I . . . well, I took a look at myself the other night and decided I'd had all I wanted. So, I've quit."

"Sounds to me like you're getting ready for something."

"What the hell do you mean by that?"

"Oh, just thinking out loud." Longarm drew a cheroot from his pocket and flicked a match across his thumbnail. When the cigar was drawing, he said, "Guess I'd better be getting back to my roll. I got the habit of sleeping light on nights like this. Don't be surprised if I come prowling around again before your watch is over."

Barns peered through the gloom at Longarm for a moment. Then, in a strained voice, he said, "No. No, I won't. But I'll be here whenever you come back, if that's what's eating you."

Well, you done what you set out to do, old son, he told himself as he walked thoughtfully back to his blankets, puffing the cheroot. *There's times when a man gets to a place where he gets tempted to do fool things, and it don't hurt a bit to let him know somebody's keeping an eye on him. Now, if you got the brains God give a spooked-up jackrabbit, you'll get back to your blankets and turn in. It's way past sleeping time, and tomorrow morning's getting mighty near.*

Morning brought the bad news Longarm had been expecting. He hadn't expected it quite so early, though. Sanchez and the *rurales* had moved faster than he'd thought they could. His morning watch was drawing to a close; the moon had set and a faint hint of gray, the illusory promise of the false dawn, was showing at the crests of the jagged peaks around him when he heard the distant drumming of hoofbeats.

Longarm had been sitting on his haunches beside the road, thinking of what had to be done in the next few days. The sound of hoofbeats came to him distantly through the gathering dawn. He dropped to his knees and pressed his ear to the hard earth. He could judge from the volume of the broken rhythms echoing in his ear that the *rurales* were still at least two or three miles away. Little enough time was left for him to get the camp's defenders into place. Longarm jumped to his feet and ran to rouse the others.

No one in the group had undressed beyond removing shoes and boots, and all of them were sleeping lightly on the hard, unaccustomed ground. They were on their feet and moving at his first warning call.

"You ladies grab the horses and lead 'em down behind that bluff yonder," Longarm said quickly. "Bobby, your job's to help the womenfolks. You keep that rifle ready, and don't let no *rurales* get close. The rest of us will be covering the road."

"How far away are they?" Julia asked.

"Far enough so we got time to get ready, but not any to waste. Now, you ladies don't worry. We ought to be able to handle the men Sanchez has got left."

"I hope you're right about that," George Blanton said. He was carrying his rifle in a manner that indicated to Longarm that he was not really skilled with firearms.

We'll get the first shots in," he reassured the missionary, "And that's half the fight won, right there."

Dodd and Ferris and Barns had joined them by then. Longarm looked at his four-man army and said, "Let's try to stay hid until they start down the slope. They won't be looking much along either side. They'll figure we'll still be moving, now that it's getting daylight."

Involuntarily, the men looked up at the sky. It was still gray and there was as yet no tinge of sunrise in the east.

"Two of us on each side of the road?" Dodd asked. "You shoot first, then we all let go at the same time?"

"That's as good a way to start as any," Longarm agreed. "I figure I'll work back up the road a ways. If you men stay here, we'll get 'em in a three-way crossfire."

"And don't stop after the first shot," Barns said. "Damn it, it's the second and third hits that takes the guts out of a bunch like the *rurales*!"

All of them stared in surprise at the usually withdrawn Barns. His young-old face had undergone a transformation. It had lost its indeterminate character and Barns suddenly looked lean and hard-jawed. Longarm picked up the conversation before anyone could comment on the change.

"You men might as well pair off the way you did last night for sentry-go," he said. "Figure out which side of the road you'll take and wait till you hear my shot. They ought to be just about to you when I pull trigger."

None of the others offered any comment. They stood up and paired off: Blanton and Barns, Ferris and Dodd. Picking up their rifles, they started for their positions.

Longarm took to the rough ground a little distance from the road. He picked his way along the rugged, boulder-studded ground, moving at a slant down the sloping shoulder that fell away from the road on each side. He'd gone only fifty or sixty paces up the slope that formed the south side of the saddle before the increasing loudness of the hoofbeats warned him to take cover. He picked a big boulder a dozen paces ahead and crouched behind it. He'd just reached concealment when the first of the *rurales* appeared, coming at a fast lope over the hump ahead.

Sanchez was riding at the head of his men. The *rurales* streamed past Longarm, their mounts gaining speed on the downward slant. He let them pass, holding his cover. To a man, the *rurales* had their eyes fixed on the road in front of them. When the last man was a safe distance past him, Longarm stood up. He hated to backshoot, but he'd counted nineteen men with Sanchez, and this was one of those times when necessity outweighed principles.

By now the sky was graying fast, shedding enough light for accurate shooting. Longarm fixed his sights on the last rider and triggered his rifle. The *rurale* stiffened and dropped from his horse.

Four rifles spoke from the cover the others had found beside the road. The *rurales* were thrown into milling confusion for a moment, but recovered fast. Longarm heard Sanchez's voice shout a command. The broken clot of riders straightened into a line and galloped up the rise on the saddle's north side. The four beside the road sent a short volley after them.

Longarm was hurrying to join the others when the *rurales* began shooting back. He'd been running down the

226

middle of the road, but when the return fire from the slope ahead began raising puffs of dirt on both sides of him, Longarm jumped off the trail and found cover behind the boulders along its side.

Behind his shelter, he raised his head to look. The *rurales* had reined in halfway up the north hump of the saddle. They had the advantage of being higher than the camp's defenders. Longarm hoped the men in front of him had been able to find cover. That was all he had time to wonder about, for Sanchez's shout of command echoed and the *rurales* spurred their mounts. They came sweeping down the hump, covering their advance with random shots as they galloped.

Longarm had seen one *rurale*'s body lying in the road just past the positions held by the others. He'd passed the man he'd brought down just before the gunfire forced him to take cover. The odds hadn't improved as much as he'd hoped. There were still seventeen *rurales* in the saddle, and they were getting close to him now, slugs whistling around him. He made himself as thin as he could in the scanty protection of the boulder.

He had no chance to shoot as they swept by him; their covering fire was too hot for him to risk raising his body from the boulder behind which he'd sheltered. The cracking of rifles from the area guarded by the other Americans, sharper and higher-pitched than the Mausers of the *rurales*, told Longarm when the riders had passed the defenders' positions. He waited and snapped off a round at the *rurales*' backs, but they had begun to zigzag their horses across the narrow roadway and the slug went wild.

Sliding down the shoulder, Longarm ran at a crouch back to where he'd left the other men. He found Dodd lying on the ground, blood staining his shirt. Sam Ferris was bending over him, trying to staunch the flow by stuffing a bandanna down the back of his shirt.

"How bad you hit, Tom?" Longarm asked.

"Bad enough to hurt. And bad enough to keep me from handling a gun."

Longarm saw that it was Dodd's right shoulder that had

been wounded, barring him from using either a rifle or a pistol.

"Feels like the slug got my collarbone," Dodd rasped as Ferris lowered him to the ground, after stuffing his own bandanna under the Ranger's shirtfront. "Sorry, Longarm. You're going to have to whip them bastards without my help."

"We'll manage some way," Longarm replied, with more confidence than he felt after having lost the skill of his most experienced combatant. He raised his voice and shouted across the road, "Barns! Blanton! You two all right?"

"Fine, Barns's voice responded. "Ready for 'em to try again!"

"Which won't be long now," Ferris observed.

Longarm turned to look. At the top of the hump, the *rurales* had stopped and turned. They were forming into a double file, one line of riders on each side of the road. Sanchez raised his arm and the *rurales* spurred down into the saddle.

Longarm took his time aiming, shifting his sights as Sanchez moved. Sure of his aim, he squeezed the Winchester's trigger. The *rurale* captain half-rose in his stirrups and toppled from the saddle. One foot caught in a stirrup. The sight of their commander being wounded and dragged first slowed, then halted the *rurales*' charge. They reined in, moving to help Sanchez.

"Hit 'em while they're stopped!" Longarm called to his men.

He stepped out into the road to get a clear field of fire, and dropped two *rurales* with as many shots. Across the road, Barns and Blanton were slow to respond. They were just coming from behind the big rocks where they'd found cover when a peppering of shots from the *rurales* sent both them and Longarm back to shelter.

Suddenly, the slugs from the *rurales* stopped kicking up dust from the roadway, though there was no slackening of gunfire from the top of the hump. Longarm broke cover and stepped onto the road. At the top of the hump, the *rurales* had wheeled and were swapping shots with a second group of riders that had come out of nowhere. Long-arm squinted through the bright, sunless dawn and began to grin. Riding at the front of the group now attacking the *rurales* were Cristobal Flores and Luís Zaragoza.

Chapter 20

After the death of Sanchez and the appearance of the *campesinos*, the battle was over. The *rurales* fought a rearguard action as they retreated down the slope, off the road, and across the rough country, and Longarm, Barns and Blanton joined the new arrivals in sniping at them. Then the retreating *rurales* scattered when Zaragoza led all but a half-dozen of the *campesinos* after them in vengeful pursuit.

"There ain't going to be many of that bunch get back to La Escondida," Longarm predicted as he stood beside Flores on the edge of the road, watching the *campesinos* riding after the fleeing *rurales*.

"There will be none, if our people catch them," Flores replied harshly. "We have suffer too much from the *rurales* and the *hacendados*. We have no love for either of them."

"Is that why you're here, chasing the *rurales*? I figured you'd decided to come help us."

"To help you, and to hurt them, *Brazolargo*. The *rurales* left the *hacienda* almost at once, to follow you. It is Luís who reminds me of the debt we owe you. To decide to ride after you and try to help you was but a small thing, after that."

"You got here at just about the right time," Longarm said. "We was down to four guns against their fifteen or so. If they'd had one more go at us, we'd have been in pretty bad shape."

"You come back to La Escondida now, no?" Flores asked.

"I ain't sure, just yet. We got a shot-up man that's going

to need doctoring. I'd say we're better off hauling him to Monterrey than we'd be going back where there ain't no doctor."

"Whichever the way you take him," Flores said, "his life will be as all lives are, *en los manos de Dios.*"

"Sure," Longarm agreed. "But there's times when God can use some help from a good doctor. Anyhow, I'd imagine Mrs. Wheatly and her mining man might like to go back with you. Let's go down to where they are and see how Tom's getting on."

Dodd's wound was being attended to by the women when Longarm and Flores rejoined the group. "But he's got a shattered collarbone," Julia told Longarm. "He'll need a real doctor to look after him, to set the bone and clean out the wound."

"I was pretty sure that'd be the way of it. And I'd imagine you and Sam will want to be going back to La Escondida, to keep an eye on your mine?"

"We'll almost have to, Longarm. The Blantons will want to go back, too. It's all the home they have right now. What about you, though?"

"I can't rightly say yet, Julia. I got to do a little talking to Tom first, then I'll make up my mind."

Stepping over to where Dodd lay, Longarm told the Ranger, "Sorry you caught one, Tom."

"Hell, any man who gets around where people are shooting at him is going to step in the way of a slug once in a while. It's not my first; I don't reckon it'll be my last."

Longarm nodded with the understanding of a fellow lawman. He said, "Flores and his *campesinos* are going back to La Escondida. I reckon you'd rather go on up to Monterrey, where there's doctors, and I'd suppose in a town that size they'd have a hospital or infirmary of some kind."

"What kind of fool question is that? Damn it, it's my right shoulder, Longarm. I need a doctor who knows what he's doing, not some country *curandero.*"

"Sure. I'd feel the same way."

"Which way's Barns traveling?"

"I don't know, Tom. Haven't asked him yet."

231

Casually, Dodd asked, "Let me know when you find out, will you?"

"Let's just call him over and both of us find out at the same time. I don't aim to take unfair advantage of you."

Longarm caught Barns's eye and motioned for him to join the two. Barns came up, his eyes questioning. Longarm explained that Julia and Ferris and the Blantons were going back to La Escondida, while Dodd would have to be taken to Monterrey for treatment. Then he asked, "Which way you planning to go, Barns? Ahead, or turn back?"

"I hadn't thought about it. Why? Is it important?"

"Just trying to get some idea," Longarm said quickly. He went on, "There's only you and Mrs. Mondragón left, besides me. She can't look after Dodd all by herself, and it's still a day and a half of riding to get to Monterrey."

"Which way are you going, Long?"

"I haven't made up my mind, either. I reckon it'll depend on who goes in which direction. All I'm interested in is seeing that there's somebody to take care of Tom the rest of the trip."

Dodd said, "It's too damn bad there's not another Ranger along. You know, Long, we've got a few unwritten rules in our outfit. If one of us gets hurt, and there's another Ranger along, that man sticks by the hurt Ranger, come hell or high water, no matter how tough it is on him."

Longarm decided he didn't need to comment on that. He said to Barns, "When you settle your mind on what you want to do, let me know, Barns. Now I got to go do some more asking. Them *campesinos* is going to want to move out sudden."

Walking over to Corazón, Longarm put the same question to her that he'd asked Barns. She did not hesitate to reply. "I have nothing but unhappy memories of La Escondida, Longarm. I have a few things there, some clothes, bits of jewelry. Let the *campesinos* have them. I will go on to Monterrey. We—that is, I—have a small house there where I will stay for a short time. Afterward, who knows? Mexico City, perhaps. Even the United States."

"You'd give a hand to helping to look after the Ranger, I guess, on the road up there?"

"Why, of course. Even if I hadn't been one of those he was fighting to protect, I would help with a man who is wounded. But you will go to Monterrey, too, no?"

"Maybe. It'll depend. Soon as I know, I'll tell you." Barns was still standing close to where Dodd lay. Longarm went back to him and said, "I hate to act like I'm rushing you, Barns, but you better decide right now who you'll be traveling with. Because if you go back to La Escondida, I'll have to try to hire one of Flores' people to see that Dodd gets to Monterrey. Mrs. Mondragón's going there, but she can't handle the job by herself."

Barns didn't reply at once. He looked at Dodd, lying on the ground a few feet away, staring up at the sky. Then he looked back at Longarm, and a frown formed on his face. With a shrug, he said, "Oh, what the hell, Long! I never pulled out of a big pot yet, even when I knew my cards weren't all that good. I'll go to Monterrey with Dodd."

"That's fine. I just made up my mind I'll be going up that way, too. Be glad to have your company, Barns."

Julia Wheatly was standing beside her horse at the edge of the hollow. Ferris had already ridden up to the road, where Flores and the remaining campesinos were waiting. Longarm saw the question in her eyes while he was still a dozen feet away from her. As he drew closer, he saw her expression change, and realized that she'd somehow read the answer in his face.

"You're going on to Monterrey," Julia said before he could speak. "I was hoping—"

"If I didn't have business that I got to tend to there, I'd go back with you, Julia. You know that."

"I wasn't just hoping you'd go back," she said. "I was hoping you'd stay."

"Now, what'd there be for me in a little place like that? You know what my job is, Julia."

"It looks as though I'm going to be a very rich woman, Longarm. Why should you worry about a job of any kind?"

"You're a fine lady, Julia. One of the nicest I ever met."

Julia met his steady, level gaze with eyes as dry and unwavering as his own. "If you change your mind, I'll probably still be in La Escondida. For a long time, at least."

"Who knows? Maybe you'll see me riding back there one of these days."

Both of them knew that was something that would never happen. Julia bent forward and kissed Longarm softly. Then, without looking back, she reined her horse around and walked the animal up to the road where the others were waiting.

In spite of his wound, Dodd insisted on riding his own horse. Indignantly, he turned down the suggestion that they make a litter for him, using the packhorses. He told them, "As long as that shoulder's bandaged good and tight, it won't hurt me any more than a bad cold. And I want to see where I'm going, not be strapped on a stretcher like a damn ninny."

Longarm rummaged in his saddlebag and brought out his bottle. It was not quite half-full. Handing it to Dodd, he said, "Have a sip of this when your shoulder begins bothering you. It's better medicine than most doctors give you."

Dodd took the bottle in his free hand. "Thanks, Longarm. I hope you got another one like this for yourself."

"I don't need another one. I can get more in Monterrey. You need it a lot worse'n I do."

"I'll save you a sip for before bed and for an eye-opener, but I sure won't turn your offer down."

Their progress through the day was slow. Longarm kept the little group moving at an even, steady pace, in spite of Dodd's protestations that he was all right and his urgings to go faster. He'd noticed the puffy redness that had begun to show on the wounded man's unbandaged right hand. Now and then, he turned to look back at the others, to make sure that either Corazón or Terrance Barns was riding beside Dodd, ready to help him if help was needed.

Evening found them still a half-day's ride from Monterrey. Longarm called a halt just before sundown, and they made a waterless camp in a stand of *ocote* pines that did little to cut the *viento septentrional* which began blowing in the midafternoon. The harsh wind skimmed the peaks that now surrounded them, and swept along the floor of the canyon into which the road had dipped.

"This is about as good a spot as we can find," Longarm announced. "We won't have to worry about nobody bothering us tonight, though. We'll get a good rest and a fresh start tomorrow, and by noon we ought to be riding into Monterrey."

It was a dry camp, and almost woodless. The few windfallen pine branches they could pick up vanished quickly in a flare of quick, bright flame and a puff of resin-scented smoke. The wind increased its force, and they were ready to crawl into their bedrolls almost as soon as they'd finished eating.

"You think we'll need to stand sentry tonight?" Barns asked Longarm, trying to peer through the darkness beyond the dying coals of the fire.

"I don't think we need to stand sentry, but somebody ought to be awake, in case Tom's shoulder gets worse. It's puffing up like he was bit by a pizened polecat. Ain't you seen how much it was hurting him just before we stopped?"

"He looked all right to me."

"Hell, Barns, Tom wouldn't complain. He's just been gritting his teeth and hanging on. If he didn't need to stop and rest, I'd have us push on tonight so he'd get to a doctor faster."

"I'll stand whatever watch you say."

"Let's split the night. You take the first half, I'll go the last part."

Rockless spots were hard to find in the *ocote* grove; the only cushioned places were at the bases of the trees where fallen needles had created thin cushions. Each of them picked one of the trees under which to spread his or her bedroll, so they were widely separated. Dodd's blankets were nearest Barns's shakedown; Corazón Mondragón had chosen a pine at some distance from the others; Longarm's blankets were under the sole remaining tree, still further from the rest.

He slept lightly, rousing and sitting up now and then, peering through the darkness to make sure that Barns was remaining near Dodd's bedroll. Once or twice while waking, Longarm thought he heard Dodd and Barns talking, but if they were, they were keeping their voices to whispers. He'd just settled back and pillowed his head on his folded coat when a soft scraping on the hard earth reached his ears.

Corazón was slipping around the bole of the tree under which he'd spread his bedroll. There was light enough for him to see that she had a warning finger pressed across her lips. Her bare feet noiseless on the baked soil, she came to the edge of the blankets and stood gazing down at him. She was wearing only a short white shift. Her shoulders gleamed softly, as white as the satin cloth that fell to her knees. Her legs and feet were bare. Longarm lifted the top blanket and she slipped under it to lie beside him.

"I intended to wait until we got to Monterrey," she whispered. "Then I saw you sit up, and knew you weren't asleep. I couldn't sleep, either, and felt I wanted to share my restlessness with you."

"Worrying about something?" he asked.

"No. I just wanted to be with you. Oh, Longarm, you aren't blind. You must've known the first time I saw you that I'd come to you the first chance I got." When Longarm made no reply, Corazón slid her hand down to grasp his wrist. She drew his hand along her body and pressed it on her breast. "I want your hands on me, Longarm. And I want you inside of me."

Corazón's body was warm against him, and Longarm could feel the nipple of the breast he held hardening under his fingers. She turned her face to him and offered her lips. Longarm bent to kiss her and she opened her mouth to him. Through the cloth of his jeans, her hand was stroking him to an erection.

"What about the others?" he asked when they broke their kiss.

"Are you worried that they'll hear us? I'm not. I have no shame for wanting you."

236

"Well, when you put it like that, I'm real proud you come to be with me. I just thought—"

"That I was a cold aristocrat? A bloodless *gachupina*? Try me, Longarm." Her hand had stopped caressing him and her fingers were undoing the buttons of his trousers. It was warm on Longarm's hardening flesh when she freed him from his clothing and closed her fingers around him. "What is it you thought?"

"Whatever it was, I don't think it no more." Longarm took his hand from Corazón's breast and lifted her, pulling the satin shift up high, under her armpits. He bent his head to caress her breasts with his lips and tongue.

Corazón arched her back as her breasts quivered under his mouth. She raised a knee and turned her hips toward him. Her hand squeezed his erection as she pushed the swollen cylinder of flesh down and twisted her body to bring him into her.

Longarm rolled as she moved and let her slide beneath him as he lowered his hips and sank into her. He felt the moist rippling of her inner muscles as he went in deeply grasping him and then relaxing to take him fully.

"Ah, yes!" she whispered in his ear. "I have wanted this, to feel you so hard and so big, pushing in me!"

Longarm felt Corazón's body grow taut as he kept up his steady stroking. She shivered once, a single convulsive shudder, and gasped urgently, "*Por el amor de Dios*, Longarm, do not stop, but close my mouth with yours or I will scream!"

Longarm found her lips, and met her darting tongue with his. She strained against him as her body shook, and then went limp. Her hands locked around his head, holding him in the kiss, and Longarm continued thrusting into her, feeling the sobs surging deep in her throat.

Moments passed and he did not slow the quick tempo of his thrusting until Corazón writhed under him again and the sobs trapped in her throat brought her breasts pressing against the hard muscles of his chest.

He was reaching for his own orgasm now, and drove into her with long, hard strokes. Then, when he felt Corazón's quivering become a series of quick, convulsive jerks, he let go and fell forward on her, still keeping her lips trapped with his until the laxness of her muscles told him that the time of her need to scream had passed. He took his lips away and let her drain her lungs of the breath trapped in them.

"Such a thing as this has never happened to me before," she breathed. "Ramón was the only man I have known, and with him it was never like this. With him, it was *la leche comparado con tequila*."

"It happens that way," Longarm said.

"Are you glad I came to you, Longarm?"

"Why, sure I am. Surprised, but proud you did."

"And you will regret that I go now? Because I must. I know you are to watch soon, for the rest of the night. But I will think of tomorrow night, when we will be in Monterrey, and by ourselves. It will be nicer then."

Before Longarm could reply, Corazón slid from the blankets and was gone, a white shape quickly lost among the trees. Her movement, heard or sensed, must have roused Terrance Barns. Longarm heard his boots scrape on the ground as he stood up, and the grating of their soles as Barns came toward him.

"I'm awake, Barns," Longarm said. "Just about to get up and spell you. How's Tom doing?"

"He's asleep now. Took him a long time to drop off, though. And I guess I must've dozed too, for a while."

"Well, you turn in. The night's half gone, and I'll get us waked up early and on the road." Longarm was on his feet now, reaching into the pocket of the coat he'd picked up to find a match for his cheroot. "We'll get started early. This time tomorrow, all of us will be sleeping in real beds, in Monterrey."

Longarm was frowning angrily when he came out of the Posada Ancirra and looked along the Avenida Hidalgo. His frown did not reflect his physical feeling. After finding a doctor for Tom Dodd and seeing the Ranger safe in the hospital, he and Barns had ridden with Corazón to the Mondragón town house, and had then checked into the hotel.

Barns had gone to his room yawning, declaring himself ready for a siesta, but Longarm had lain soaking in a tub of hot water after the hotel barber had shaved off his three-day beard. After his bath, the time of the siesta had passed, and Longarm had tapped on Barns's door. When there'd been no answer, he tried the knob and the door swung open. Barns was not inside. Longarm dressed hurriedly and went to the small, crowded lobby.

"My friend Barns," he said to the clerk. "He ain't in his room. You got any idea where he went?"

"*Señor* Barns? Ah. He is go out soon ago."

"I figured that out myself, sonny. What I want to know is where he went. Did he ask you where there's a good cantina, or anything like that?"

The clerk shook his head. "He do not need to ask that, *señor.* Is in Monterrey many cantinas. But the *estación de ferrocarriles, sí.* That he is ask how to go to."

"Let's see if I remember where it is myself. Down that street in front of the hotel to the square and turn north. Is that right?"

"*Sí, señor,*" the clerk beamed. "A small way, along Avenida Zaragoza."

There was no sight of Barns on Avenida Zaragoza when Longarm swung into it. He looked across the square, not expecting to see Barns there, and not being disappointed when there was no sign of him. In long strides, Longarm covered the short distance to the raidroad station. He stopped just inside the door. Barns was just turning away from the ticket window. He saw Longarm and hesitated momentarily, then kept walking toward him.

"You didn't mention you was planning to go on someplace from here," Longarm said casually.

"I made up my mind unexpectedly. It didn't occur to me you'd be wanting to buy a ticket home."

For a moment the two men locked eyes. During their stop on the way from La Escondida, Longarm had noticed the change in Barns, but until now he hadn't realized how complete it had been. Barns's eyes were clear, and their pale gray pupils seemed even lighter than before. The liquor-fed puffiness of his flesh had melted away; Barns's

239

jawline was clean, and the muscles at his earlobes bulged in firm knots. Before the strain of their stares grew too intense, Barns grinned.

"You can put off getting your ticket for a while," he said. "I owe you a drink, if I remember rightly. Why don't I buy it for you now?"

"Thought you was off liquor."

"Call this a special occasion, Long. One more drink's not going to hurt me. Come on. I noticed a saloon just down the street that looked pretty good."

Side by side they walked through the sun-washed air. They pushed through the swinging doors together, brushing their sides, and Longarm felt the bulge of the revolver on Barns's hip. Barns motioned to a table near the wall.

"That one looks all right, don't you think?"

"Good as any, for just a drink or two."

"Only one, for me," Barns said as they sat down. "You're partial to Maryland rye, I remember." He turned to call to the barkeeper, *"Un botella de* whiskey *centeno, por favor!"*

"Sounds sort of funny, when you call it that." Longarm smiled when he made the remark, but there was no mirth in it.

"A lot of things sound funny in Mexico, even after you've learned the language."

Barns fished a five-peso gold piece out of his fob pocket and laid it carefully on the table. The barkeep brought the bottle and glasses. Barns poured for them both and raised his glass.

"As they say down here, *salud y pesetas,*" he said. He downed the rye and shook his head. "A real man-sized drink, that is. Especially after the stuff I've been swilling." He motioned to the bottle with his empty glass. "Pour yourself the other half. I said one drink, and that's all I'm going to take."

Longarm lifted the bottle and held his glass up to it while he poured. He did not watch Barns, but noticed when he shifted slightly in his chair. Longarm kept his eyes on the neck of the bottle, filling his glass to the brim. He set the bottle down and raised the glass to sip from it.

"I don't guess I need to tell you, do I, Maddox?" he asked.

"No. I was pretty sure you'd tumbled to me even before we left La Escondida. But you're a federal man, Long. I can understand Dodd looking for me, but why in hell did they send you after me?"

"It goes back quite a ways. Seems you've got some papers that a few big men in Washington don't want to see daylight. And there was something about a few million dollars in gold that stuck to your hands back when Reconstruction ended in Texas. They'd like to have that back, too."

Maddox nodded slowly. "It's clear now. I guess you figured out where I was from that postcard I sent Amy?"

It was Longarm's turn to nod. "It wasn't much of a trick. That card had to be more of a message than it looked like. Took me all of ten minutes to figure it out."

"Too bad it won't do you any good. Keep your hands up in plain sight now, Long. I've had you covered from under the table ever since you poured that second drink."

"It won't do you any good. I don't hand my gun over just for the asking, Maddox."

"I didn't imagine you would. You'd draw when I started for the door, so I can't just let you sit here. But, damn it, I hate to have to kill you."

"Comes sort of tough when you've fought beside a man, don't it?" Moving his hands carefully, Longarm downed the rest of the rye that was in his glass. He put the empty glass on the table and said, "You don't have to kill me, you know. You can hand your gun over, and let me take you back."

"Like hell I will!" Maddox said pleasantly, but forcefully.

Longarm had no doubt that the renegade Ranger meant what he'd said. He raised a finger to point to the whiskey bottle.

Maddox nodded. "Help yourself." While Longarm was pouring, he went on, "I can't walk away from you, Long. You strike me as being pretty much like the Rangers.

When you start out after a man, you don't give up until you've got him."

"I try." Longarm stopped pouring, his glass only half-filled, and asked, "You mind satisfying my curiosity, Maddox? You must've done a pretty good job of hiding that stuff the men in Washington are after, for it to stay hid so long. How'd you manage that?"

"If you stopped by to see Amy, you were within fifty feet of it," Maddox grinned. "The last place I hid it was in the well, there at the house in Georgetown, with the papers all sealed up in oilskin. Too bad you didn't think to look. It'd have saved us both a lot of trouble." His grin vanished and his eyes hardened. "Now finish pouring your last drink, Long. It's too risky for me to keep holding a gun on you this way. I'm going to have to put an end to it."

"If it's going to be my last drink, I guess I'm entitled to have a cigar with it. Ain't that the custom down here?"

Maddox nodded. Longarm slid his hand inside his coat lapel. He twisted out of his chair the instant he triggered the derringer, and was falling to one side when Maddox's finger closed on the trigger of the gun he was holding under the table.

When the slug from Maddox's pistol splintered the tabletop and broke the bottle of rye, Longarm was well out of its path. He got his feet under him and stood up. Maddox was still crumpling to the floor.

There's times when it's too damn bad, Longarm told himself as he looked down at the renegade Ranger settling to the floor to lie in the stillness of death. *If things hadn't been the way they was, him and me might've been friends, one time.*

Thoughtfully, his eyes still on the dead man, Longarm fished out a cheroot and lighted it while he waited for the *Policiá Federal* to show up so that he could explain things to them. By suppertime, he thought, he'd have his appetite back and enjoy the dinner he'd promised to have with Corazón. There'd be plenty of time afterward to send a wire to Billy Vail and tell him to look for him back after he'd stopped in Georgetown.

As he turned his chair back onto its feet and settled into it, the last verse of the old song floated unbidden into his mind:

"And now my song is ended, I guess I've sung enough;
The life of a Texas Ranger you see is very rough;
So if you have a mother who don't want you to roam,
I advise you by experience, you'd better stay at home."

SPECIAL PREVIEW

Here are the opening scenes
from

LONGARM ON THE HUMBOLDT

twenty-eighth in the bold
LONGARM series from Jove

CHAPTER 1

The first time Longarm saw her, he felt as if someone had tied a wicked half-hitch in the taut nerves deep in his belly.

Until now, the long stage ride north to Denver had been tiring, tedious, boring, and monotonously uncomfortable. At Devil's Gorge station, things looked up. Way up. All the way up.

"Board. All aboard." The driver came out of the way-station cafe, still chewing his steak and potatoes.

She stood near the brink of the platform, regal, yet somehow helpless, as if she were used to people jumping to wait on her. She wore—and it wasn't so much *what* she wore as the *way* she wore it—a tan traveling suit which appeared, from Longarm's vantage point inside the shadowed coach, to have been more sculpted than tailored to her stunning form. Though her fur-trimmed jacket was severely plain, her ruffled white shirt pinned primly at the base of her throat, and the hem of her pleated skirt revealing no more than the color and shape of her high-button shoes, the total effect was devastating. A man looked at her and thought, between sweet anguish and bitter delight, "Oh, damn."

She didn't move. Obviously, she was waiting for someone to stow her bag and hand her inside the coach, which was already crowded with two middle-aged men, Longarm, and a sour-faced woman in her forties. The gal on the platform didn't have to worry about being ignored. She stood there and stopped traffic in every direction. Men bumped into each other and into uprights and baggage, ogling her.

Longarm grinned. He didn't blame them. She was somewhere in her twenties; hard to tell exactly about

247

women's ages these days. Anyway, it was difficult to determine because you couldn't see her eyes. She wore dark brown smoked glasses, almost as if she were hiding something, or hiding from somebody. And with a shape like hers, that wasn't easy. Tall for a woman, every inch was stacked like silver in a poke. It was mostly an essence of beauty—some aura emanating from inside her. Someone had told her once that she was beautiful, and she'd never forgotten it. By now, nobody around her could forget it.

Her hair was blonde, piled fine-spun and pleated and twisted in a rich old-gold color and caught in a thick bun at the nape of her slender neck. Her lips were perfect, like chiseled red shards of precious jewels, and her skin was as smooth as molten gold. She was slim, but her high-standing breasts bulged elegantly, her waist was flat and trim, and her hips plunged to long legs that wouldn't stop, outlined under that restraining outer garment. Looking at her, you got the intoxicating feeling that she wasn't wearing *anything* under that traveling suit. Or maybe you just hoped she wasn't. Like you wondered what color those eyes were, and why she hid them.

The driver caught the rest-iron to swing himself up on the boot from the raised platform. He stopped as if pole-axed, gawking at the slim, trim-waisted gal. There were few women in the West, and almost none who grabbed your eyes and held them until they burned and hurt.

"You going on this coach, miss?"

"Yes." Her voice was as lovely as she was, modulated and throaty. A voice meant to whisper caresses. "Would you take care of my bag?"

"Yes, ma'am. Where you going?"

"Denver. This is the stage to Denver, isn't it?"

"Sure is." The driver spoke as though these were the proudest words he knew and he was happy to be able to speak them. He might have lied to please her. He secured the bag and then stood grinning, ox-like, at her.

She favored him with a dazzling smile and lifted her arm. "If you'll help me, please?"

He leaped to obey, forgetting to chew, suspending respiration. Who could blame him? How many times did

248

a rough, horse-smelling fellow like him get invited to touch such a beauty?

He held open the door and she stepped into the cab. She caught her shoe on the step and stumbled slightly, but he grabbed her adroitly with both hands. "You're all right, miss," he assured her.

"Of course I am."

Longarm grinned faintly. She would have gotten three votes on how all right she was from within the coach. The elderly woman, with that evil instinct sometimes native to aging females, got up and plopped herself into the seat facing to the rear beside Longarm, making room for the girl at the window beside the two older men. One could see them mentally burning candles to the old biddy.

The driver and the two male passengers beside the girl made her as comfortable as possible. The driver grinned helplessly at her, totally enchanted. "Nothing else I can do, miss?"

Her smile was rarer gratuity than a gold piece. "No. I'm fine, driver, thank you."

Reluctantly, the stout, bearded driver slammed the cab door and swung up on the boot. He pushed off the hand brake and cracked the whip, and with that jostling, camel-like motion, creaking of metal and squealing of thorough-braces, the four-span coach headed northward through the pine forests toward Denver.

The stage swayed and rocked worse than a boat battered in a gale. The woman beside Longarm went deathly pale and bit back bile gorging up into her throat, already sick at her stomach.

The beautiful blonde remained cool, self-possessed, regal, and serene. Dust clouded past the windows, but she ignored it, glancing warmly at the people inside the cab. "My name is Alicia Payson." She turned, dazzling the man beside her with a smile.

He introduced himself in turn, shaking her hand and giving her a thumbnail sketch of his life until this moment. The fat man was next. He told her his name and where he was from and how long he'd been selling leather goods in this territory.

"I'm sure it's very exciting," Alicia Payson said. "You both sound as if you lead stimulating lives. I envy both of you."

"I'm Emma Frye," the woman beside Longarm said. "I'm not usually this morose, but I've been ill since this terrible contraption took off from the station. Does that man have to drive so fast?"

"I imagine he has a schedule he has to keep," Alicia said. She reached across and patted Emma Frye's hand. But her head was tilted, her nostrils flared slightly, as if she were studying Longarm minutely.

Longarm remained slouched in the corner of the cab. He kept his snuff-brown Stetson tilted low over his forehead, shadowing his eyes, his face in repose, an unlit nickel cheroot clenched between his teeth. His features appeared hewn from stone in his deeply tanned face.

He was a tall man, exceptionally tall when the average height for American males was five feet six inches. He towered almost ten inches above that, lean, muscular, and rock-hard, his body conditioned by the demands of his profession. He was on the downhill side of thirty, but there remained nothing youthful in his rugged face. It was braised and cured to a saddle-leather brown, and she could not see his gunmetal-blue eyes in the deep shadow of his flat hatbrim. He touched at his drooping longhorn mustache and returned her gaze with a faint, teasing smile, but he did not speak.

He supposed he didn't appear too prepossessing to Alicia Payson, and it was just as well. There was something of the pampered aristocrat about her. She had the thrilling beauty of a well-made fantasy, but there was about her the sort of scrubbed purity that warned that the trail into her bedroom led past the altar, and Longarm was not at that place in his life where he could get involved in cottage talk.

He sighed and sank deeper into the uncomfortable seat, aware that Emma Frye was getting paler and sicker by the mile. He stretched out his brown-tweed-clad legs and wriggled his toes inside his low-heeled cavalry stovepipe boots. These, he'd discovered, were far more suited for running than for riding, which was just what he wanted. He spent at least as much time out of the saddle as in it, and in these boots he could outrun almost any pursuer, except maybe the rare bad dreams that chased him in the night.

He shifted his cross-draw gunbelt, moving the double-action Colt Model T .44-40 to give the ailing Mrs. Frye more room.

He sweated under his brown coat and gray flannel shirt. He wanted to loosen the string tie at his throat, but did not. His sweating didn't make sense, because every roll of the stage carried them higher into the afternoon mountain chill. He decided he was uncomfortably hot either because that girl was lovely beyond compare, or because she stared at him, smilingly yet intensely, across the narrow space.

"Don't you want to tell us who you are?" Alicia Payson asked. "It makes traveling together so much more enjoyable if we know each other."

Longarm grinned at Alicia tautly, thinking, *You know damned good and well, lady, you don't care who I am—a tough and ordinary lawman, fated to prowl forever like a hungry cat in the shadows.*

"I'm Custis Long," Longarm said. "They call me Longarm."

"I'll bet they do," Alicia said. She gave him a faint, wry smile. "Do you want to say why?"

Longarm shrugged. "Everybody's got to be called something."

She smiled, as if pleased about something. "Don't they, though?" Her head tilted slightly. "Could it be because you are somehow involved with the law? Oh, not against it. In it. Do they call you the Longarm of the Law?"

He laughed. "How did you know that?"

But she did not smile. "I have special—powers—like that," she said. "For instance, I could have told Mr. Beale he was a leather salesman before he told me. And I knew Mr. Jacob was a clothing representative."

"Ladies lines," Mr. Jacob said.

"And Mrs. Frye," Alicia began, and then she stopped,

251

a look of alarm in her face. She leaned forward, taking Emma Frye's hands in her own. "Are you all right, Mrs. Frye?"

Emma Frye tried to smile, but failed. "If I were on the ocean, I'd know what was wrong with me—I'd know I was seasick."

"I do think it's riding backwards," Alica Payson said, her voice gentle and throaty with concern. "Sometimes riding facing the wrong way can be very upsetting. Wouldn't you like to trade places with me?"

Emma Frye thanked her gratefully, and they exchanged places in the bouncing cab. Both Jacob and Beale were so busy supporting Alicia that they were unable to lend any assistance at all to Mrs. Frye. Emma sagged her head against the windowsill, sucking in fresh air. Alicia Payson fell hard against Longarm, and for a long moment the full insulation of her spectacular breasts stabbed him. She sank back in the seat, smiling. "There. Isn't that better now?"

Alicia asked him the usual casual traveler's questions, and he gave her polite answers. He'd been born in West-by-god-Virginia, had lived through the troubled times leading up to the late War, had suffered during its battles, and had grown up in the tragic Reconstruction years that followed. He'd drifted west a long time ago for unspoken reasons. In his time he'd been a soldier, a cowboy, a rail-roader, a hard-rock miner, and for the past eight or ten years, a lawman.

He remembered for her the Corner Society back home in his native village, where reformed or dissident Quakers had settled and grown rich from the rocky ground. The town elders met weekly at the same corner of the same snake-rail fence to settle community matters, punish its offenders, levy its tariffs, and run the moral lives of its people. Maybe this was where he'd developed his own strange sense of responsibility toward law and order. There had to be law. Laws had to be obeyed, but some-times the ends justified the means and other laws had to be bent, or even broken. This was the unyielding credo of the Corner Society, bearded men who'd strayed from the Church of Friends. Vigilantes without horses. Lawmen without badges. Prosecutors without mercy. Judges without sanction. Jury without appeal. He laughed and shook away the memory.

As for Alicia, she'd lost her father tragically when she was six years old. She'd been in Texas most recently, and was traveling alone from necessity, though this was unheard of. It had to be done. It was urgent that she get in touch with a certain man in Denver.

"Maybe I can help you find him," Longarm offered idly, being polite, not really meaning it, chatter passed between strangers.

"Maybe you can." The way she spoke, with steel ribbing underlining each word, charged through Longarm. Even when she smiled, this girl was serious. Deadly serious.

As the westering sun set behind the Colorado foothills in the long climb to the Mile-High City, a bone-chilling cold permeated the coach. At the next stage way station, the driver thrust three heavy buffalo robes through a window. "You folks snuggle down under these," he said. "You'll think you're a-settin' before a roaring fire at the Ritz."

Darkness smoked down upon them, and the horses settled to a steady pace. The blonde remained sitting straight, but she shared one huge robe with Longarm. Its lining was pleasant against his hands. He heard her teeth chatter, but she said nothing. But before they'd traveled five miles, she'd shifted until her trim thigh and shapely leg rested hotly against Longarm.

Longarm kept his flat-brimmed hat lowered and straight on his head, cavalry-style, and said nothing. The darkness flooded the interior of the cab, making a stygian grotto of it with the oil-cloth curtains secured at the windows. Emma Frye, slightly recovered, was the first to surrender to sleep, snoring loudly. Soon Jacob had sunk against her, almost pulling the shared robe off Mr. Beale. But this worthy gentleman was obviously sleeping quietly too, for he did not even protest, blowing tiny bubbles between parted lips.

Longarm was tired, but knew he was not going to sleep

this side of Denver, never again as long as this heavenly body jostled so intimately against him. He found his mind and senses totally preoccupied by this blonde beside him. She sagged more and more upon him, her head bobbling tiredly. He felt his heartbeat increase as the faint, clean-scrubbed scent of her body attacked his nostrils.

When finally she let her head fall upon his shoulder, he reckoned she was asleep and pulled the heavy buffalo robe up closer around her. In doing so, his hand brushed the upthrust resiliency of one of her breasts. He moved his hand away quickly. Rather than retreating, the blonde turned a little more toward him. He allowed her to snuggle her head into the less bony area between his shoulder blade and his neck. She pressed down into its softness as if it were a pillow.

Now Longarm was in trouble. Her rich, spun-gold blonde hair lay within inches of his nostrils. The strange, warm musk of her hair assaulted and intoxicated him and, believing her asleep, he let his cheek rest against the fragrant crown of her head, and drank in the rich incense of her.

Across the well of darkness, the other three passengers slept soundly, bouncing and tumbling with the sway of the coach. Longarm felt as if he were neither fully awake nor completely asleep, but rocking in sweet discomfort in some netherworld.

He grinned tautly. Even had he created this fantasy, it was unlikely he would have peopled it with such an incredibly lovely creature. She pressed closer and her lips brushed his throat, a touch as light and random as the flitting of a butterfly, but as hot as sparks of hellfire. His heart thudded raggedly. Was she nuzzling his throat in her sleep? Was it entirely accidental or on purpose that she raked his sensitive skin with her perfect lips?

She did not move for a long time, and when he decided she *was* asleep, she slid her arm across his chest. Now her breasts, like gentle lances, impaled him, and he wondered if she felt the fusillading thunder of his heart?

Slowly, almost imperceptibly, her hand loosed its tenuous grip on the upper pocket of his vest. Her fingers shifted downward, with the terrible slowness of an ice floe, to the gold chain that linked his watch in one vest pocket to the double-barreled, .44-caliber brass derringer in the other. She shifted her hip, bumping the Cold .44-40 in its holster. He grinned tautly. By now, these were not the only guns loaded and primed for action under that buffalo robe.

He began to sweat, but he would not have moved the robe even if he melted down. That slowly drooping arm was driving him loco, and he waited with bated breath to find where it would finally settle. Every time they struck a bump or a pothole, or rounded a curve in the darkness, that hand lost a little of its battle against gravity. It rested now against the heavy brass of his belt buckle.

When he was certain she must be asleep, he was sorely tempted to place her errant hand gently where it would be warmest and do the most good. She spoke suddenly in a throaty whisper, and he started, literally shocked.

"Do you mind if I move closer, Mr. Longarm? I—want to have a—private—talk with you."

Longarm tried to keep his voice level, but his heart pounded so that he felt breathless. With that throbbing eminence poised just below his belt buckle and her straying hand, he could not see how there could be any mistaking her meaning in using that word *private*.

"Talk," he invited. "I'll lie and say I'm all ears."

Instead of speaking, Alicia let her hand move down over the buckle. Unable to credit what was happening, he felt her fighting the buttons on the fly of his skin-tight, brown tweed pants.

He wondered if he was asleep, lost in the kind of fantasy that attacks every man traveling alone. Had he fallen asleep hours earlier? Was he doomed to awaken any minute, throbbing and in pain—and alone?

He bit down hard on his underlip. This blonde knew what she was doing, with a wisdom as old as womankind. She knew what she wanted. She had far less trouble loosening his buttons than he'd had cursing them closed.

He sucked in a deep breath, feeling her clasp his

throbbing erection in her fist, and he was rewarded by hearing her delighted and shocked intake of breath.

"I had—no idea," she whispered, awed, against his chest. Her head was well under the robe now. He moved only enough to slip his hand beneath the fiery heat of her upper arm.

Her hand moved faster on him, and he could feel the fire of her rasping breath. Closing his eyes and praying that he would never wake up, he let his seeking hand cover the fevered rise of her breasts. She let him force her head down to the flat plane of his stomach with his kisses against her sweetly fragrant hair.

To preserve his sanity as long as possible, he tried to keep his mind from considering directly what she was doing to him under that robe. She was fierce about it, dedicated to pleasing him right out of his skull. He didn't know if she wanted it all, but he did know that any minute, unless she moved quickly, she was going to get it.

With one hand, he gripped her head as if in a vise. She sent him spiraling mindlessly out of himself. He was aware of unbuttoning her shirt, fondling and caressing the smooth, burning flesh. He even pulled her skirt up around her hips and verified what he'd suspected to be true. She was absolutely naked under that elegant tan traveling suit!

"Mr. Long?"

Longarm straightened, trembling, as if someone had ambushed him.

He jerked his head up. Disoriented for a moment, he gazed at Emma Frye, sitting forward in the seat across from him. He knew what was happening to him, but he almost didn't know where he was. "Ma'am?"

Mrs. Frye nodded. "Just woke up. Is little Miss Payson all right?"

"Oh, she's—just great." He lowered his voice, feeling Alicia's frantic caresses under that robe. "I think she's trying to get—some sleep."

"Poor little thing, she should be whipped."

"Yes, ma'am, reckon she ought to." Longarm winced as Alicia bit him mercilessly.